TERENCE BAILEY

DEAD IN TIME

THE SARA JONES CYCLE BOOK ONE

Published by Accent Press Ltd 2017

ISBN 9781786153876

Copyright © Terence Bailey 2017

For Janet

Acknowledgements

Thank you to my editor at Accent Press, Greg Rees, for guiding Sara Jones along her path. Thanks also to my old friends Dr David W. Grossman and Inspector Alun Samuel for their long-term help and support, and Ifan Elias and Annemieke Fox for their kind assistance.

ONE

'D'you know what, Detective Inspector Harding?' Inspector Ceri Lloyd glowered at the Englishman. 'There are windows in this building harder to see through than you.'

James Harding smiled tightly and straightened his shoulders. The way to win with this old bird was to stay stiff. Be blandly professional and don't play her game. That should have the added attraction of annoying the hell out of her.

'I'm sorry,' he said, 'I'm rubbish at innuendo. Exactly what are you saying?'

Lloyd's eyes narrowed in contempt. 'I am saying I don't want you to contact her. I don't want her to hear anything about this investigation she can't read on *Wales Online*.' She shoved open the double-glazed window, inviting a waft of air into the room. 'I do not want her involved in this. And I don't want you involved, either. I question your motives, Detective Inspector Harding. Is that clear enough?'

Harding raised his eyebrows with what he hoped was studied speculation. Coolly, he nudged back the vertical blinds on the interior window overlooking the corridor. 'You run the Penweddig police station, don't you, Inspector Lloyd?'

'When it's open, yes – but I'm spending more and more time up here.'

'I imagine they need you in Aberystwyth, considering all that's happened.'

She furrowed her brow. 'We're coping perfectly well. Officers from all over Wales are assisting.'

Out in the corridor, a young constable approached a photocopier. Through the glass, she nodded cordially to Harding.

'Let me put your mind at ease,' he said. 'I'm here because of my expertise in this area; nothing more.'

Lloyd snorted. '*Malu cachu*,' she swore.

The detective inspector drew a steadying breath. He didn't know what she'd said, but it wasn't a compliment.

'Harding, you don't have any expertise! All the attention you've had in the last couple years is a result of the help she gave you.'

Harding felt himself flinch, and watched Lloyd's eyes twinkle in response. She seized her advantage.

'Without her, you'd still be chasing iPhone thieves in Hammersmith, and you know it. So enjoy your reputation while it lasts, Detective Inspector Harding, because you are now on your own – professionally *and* personally.'

She moved to the door, and jerked it open. The constable at the copier looked up, startled.

'As for Sara Jones,' Lloyd said, 'she's finally back where she belongs.'

Even with a steady sea breeze and two electric fans whirring, the room felt oppressive: too many bodies crammed into too small a space, the fug of heat raised faster than it could be expelled.

The Mid Wales Task Force on Mental Health met here, in this Aberystwyth seafront flat that served as a drop-in centre, once a month. The local worthies who comprised the board converged from all over the county of Ceredigion, and rarely saw each other between meetings. Most were retired, and looked forward to these monthly conclaves for gossip. Although they never failed to discuss actual business – how to get a Lottery grant, whether to launch a new Children's Club – they also compared illnesses, and shared intelligence about who had passed away, or might be about to.

This evening, however, their standard topics had been shelved; in hushed tones; they were discussing murder.

A skeletal woman scanned the others with bright, clear eyes. 'The police didn't want anyone to know the body had been burnt,' she said, 'but my son told me. He works for the *Cambrian News*. He hears the most awful things.' At her feet, two bug-eyed Chihuahuas quivered.

'Everyone knows the body was burnt, Mrs Davies,' huffed a retired English solicitor. 'It happened in the fellow's car, for heaven's sake. Right out in the street.'

'The second body wasn't burnt,' offered someone else.

'No, not the second,' agreed the solicitor. 'It was the first fellow who was burnt.'

'Honestly, I'm terrified to be alone,' Mrs Davies added. 'I know there's been a prowler in my garden. I rang the police two nights running.'

'Find anyone?' someone asked.

She shook her head. 'That doesn't mean no one was out there. I heard what I heard.' She dropped her hand and snapped her fingers. Both Chihuahuas leapt to their spindly legs and snuffled at them. 'Aglaea and Thalia were so frightened they hid under the bed.'

At one end of the table, the charity's newest employee, Dr Sara Jones, sat with a fixed expression, trying to mask her discomfort. At thirty-four, she was the youngest board member by half her age; a qualified GP and psychiatrist, she had been hired three months earlier to run this mental health drop-in centre.

Mrs Davies craned her neck and raised her pencilled eyebrows. 'How have the murders affected our clients, Sara?'

Sara glanced up from her paper. 'Well, when the first one happened,' she said, 'everyone assumed it was a single, horrible event. Now there's been a second, they're starting to get frightened.'

'I imagine they are,' Mrs Davies said. 'And what do you know about the murders?'

Sara blinked. 'Nothing. Why should I?'

The old woman shrugged coyly. 'Everyone knows you're an expert on this sort of thing.'

Sara closed her eyes wearily. When she'd lived in London, she had been an occasional consultant on certain types of crime – but she had hoped to escape those conversations when she fled her old life. 'Sorry, I don't know anything.'

The English solicitor frowned. 'Surely you must have an opinion?'

Sara remained silent, reluctant to feed their speculation.

'Just from your experience,' someone else prompted. 'What kind of person could have done it?'

'Without knowing the motive,' she said haltingly, 'that's hard to answer.' They waited for her to continue, and she sighed. 'Murder can be the result of different drives. There's crime, such as robbery. Then there's sex, or some personal reason. Sometimes it's a group cause. Each motive suggests a different kind of killer.'

The solicitor encouraged her with a nod.

'As I said,' Sara concluded, 'I don't know enough to speculate. I'm not involved in the case. Inspector Lloyd has not discussed it with me.'

Nobody looked convinced; they all knew that Ceri

Lloyd was Sara's closest friend.

'Now,' Sara said sharply, 'it's late, and there are three items left to cover. We ought to rush through them.'

To her relief, Mrs Davies nodded. 'That would be sensible,' the old woman agreed, and looked down at her feet. 'My babies would feel safer if they could walk home while it's still light.'

Jamie Harding had thought this would be easy: he'd pay Lloyd the visit required by protocol, glide over her rudeness with cool detachment, then move on to the seafront, and Sara's office. Trouble was, they were arguing about too many things at once. This woman could not separate the personal from the professional. It was time to turn the tables.

'Inspector Lloyd,' he said, 'I've worked with forces all over England, Scotland and Northern Ireland.' He glared into her implacable face. 'Everywhere I go, I find that professionals don't let their personal lives threaten an investigation. If you trust Sara's abilities, then I'd say you should have had the professionalism to hire her yourself.'

Lloyd stiffened – then without warning slapped her hand against the wall. '*Pisho bant*,' she snarled, locking her eyes onto his. 'You know full well why I haven't called her – and why I won't let you do it either.'

He felt a pulse of satisfaction at her loss of control, but when Lloyd spoke again each word was like a bullet fired with deadly precision. 'Sara doesn't need this right now,' she said, 'and she doesn't need you either. If you had any decency, or morality, or willpower, you'd realize that. And you would never have come here.'

She tugged at her uniform, drew herself up to her full five feet, six inches, and stared into his tie. 'Your presence on this investigation is not required. I'd be grateful if you'd leave now.'

She gazed into the again-empty corridor. Waited.

Harding listened to her laboured breathing; in the wake of her words it sounded unnaturally loud. He swallowed; in a battle between the personal and the professional, the personal usually wins. 'Shut the door,' he whispered. 'We need to talk.'

Lloyd remained still. Harding closed his eyes. 'Please, Ceri.'

She started, then glared. Somehow the presumption of using her first name changed the ground rules. Reluctantly, she pushed at the door; it clicked gently. Harding shrugged helplessly. 'I should've expected I couldn't come in here and get my way by insulting you. It was stupid of me.'

Lloyd nodded once.

'People say you can be difficult.' He tried to smile. 'And I have a feeling you're rather proud of that reputation. But I've heard other stories too. About the acts of kindness you perform all the time without hesitation, and later deny.'

He waited for a response, and Lloyd tongued her teeth with bland deliberation. She'd been flattered before.

'You question my motives,' he continued. 'Let me be honest – I'm not really sure what they are either. Maybe they're so tangled, it's hard to see where one ends and the next one begins. But I do know one thing: you won't let more people die just because you don't like me. You're not like that. She's told me.'

The Inspector's frozen stare melted slightly.

'As for my reputation,' he added, 'maybe it's true. What if I do need help on cases like this? We both know that there's only one place for me to get it.'

He held out his hands. 'Let's face the truth, Inspector Lloyd … maybe both of us need Sara Jones.'

In the past half-hour, the Steering Committee had, with painful deliberation, agreed the contents of a report to the Bronglais Hospital, and Sara had completely covered her agenda paper with spirals. Now, Mrs Davies held court about a meeting she'd had at the University's Student Centre.

Sara paid her little attention; the details of the murders were nagging at her. According to reports, both dead men had almost certainly been victims of the same killer. They were murdered within two miles of each other, and each had had his throat cut cleanly. There were few signs of a struggle in either case, indicating planned and carefully executed assaults. Yet the first body had been burnt, and the second had not. Had the killer meant to incinerate the second man, but failed? Why burn them at all? To remove evidence? That was the speculation after the event, but it seemed a crude attempt for someone so meticulous …

Sara drew a slash across her doodle, and dropped the pen onto the Formica tabletop. *Stop it, Sara, it's not your responsibility.*

The meeting room door creaked open a crack, and Mrs Davies' precise words faltered, then faded. The hesitant face of Inspector Ceri Lloyd peered into the room. Sara raised her eyebrows to the older woman. Ceri had been one of the few unfailing sources of support in Sara's life, and was the main reason she had been able to leave her old life in London for this new one in Wales. Not only had Ceri recommended Sara for this job, she had also found her an inexpensive farmhouse in Penweddig, a town just down the coast. Now and again, Sara would spend time with a group of community psychiatric nurses and social workers who enjoyed a night out, but Ceri was the only true friend she had in Wales.

Ceri spoke with an unsettled smile. '*Maen ddrwg*

gennyf dorri ar draws pawb,' she said. *Sorry to interrupt, everyone.* The English solicitor furrowed his thin white brows in irritation at her speaking Welsh. The rest of the group waited with prurient interest to hear why she had come.

'Sara,' she continued, in English now, 'there is a gentleman looking for you.' She placed a flat emphasis on '*gentleman*'; in her eyes, there was a trace of annoyance and distaste. 'He says it's important.'

Before Sara could respond, the door swung open and Detective Inspector Harding breezed past Ceri, striding into the room.

'Evening, Sara.'

She caught her breath, and groped stupidly for her pen, as if it could give some sort of support. *What is he doing here?*

Jamie worked for the Metropolitan Police's Special Branch. Although multiple murder was virtually non-existent in rural Wales, it was still unlikely that the Dyfed-Powys Police Authority would have requested assistance from Scotland Yard. As far as Sara knew, they had never done so.

And even if they had, the odds that the Met would send Jamie were astronomical.

And yet here he was.

Sara lowered her gaze, and crumpled her agenda into a ball. 'I think that's all for tonight,' she whispered to the other board members. Hesitantly, they began to rise.

Jamie smiled kindly as they drifted from the room, silently thanking them for their understanding. Soon, only Mrs Davies remained, placing documents in a plastic file folder one by one, then removing them again as her dogs trembled at her feet. She blithely ignored the room's hollow silence until Ceri Lloyd intervened.

'Mrs Davies?' she said respectfully. 'Why don't we go

outside? I need to ask about that prowler you've been hearing.'

The old woman pursed her lips in disappointment, then nodded, scooping up Aglaea and Thalia. The door squeaked as it swung shut and closed with a muffled rattle. Sara was alone with Jamie.

He slid into a chair opposite her, and smoothed out the balled-up agenda, staring at her scribbles.

'Interesting,' he said with a smile.

Sara reflected on how she had only just begun to enjoy her life again. Finally, she raised her eyes to connect with his. Their silence lasted longer than was comfortable, until Jamie's grin finally melted into a look of hopeful trepidation. Finally, Sara sighed.

'What?' he responded, too quickly.

'You have to admit,' she said, 'your timing has always sucked.'

TWO

An iPad sat on the tabletop, showing a grid of thumbnail photos. They revealed wide shots of a street, which Sara recognised as a residential area up the hill, behind the University. A car could be seen parked alongside a pavement; it became more prominent with each photo, the series ending with close-ups of the sooty black interior, a charred corpse in the driver's seat.

Jamie ran his fingers through his copper hair, and tapped on one of the photos, which enlarged to fill the screen. 'This was Navid Kapadia,' he said. 'Married, with two children. He lectured in Geography at the University. He was well-liked, and had no enemies that we've heard of.' He looked down at the photo, and Sara's gaze followed; even upside-down, she could see that the body's chest and stomach had been burned completely black. The charred tissue had hardened into a shell of stiff sheets, separated by wide cracks revealing shiny gullies of drying blood. Congealed white fat clung to the edges of the eschar; in the heat of the blaze, it had bubbled up through the fissures in the cracking skin, and dried once the fire had died out.

Despite Jamie's years of professional experience, the skin of his face tightened into an expression of pity and distaste. 'We're pretty sure his death wasn't the result of a mugging,' he continued. 'He was still wearing some gold

11

jewellery, and Dr Hefin, the forensic pathologist, found about sixty pounds in his wallet. It was in his back pocket, underneath him, so it survived.'

Sara slid Jamie's iPad closer to her, and enlarged the section of photograph that revealed Mr Kapadia's face. The man's head lolled to the left, against the blistered leather head rest of his car. The right side of his face was as badly damaged as his torso: the eyelid had been burned off, making the eye appear to bulge. Sara noted that the heat had turned the pupil an opaque, creamy colour. Mr Kapadia's cheek had been burned through, exposing shining white molars, and his right ear had been entirely consumed by flame, leaving only a remnant of the auricular cartilage ringing the naked otic canal. The left side of the face had been largely spared, with parts of it bright red from second and third degree burns. The contrast between the two sides of the face made the corpse's appearance even more horrific.

Sara returned the photo to its usual size, so she could see all of Mr Kapadia. His posture revealed no signs of the usual agony that accompanied death by fire: the arms were not raised before the face, the fists weren't balled, the teeth weren't bared. He had not suffered, because he had already died before being set alight.

'From the appearance of the body,' Sara said, 'I'd guess the offender killed him, doused him in petrol, dropped a match in his lap, and then closed the car door. That's why part of the face is intact – the fire burned up all the oxygen in the car and died before it could consume the corpse completely.'

'That makes sense,' Jamie said, nodding. 'So now we know how it was done. What about the why?' He dragged the iPad back across the table towards him. 'At first,' he added, 'the police wondered if it might be a racist killing.'

Sara shook her head. 'That's unlikely. He died from

one slash to the throat, right?'

Jamie made a small sound of agreement.

'Hate crimes are never that meticulous.'

The detective nodded once. 'We've already come to that conclusion. Aside from a few troublemakers, racist incidents are uncommon around here. Surprisingly, Aberystwyth has quite a cosmopolitan attitude to outsiders.'

Sara smiled. Why was that surprising? Years of experience had given Jamie the ability to speak with certainty about things he had only just learned. Sara knew that there was no real arrogance in it: it was an occupational hazard, and he did it unconsciously.

'The second victim was Dan Williams,' Jamie said, swiping the screen to get past Mr Kapadia to another collection of images. 'Murdered four days later, on the evening of July twelfth. He was an English builder, working on a site next to the harbour. He'd hired a small holiday cottage in Llanfarian, just south of here.'

The photo Jamie had chosen showed a well-furnished living room. The body could be seen in the far corner, lying against an ivory-white wall, on beige carpet stained maroon with drying blood.

'No sign of forced entry. The offender probably talked his way into the house. It looks like he grabbed Mr Williams when his back was turned, and slashed his throat with one clean cut. Mr Williams stumbled forwards, hitting his head on the fireplace.' Jamie rifled through the images as he said, 'The assailant waited until he had bled to death, turned him over … and did this.'

In the photo Jamie had selected, the focus was on the groin. Sara raised her eyebrows speculatively: the man's penis had been severed with a single clean slice, and the skin of the scrotum had also been peeled away. The left testicle dangled from the body, still attached to the spermatic cord.

'There's very little blood,' she murmured. 'Has the pathologist confirmed that this happened after death?'

'Yes,' Jamie said. 'There's a shot of the severed penis, if you'd like to see it.'

'Err, no thanks,' she replied 'I think I can imagine it.'

Jamie nodded agreeably and covered the screen. 'So,' he asked, 'any thoughts?'

Sara straightened her back, levelled her shoulders, and took a breath. 'Let's start with the murders themselves,' she said. 'He killed each of them quickly with one clean slash to the throat. That's significant, because it doesn't fit the traditional profile of a serial killer.'

Jamie raised his eyebrows but said nothing. Sara knew that such a simplistic exercise in profiling came second-nature to him, and wondered why he was making her start from square one.

'Serial killers,' she continued, 'are after control. If this one were typical, he'd want to dominate his victims. He'd keep them alive, and in terror, for as long as possible, and then kill them as slowly as he could. But this killer wasn't interested in toying with either man. He didn't even want to cause them physical suffering. It appears he just wanted them dead.'

She stared into Jamie's green eyes, and saw a gleam of admiration. She lowered her gaze, and stumbled slightly on her words. 'Moving on to the time frame ... serial killers also follow a certain cycle. You'd think this guy's need to kill would grow until it became intolerable, and that's when he'd strike. Then he'd calm down, cool off for a while, before he started to feel the prick of desire again.'

She waved to the photographs on the table. 'Instead, he attacked both of his victims in the same week.'

'Okay,' Jamie said, as if he were playing along, 'if he isn't a serial killer, what is he?'

'In profiling terms, I'd say he's an assassin. He's got a reason for doing this; he thinks he's on a mission.'

Jamie pondered her words before speaking.

'What about the mutilation?' he countered finally. 'An assassin usually doesn't want physical contact with his victims.' He picked up a close-up of Mr Williams' mutilated groin. 'He certainly wouldn't entertain any sort of castration fetish.'

Sara shook her head. 'I don't think it's a fetish … I think it's a message.'

Jamie raised his eyes sharply to her. 'A message?'

'Both Mr Williams' castration, and the burning of Mr Kapadia. He wants us to figure out why he killed these men.'

Jamie stood, and slipped the iPad into his leather briefcase. 'Excellent work,' he said happily, 'that's what we think too.'

Sara frowned in annoyance at his offhand manner. If this investigation was all so cut-and-dried, then why was he here? She pushed her chair back and stood, resting her palms on the table. 'Jamie, any good forensic psychologist could help you get into this offender's mind – and you know every one in Britain. I am not a professional forensic psychologist, and have never wanted to be one.'

Jamie smiled as if she were being modest. 'You've helped me solve some of my most difficult cases,' he said, deliberately missing her point.

'They were all of a specific type. For my own reasons, I used to consult on certain types of crime –'

'Ones linked to the occult, fringe religions, bizarre rituals –'

'All the weird stuff, right. So clearly, there's nothing here to interest me.' Sara shook her head in frustration. 'Jamie, if you wanted to talk to me, why didn't you just ask?'

He frowned, and looked past Sara, out of the window and over Cardigan Bay. 'Maybe because it hasn't worked for the past six months,' he said, his voice quiet and firm. 'That's a long time to wait for a conversation.'

Sara pursed her lips, and dragged the tip of her pen through a splash of coffee on the table, making a thin wet swirl. 'I can't even get a grip on why you're here in the first place,' she muttered.

'What do you mean?'

'Why would the Detective Chief Inspector at Carmarthen draft in someone from two hundred miles away? You must be costing him a fortune. And why would your chief at the Met agree to lose you? It doesn't make sense.'

Jamie snorted. 'The head of CID isn't happy about it ... but Aberystwyth needed my experience. Just as much as I need yours.' He reached out across the table, as if to grasp her hand, but hesitated, and then withdrew.

'I promise you,' he said, 'that our past has nothing to do with why I'm here. There is a lot more to this case than I've told you.'

Sara's eyes narrowed. 'Go on.'

Jamie slipped both stacks of crime scene photographs back into their envelope, and stretched languidly. 'This place is uncomfortable. Where else can we go?'

Sara hesitated, but a rush of curiosity overwhelmed the dim pang of caution that pulsed in her chest. 'Where are you based?' she asked.

'Tonight? In Carmarthen.'

She sighed. 'My place is on the way. I don't mind you stopping by – so long as we keep this professional.' She raised her eyebrows, seeking agreement.

Jamie handed her the envelope of photographs. 'I'll follow you in my car. Where did you park?'

*

Eldon Carson lounged on a wooden bench and gazed at the building that housed Aberystwyth's mental health drop-in centre. His nausea was dying down now, but his heart still beat rapidly; he took long, deep breaths, and willed the adrenaline to stop pumping.

Carson's back was to the sun, which sank rapidly into Cardigan Bay, pushing his shadow, long and narrow, across the flagstones. The shadow pointed to the other side of Marine Terrace, where the buildings glowed burnished orange. Everything looked so different here. Not at all like the wide roads and stately high-rises of Eldon's hometown: Raleigh, North Carolina.

A short time earlier, Carson had watched a police car and a blue Range Rover pull over on the side of the street. One person climbed out of each: a stocky lady cop and a guy in a suit. He looked like a cop, too – and the lady cop didn't approve of his presence. Carson was good at picking up that sort of thing, and the emotional frisson made the couple more interesting to watch. It lent special meaning to the guy's stiffened back, the woman's turned shoulder, their lack of conversation as he followed her into the drop-in centre.

Although Carson was on edge, the presence of two officers of the law did not contribute to his nerves. He didn't expect they would notice a short, muscular, casually dressed young man on the promenade, where so many college kids lived. At twenty-three, Carson blended in; he could have been a graduate student, waiting for friends before a night of drinking.

When Irene Davies emerged from the building, she was with the policewoman. Carson tensed, and watched the older woman intently. The two lingered on the sidewalk for several minutes, Mrs Davies doing most of the talking as the cop listened indulgently. Finally, the uniformed cop gestured goodbye, and walked down the street, in the opposite direction to where her car was parked. The old lady watched her go, then led her little dogs briskly towards Terrace Road.

Carson drew a breath and began to stroll after her with studied nonchalance. He followed her all the way home, as the last ember of sun was extinguished behind the watery horizon.

Sara had left her red BMW in front of the Chinese takeaway down the street. As she and Jamie went in opposite directions on the pavement, she told him to join her there.

As she approached the car, Sara noticed a uniformed arm dangling from its open window, fingers scissoring a cigarette, blue smoke curling into the cooling summer evening. Her radio was on – tuned for the first time ever to a country music programme. Ceri Lloyd sat in the passenger seat.

'You should have locked up,' Ceri murmured as Sara climbed in behind the wheel. 'Car crime does happen in Wales, you know.'

Sara smiled. 'I've left the back door of my house unlocked, too. I suppose it's the contrast with London – I just can't imagine anything bad happening here.'

Ceri glanced in the direction of the drop-in centre and snorted grimly.

'Well,' Sara added, 'I couldn't until recently.'

'Police in this region handle something like three thousand crimes a month,' Ceri said, 'and it's not all simple stuff like burglary. I've personally dealt with violent assaults, rapes, and murder. Maybe this isn't London, Sara, but even here we've got our share of serious crime. Nowhere's safe these days, and it doesn't pay to take chances.'

Sara smiled indulgently, but she knew that Ceri was

right. People around here were frightened out of their wits at the thought that a killer might still be in their midst, and it was making everyone feel like a potential victim. Even Sara felt vulnerable alone in her farmhouse, isolated at the end of a lane in a thicket of trees.

'Do you need a ride home?' she asked.

Ceri shook her head. 'I just wanted to make sure you were all right before I left.'

'All right?' Sara asked. 'Why wouldn't I be?'

Ceri smiled thinly, and took a long pull on her cigarette. 'Because of him … the father.'

'I'm fine,' Sara said, too harshly. She looked down the street for Jamie's car.

'You're well rid of him,' Ceri muttered.

Sara rubbed glumly at a smudge on her steering wheel. 'Why is he working on the case, anyway?' she asked finally. 'Do you know?'

Ceri drew in a deep breath, as if she had been wondering that, too. 'After the second murder,' she said, 'CID sent out a confidential email to all the Special Branches force-wide, requesting information. Detective Inspector Harding saw it … and volunteered his services.'

Sara blinked in surprise. 'He volunteered? Why on earth?'

Ceri adopted an expression of naïve innocence. 'I have absolutely no idea,' she said flatly. 'You'll have to ask him.'

Sara remained still, then said, 'He's not such a bad guy.'

'It would take a lot for him to prove that to me. Everything about him sets my teeth on edge. He did nothing – nothing – to help you when you lost the baby.'

Sara gasped. 'That is simply not true!' She felt herself blushing. 'He wanted to help – in fact, he was desperate to. I left him, remember? And with your encouragement, if you'll recall.'

Behind them, Jamie's Range Rover crept up and pulled to the curb, waiting for Sara to pull out and take the lead. Ceri pinched her lips together in a sad smile. Sara's anger broke and retreated.

'Please don't worry about me,' she said. 'I really am fine.'

Ceri opened the passenger door and dropped her cigarette butt on the street, but did not climb out. 'Remember that night you phoned me? The night you decided to leave? I don't know what prompted you to do that, but it was the right decision. Believe me, Sara, you needed to be back here.'

THREE

Sara had met Jamie just over a year earlier, on a warm summer's day in London. It had been an uneventful morning at the Harley Street clinic where Sara was a junior partner: she had been curled into her favourite batik chair with her Burmese cat, Ego, purring on her lap. Yet another session with her oldest client, Andrew Turner – a successful defence lobbyist, whose business card read 'consultant'.

A quick glance at the clock behind Andy: only six minutes to go. He was rabbiting on about the best ways to promote European battle tanks to military dictatorships – the kind of flak he deployed to dodge talking about his problems.

'Do you know why weapons platforms look the way they do?' he asked with ironic amusement. 'Simply to flatter the generals' egos. They want their armaments to look hard, these lads.'

Although Andy Turner was wealthy and powerful, he spent his days feeling like a failure. Since childhood, he had harboured an impossible yearning to be a great military hero; he had even done a stint in the Territorial Army, but had shown little aptitude.

'Think of a tank as a trophy dog for military kleptocrats …' Andy went on.

Sara was not surprised he had proved unfit for military

rigour: at heart, Andy was an aesthete, as fond of luxury as of military lore. Once, he had said he came to Sara because he liked her office, and meant it as a compliment. He was fond of bold fabrics and ethnic patterns, and Sara's room had both: paintings by a recently famous Aboriginal artist, a beaded Sioux throw rug, and several Inuit sculptures. The theme that unified her eclectic decor was expense; it had taken money to make things look this primitive.

'Thing is,' Andy was saying, 'these countries throw their peasants' dosh at the products, but they don't know how to use them. They waste more missiles on a training mission than the Yanks did in Afghanistan.'

In treating Andy's long-term depression, Sara was relying on a two-pronged strategy of drugs and therapy. An antidepressant dealt with the biochemical imbalances that stoked his negative feelings, while she tried to resolve his underlying issues through Cognitive Behavioural Therapy. Sara knew from experience the positive effect such a regimen could have: her own psychiatrist, Dr Shapiro, had been using the same combination on her.

'Oh well,' Andy muttered, 'it's all a game, really. Keeps our chums in the defence industry solvent – and me too, I suppose.' He peered at her for the first time in several minutes. 'So,' he said, 'how are you?'

Sara's eyes refocused, from the clock to Andy. 'Me?'

'I haven't seen you on telly recently. Not even a word in the papers. Has your work with the Met dried up?'

She sighed. 'Mercifully, yes.'

He shook his head sympathetically. 'You must see some ghastly things. Does it bother you?'

Sara puckered her lips and raised her eyebrows contemplatively. She didn't feel like baring her soul to a patient. She put a layer of mock offence in her voice: 'Andy, who's the therapist here?'

Andy shrugged. 'It would bother me,' he said simply.

At two o'clock, the office door opened and Emma, the clinic's secretary, leaned into the room. Ego stood with a quivering stretch and jumped from Sara's lap.

'Sara?' Emma said, 'I'm afraid Mr Turner's time is up ... and there's a police inspector in the waiting room.'

Andy Turner grinned archly. 'Speak of the devil.'

Sara looked up quizzically. 'Anyone I know?' she asked.

'I don't think so,' Emma said. Smiling slyly, she mouthed, 'But he's absolutely gorgeous!'

Andy rose. 'I'll shuffle off now,' he sang. 'Wouldn't want to keep you girls from the serious business of fighting crime.'

James Harding was a handsome man in his mid-thirties, six feet tall with an athletic build, sharp green eyes and a shy smile. Although he had tried to comb his copper fringe off his forehead, it had fallen into his eyes. Probably, it always did. Sara noted he was better-dressed than most of the police she knew, without looking vain. He wasn't wearing a wedding ring.

He sat on the edge of the chair that Andy Turner had just vacated. Ego occupied the rest, rubbing his chocolate-brown head against the detective inspector's back. 'You're an expert on the occult, is that right?' he asked, trying to ignore the cat.

'It's one of my areas of study, yes: why some people are attracted to fringe belief systems, how they integrate these world-views into their lives – and what can happen when they fail to. I teach a course on it at UCL.'

The detective nodded. 'I know – someone lent me one of your books.' From his leather attaché case, he took a copy of *Magical Thinking in the Secular World*, by Dr Sara Jones.

Sara wrinkled her nose. 'Your friend has odd taste in reading material. What did you think of it?'

'To be honest, I haven't opened it yet.'

'For heaven's sake, don't!' she chuckled. 'It's a bit of a slog.'

He mimed tremendous relief. 'I think I prefer talking to you in person.'

Sara smiled, and decided she liked this detective. 'Then let's talk.' She leaned forward. 'Who gave you my name?'

Harding's cheer evaporated as he pulled out a file folder. He didn't open it, but simply held it tightly, as though it would get away otherwise. 'Former patients of yours. The Loxley family. They live up in Finchley.'

Sara stretched her mind and remembered. A couple of years ago, she had given the couple and their thirteen-year-old daughter family counselling, and had also seen the girl, Vivian, on her own. She had not had word of them for eighteen months.

'You've heard about yesterday's stabbing in Mill Hill?' the detective continued. 'A secondary school student, now on the critical list. He was attacked by a sixteen-year-old classmate named Paul Sullivan, who has since gone missing. Sullivan is probably with Vivian Loxley. She's his girlfriend.'

Sara felt a sudden weight in the pit of her stomach. 'I see.' She twirled a length of spiky hair, and chewed absently on her lower lip.

Sara remembered a few things about the young teenage girl. Once, she told Sara how a friend had taught her to read Tarot cards, and said that sometimes they played with a Ouija board. Vivian had been delighted with Sara's understanding of such things – her parents didn't have a clue, she'd said – and she enjoyed baiting Sara with messages from other world. Sara would laugh and tell her it was all nonsense. Now, she hesitated before saying to the detective, 'I hope you came to me because I was Vivian's therapist, not because of any occult connection.'

'Sadly, both.' Harding offered the folder to Sara. 'The Sullivan boy considers himself a Satanist.'

Sara accepted the file, laid it on the coffee table, and closed her eyes. She was starting to get a headache.

'His parents, meanwhile, are devout Baptists. You can imagine the Battle of Armageddon that's been going on in Mill Hill. In the last couple of months, the boy's been dragged to church, prayed over, confined to his room – everything his parents could think of. He responded by getting weirder. By all accounts, he's not a strong boy, physically or emotionally. He was being bullied at school.'

'Let me guess: his victim was the chief bully.'

Harding inclined his head deferentially. 'Spot on. There's no indication that Paul meant to stab the victim until it happened. But he'd taken to carrying a ceremonial dagger, and when he was cornered in the lavatory ...'

Sara shuddered. 'I can imagine.'

'He fled the building, then Vivian Loxley failed to return home from school in Finchley that afternoon. Neither one's been seen since.'

Sara gazed at a wall hanging, losing herself in thought. Eighteen months ago, Vivian had been a bright thirteen-year old with long brown hair and a taunting smile. She had seemed smarter than her parents, and took pleasure in driving them around the bend. She reminded Sara of her own brother, Rhodri, at that same age. Through a combination of family counselling and individual sessions, Vivian's relationship with Mum and Dad had started to warm. As soon as that happened, the family stopped coming. Sara never found out why – it might have been the cost, or exaggerated optimism on their part – but Sara had not worried about the girl's future. She was a bright spark, Sara had thought. She'd pull through.

She watched her cat as he edged around Harding, leapt gracefully over his knees and onto the coffee table, settling on the agent's file folder. Harding smiled and attempted to stroke him. He said, 'Nice kitty,' without conviction.

'You say he considers himself a Satanist. Any idea what he means by that?'

'Is there more than one way to worship the devil?'

'Several. I assume he's more than just a fan of death metal?'

Harding nodded. 'Full-blown devil worshipper.'

'Okay,' Sara said, 'but what you call "the devil" depends on your point of view. The boy might be associated with one of the Satanic churches – the Temple of Set or the Church of Satan ...'

Harding gave a sardonic snort. 'I doubt it. This kid isn't a joiner. He spends most of his time in his room.'

Sara shook her head. 'That wouldn't matter. Those groups tend to be American anyway, and much of their interaction is online. In a sense, it would be better for him to be part of a cybersect than to be a complete Solitary.'

'Why?'

Sara patted her lap and Ego jumped from the file folder. 'Think of it like this: some of the well-known, public groups practice what you might call philosophical Satanism. They preach a kind of self-centred individualism, as well as contempt for most other people. It can seem antisocial, but it's not usually violent. For the disturbed types they often attract, these groups can be a form of social constraint. They offer a world view, such as it is, that boosts self-esteem and keeps misfits from going completely off the rails.'

Harding nodded slowly. 'Like a pressure valve. Which

would be denied to a troubled kid who's making it all up by himself.'

'My guess is, he's looked at Satanist websites, but takes a syncretic approach – blending whatever bits feed his fantasies, and using them to escape the things in life that scare him. Problem is, without guidance from a community, there's nothing to anchor himself to. Just a constant flood of poisonous thoughts.'

Harding took a slow, deep breath. 'So you're saying the boy is dangerous.'

'Oh, there's no doubt about that. The real question is, to whom?'

'You're worried he might hurt Vivian?'

'I can imagine a lot of outcomes.' Sara glanced at the file of documents on her lap. 'Can I keep this?'

'Long as you like.'

She looked at the clock behind Harding. 'I have another patient coming, but I'll find time to look at it this afternoon. Would you like to meet for dinner?

Harding stood. 'If it's not too much trouble.'

'Seven o'clock?' She smiled and added, 'And don't worry – I can tell you don't like the cat. I'll leave him here.'

That afternoon typified feelings that would soon be common in her relationship with Jamie Harding: a blend of emotional turmoil and attraction.

The turmoil came from knowing that a former patient of hers – someone she'd let slip away – was in trouble. What detail had she missed eighteen months ago? In her heart, Sara knew the question wasn't rational. Kids change between thirteen and fifteen ... but should she have convinced the family to keep coming? Should she have offered free sessions? These thoughts tumbled pell-mell through her brain as she reviewed the detective's papers, as well as her own file on the family. Vivian's story was resonant of Sara's own miserable past: young people mixed up in strange beliefs, ending in violence. It sent her down well-worn mental pathways, into areas of thought better left unvisited.

But along with the bleak mingling of past and present, there came a small caress of desire. She realised she wouldn't mind spending time with this new policeman.

At the pavement café, they had chosen a table in the sun, away from the shade of a large canopy, as well as the other diners. Furtive as secret lovers, they had not wanted their conversation overheard.

'I've studied the file and I think we can guess that the boy's do-it-yourself Satanism results from a rift with his parents,' Sara said in a quiet voice. 'It's been his way of rejecting, even hurting, them.'

'I suppose if your parents are deeply religious, devil worship will do it.'

'It does have implications for the present, though. It suggests he won't run home to the loving support of Mum and Dad. He'll want to get far away.'

Sara's mind harked back to the epilogue of the horrible events of her own childhood: Glyn Thomas gone and Rhodri's motor scooter found abandoned. A flush of fury always surfaced when she thought of Glyn Thomas. She forced herself to concentrate, and pressed on.

'I'd suspect that in Paul's state of mind – and having already wounded somebody – he'd do almost anything to escape.'

Harding nodded. 'There are plenty of ways to do that.'

'The wild card is Vivian Loxley. Her reaction will be critical to what her boyfriend does next. I don't know what she's like any more. Does she share any of his beliefs?'

'As you've noted, it's hard to pin down what his

beliefs are, other than a rebellious sort of hatred for everything his parents stand for.' Harding shrugged. 'We know she's a bit of an oddball, but does she call herself a Satanist? She didn't before she got involved with him. Now, who knows?'

'People adopt new beliefs for all kinds of reasons,' Sara said. 'Sometimes, it's because they admire the people who hold it. That's called Affectional Conversion.'

Harding pursed his lips. 'So Vivian Loxley might call herself a Satanist just because Paul does?'

'Possibly.' Mentally, Sara kicked herself for not staying in touch. 'How loyal is she to him?'

He smiled. 'I'd imagine you know more about the love life of a fifteen-year-old girl than I do.'

'Don't be so sure. I was an insular child.'

'I'm inclined to doubt that.'

Sara grinned, then checked herself. 'We need to talk to the Loxleys,' she said.

Harding nodded once. 'They're expecting you to come.'

Sara pushed away her plate. 'Eat up.'

Harding looked shocked. He had barely touched his food. 'You want to go now?'

She pulled out a debit card and signalled to the waiter. 'Did you have anything else planned?'

In her time analysing the family, Sara had never seen the Loxleys' house. Part of a terrace off Finchley High Road, it was comfortable, casual, and dishevelled. Their leather recliner sofa was strewn with mismatched pillows, two iPads, three remotes, and a cat toy. The place smelt of pipe tobacco. Mr and Mrs Loxley were a short couple in their mid-forties, as lumpy as their furniture. Clearly, they hadn't slept much since their daughter's disappearance the previous afternoon; their eyes were bleary, their faces slack with weary bemusement.

'School?' said Mrs Loxley. 'Vivian's never been particularly academic. Lately, her grades have been getting worse.'

'Much worse,' said Mr Loxley. 'And it's because of him.'

Sara nodded. 'Paul.'

The very ordinariness of their home filled her with wracking pity: the knick-knacks, the hangings, and the nest of rosewood tables seemed entirely too safe. It reminded her of something she had already learned in her studies of the occult: the bizarre can creep up on the most banal of family stories.

The couple showed Sara and Jamie around the house. They spoke of Vivian's recent worsening attitude.

'You could have called me, you know,' Sara said. 'I would have spoken to her at any time.'

Mr Loxley shrugged helplessly. 'She wouldn't have come.'

'How long has your daughter been seeing Paul?'

'A few months,' the woman sighed distractedly.

'We knew he was odd,' Mr Loxley said, 'but we didn't know about the – you know, the devil business.'

They climbed the stairs to the second floor. On a landing, Mrs Loxley picked up a small framed snapshot. 'This is what Vivian looks like now.'

Sara took the picture and released an audible gasp.

The difference between the teenager now and when Sara had known her was startling. Then she had been fresh-faced and impish, not pretty, but attractive in her own way. Now, her style was a jarring contrast to the high street anonymity she had sported eighteen months ago: her make-up ghostly white, her hair dyed coal-black, which was also the colour of her clothing. She wore chunky silver jewellery, mostly crosses and skulls.

Although she smiled for the camera, a glint in her eye suggested this commonplace act could only be submitted to with heavy irony. What had happened, Sara wondered, to make this girl show such contempt for the mild manners with which she had been raised?

'How did you get along with Vivian just before she met Paul?' Sara asked.

'As you know, Dr Jones, she's always been unusual,' Mrs Loxley said. She had misread Sara's question and was apologizing for her daughter's transformation. 'Things were pretty good for a while, after we saw you. Then they slipped again.'

'When she met him,' said Mr Loxley. 'We did the best we could.'

'Do you think she was influenced by Paul's beliefs?' asked Jamie.

'I told you,' the father said, 'we didn't know about his beliefs. But I'll say one thing: she got stranger once she started hanging about with him. All her old friends – her normal friends – she just shut them out.'

Mrs Loxley shook her head in puzzled wonder. 'But it's odd. When they're together, it's always Viv who tells him what to do. Sometimes she walks all over him. Still, he has this influence … it's hard to describe.'

She paused, and added, 'His parents are ever so religious, you know.'

They climbed the remaining stairs to Vivian's room. What Sara saw caused her to shudder; it was like an obscene parody of her own room as a child – but with the *Take That* posters replaced by death metal bands Sara had never heard of. One wall was painted matt black, and black candles dripped from wrought-iron candlesticks.

'What can you do?' Mrs Loxley asked. 'Kids go their own way.' Tears welled in her eyes but she did not sob. 'I'm sorry she's turned out this way. You *will* find her, won't you?'

'We'll do everything we can,' Sara said. 'And when we do find her, I'll want to talk to her regularly. There'll be no charge.'

They took their leave of the distraught couple, and climbed back into Jamie's Range Rover. 'What do you think?' he asked as he pulled away from the curb.

'I think Paul Sullivan will regret taking his girl along for the ride,' Sara said. 'She won't be a silent partner.'

'Do you think there's a chance she might get fed up and leave him?'

Sara pursed her lips, then sighed. 'There's a chance, but it's slight. His desperation, combined with whatever power he has over her ...' She lowered her head. 'I think it's more likely that Vivian Loxley is in terrible danger.'

The detective inspector pondered her words before muttering, 'Well, thanks for talking to them, anyway. I'll call you if we learn anything.'

'You'd better call me anyway,' Sara said.

'Why?'

'Because I'm not going to let you waltz into my office, dump a load of unpleasant news on me, then walk away, that's why. You've depressed me, Inspector. Now it's your job to cheer me up.'

He smiled. 'Ah.'

'So call me tomorrow, no matter what happens. I know you'll be busy – but it's your turn to buy dinner.'

FOUR

Once they had called him Taffy, because he was Welsh, and that had been demeaning. He had hated it the same way an Irishman might object to Paddy. The name's biggest insult was its lack of imagination, the idea that he wasn't even worth original condescension. When you're a street person, any nickname will do, even when you're talking to other street people. Somewhere along the line – he could never remember when or why – someone had changed it to Daffy. Maybe because it sounded like a Welsh emblem – the daffodil. Whatever the reason, he had kept the name.

Daffy stood in the maze-like queue of London's Victoria Coach Station ticket hall, fifth from the front. *Sell me a ticket, sell me a ticket, sell me a ticket …* he repeated those words as if they were a form of magic, as if his will power alone could compel the people behind the wickets to overlook his clothes, his face, his hair, and sell him a ticket to Aberystwyth.

Sell me a ticket. For God's sake, sell me a ticket.

An hour before, he had washed himself at a McDonalds loo, and tried to slick down his hair. Daffy wore a worn brown sports jacket that had once been expensive, but now was unravelling at both elbows. The fabric was shiny, and so was the cloth of his trousers and the polyester of his shirt. He couldn't hide that, but he had hidden his bedroll and dingy canvas bag in the corner, where he could keep an eye on it, but the ticket-sellers couldn't see.

It was his face that really gave him away. Years of living where he could had told their story there. That was why he could no longer hitchhike; nobody would give him a ride. That was why he'd had to beg for the money, and steal the last eight pounds from a naïve young lad new to life under Waterloo Bridge.

Daffy was ashamed of having done that. But his desperation outweighed his shame. He needed the money more than that kid.

The person in front of him loped towards a free window, and he scanned the row of wickets nervously, wondering which one would be free first. This would never have happened if he'd just kept his mouth shut. He should never have gone to that man. He should have never said what he said. That bastard was cruel, brutal, and Daffy knew that. He had always known that.

A window became free, and he shuffled towards it, the broken soles of his shoes scuffing against the dirty floor.

Sell me a ticket. If you don't, I'll ...

'One ticket to Aberystwyth,' he said.

He held his breath, sensing that the woman was staring at the dirt under his fingernails – the grimy layer he had not been able to remove.

'Return?' she asked.

'Yes,' he said, nearly barking in his enthusiasm. 'Return.'

He wished he could truly be so certain about his future. He released the crumpled bits of money from his sweaty palm, and pushed them forward.

Jamie sat at the large pine table in Sara's kitchen in Penweddig, a mug of coffee at his elbow. He looked around the large room, an extension to the original farmhouse. 'Cosy,' he said.

Sara smiled lopsidedly. Jamie was being polite; the kitchen was a mess. 'It will be cosy. Just give me more time.'

Because everything in Sara's life at the moment was subject to change, she had intended to make as few renovations to her newly purchased farmhouse as possible. She didn't even know whether she planned to live in it for long. Yet once she had actually moved in, she found herself unable to accept the old stone house as it was. She had been aghast that the place had actually used a solid fuel-burning oven for heat and hot water. She couldn't imagine herself getting up in the morning and stoking it with wood or coal before she could even take a shower. She had been astonished that the attached stable – the one real storage space in the entire house –only had an external entrance. She imagined having to run through the pelting winter sleet to fetch something from a box. It would never do; within her first week, she'd had a plumber installing new oil-fired central heating, and a builder knocking a hole in her living room wall in order to make an internal entrance to the stable. As soon as the builder had finished the new door, she had set him to work in the kitchen, ripping up the hideous cork-tiled floor and breaking away the crumbling plaster. Meanwhile, the plumber had replaced the bathroom suite.

Sara enjoyed the order she had so far imposed on the house. She had hopes for this kitchen, especially. So far, it had a new slate floor, and all the walls had been re-plastered. The aboriginal paintings from her Harley Street office sat on the floor, leaning against the unpainted, putty-coloured walls. The paintings' bright colours and modern, expensive frames made a strange contrast to the bare plaster, the old, splintered wood, and the cobwebs that seemed to grow in the corners no matter how many times Sara brushed them away. Unopened boxes filled with plates and kitchen gadgets were piled in front of almost every cabinet.

Sara leaned forwards onto the table opposite Jamie. 'What have you got to show me?'

He typed his pass code into an iPad, and tapped the 'Photos' icon. 'We've kept this out of the newspapers,' he said, 'to weed out bogus confessions.'

Jamie pushed the tablet towards her, and swiped back and forth between two photos. Each showed in close-up a neatly rendered drawing of a symbol: an equilateral triangle, with its base missing. The bottom side had been replaced by two semi-circles, each seeming to hang from one of the sides of the triangle. Inside this unusual glyph stared a single eye, and radiating from it was a series of lines.

'Where were these found?' Sara asked.

'The first was drawn in chalk on the pavement of Mr Kapadia's house. It didn't appear until two days after his murder. The second was drawn in ink straight onto Mr Williams' skin.'

'His skin?'

'His stomach, to be precise. What can you tell me about the symbol?'

Sara looked at one of the photos and shrugged. 'It's the All-Seeing Eye … a common enough mystical motif. To some, it represents the omnipresent nature of God, but it can also signify spiritual knowledge or abilities: the "third eye" of an enlightened individual.'

Jamie nodded, scratching notes into a small booklet. 'What about the pyramid?'

'It's a sign of durability. It can illustrate the unchanging nature of God's protection, or the age-old wisdom possessed by the elect.'

'You said this thing is common?'

'Quite common. Freemasons in the late eighteenth century were especially taken with it – that's why you'll find it on the back of every American dollar bill.'

Jamie raised his eyebrows. 'Interesting.'

Sara tapped her Mont Blanc fountain pen on the edge of the iPad. 'What makes this one unusual is the bottom of the pyramid,' she said. 'There are semi-circles where the base should be. My guess is, they have special significance for the killer.'

Jamie nodded. 'We found things written under the symbols. Look at the next four photos.'

Sara swiped. Two of the next photographs displayed the pyramids from a wider angle, and words were now visible under each symbol. The other two photos were close-ups of the writing itself. In one photo – the words rendered in chalk on pavement – Sara read:

Jamila

Yusuf

In the second – ink applied neatly to flesh – only one name was inscribed:

Carol Ann Elliott

'In Mr Kapadia's case,' Jamie said, 'the names are of his children. Carol Elliott is a woman Mr Williams didn't even know. She's nineteen years old, lives with her parents, and works at a Spar shop in Aberystwyth. Her only connections to the victim are that she lives a half-mile from his house, and he used to purchase cigarettes at the shop.'

Sara stared pensively at the names. 'Could they be the killer's next targets?' she asked.

Jamie nodded 'We've got to assume that. He may be leading us on an Easter egg hunt from one victim to the next, daring us to protect them.' He sucked thoughtfully on his upper lip and added, 'It's interesting that he included Carol Elliott's middle name – she never uses it.'

'So why did he put it there?'

'Because there are two other Carol Elliotts in Aberystwyth, but she's the only one with the middle name Ann. He was concerned that we find the right woman.'

Jamie dug out some papers from his briefcase and slid them towards Sara. 'We've drawn up a contingency plan for each of the potential victims, so that everyone agrees on how to deal with them. These are now posted in the control room of every station in the area.'

Sara cast her eye swiftly over the documents. 'I see you've re-housed the Kapadias, but not Carol Elliott.'

'Her parents refused to let her leave. We've alarmed their home, and we're keeping it under surveillance.' He shook his head. 'Still, I'm not convinced that they *are* intended victims. Why would he have chosen them? Why select the family of his first victim, and a complete stranger to the next? The combination doesn't add up.'

Sara glanced at one of the photos of the symbol. 'Quite possibly, it's got something to do with this. Whatever this Eye in the Pyramid means to him, it's what links all these people.'

Jamie reached across the table and pulled away his iPad. 'Then you know why I volunteered for this job. There aren't many people in the country who've dealt with cases like this. If he is on some sort of mission, then his personal safety isn't important to him. He's willing to take chances, and he'll keep killing until we stop him.'

Jamie's pale green eyes seemed to cut into Sara. 'I've got to understand what this man is thinking, what he's trying to achieve. This investigation needs both of us.'

Sara nodded, and they sat in silence for several seconds. Jamie took a deep breath, then bit his lip, as if trying to hold back a torrent of words that were trying to escape. Abruptly, he stood up. 'I'll go now,' he said.

'Thank you for the coffee.'

He slid the iPad into his briefcase. 'I'll email you copies of the photos. Just let me know what you think.'

Sara looked into his eyes, sighed, and accepted the envelope. It felt heavy in her hand, as if it carried the entire weight of her past.

Thirty minutes later, the aroma of coffee had been overpowered by sharp fumes from a freshly opened tin of paint. Sara had changed into her oldest clothes, moved the aboriginal paintings, and shoved the pine kitchen table to the far end of the room.

She had always planned to decorate her new farmhouse by herself. After two months' worth of builders, the thought of opening her doors to decorators had been unbearable. The work had not been on tonight's agenda, but Sara found herself pouring a dollop of honey-yellow paint into a tray. It plopped out in a wobbling mound, into which she eased a roller, levelling it out across the tray's shiny black plastic. At random, she selected a space on the longest wall, and began to cover it with a strip of bright colour. Paint leapt onto her sleeve and sprayed droplets into her eyes.

'I thought this was supposed to be non-drip,' she muttered to no one.

The sound of her own voice intensified her sense of being alone, which had curled around as soon as the rear lights of Jamie's car had disappeared down the lane. Sara was sharply aware that the nearest house was half a mile away. It was silly to be frightened, but she couldn't help it. The murders were fresh in everyone's mind, and most single women in the area felt like this now, even without being exposed to crime scene photos. At least physical activity kept her from jumping at every noise she heard.

And yet, she reflected, it would take more than a spot

of decorating to make sense of the major new complication that had entered her life, inconveniently, at a time when she had only just begun to enjoy herself again. For months, she had carried with her a numb feeling, punctuated by the image of a living, vibrant baby girl – the child she would never know. It was only in the calm of Wales that Sara had been able to think of the daughter she had never named, and feel no emotion stronger than fond melancholy.

Sara held the roller over the tray and allowed some droplets to fall. She wondered what might have happened between her and Jamie if she hadn't fled London. What kind of intimate détente might have been possible? For a moment, she felt a pang of pity for her ex-lover: Jamie still believed she had run away to Wales because of him. Of course, their affair, and the small demise it had left in its wake, had been the melancholy background to her decision. But Jamie himself had little to do with Sara's actual flight. The dark catalyst for that impulsive move had been her brother, Rhodri.

Sara began to roll paint onto the wall with grim concentration. She did not want to relive the day, last winter, when Rhodri had rung her mobile, demanding to see her immediately. But, as on so many other occasions, Sara found the memory hard to suppress.

A medical emergency – that's what he had told her. There was a medical emergency and she needed to come right away.

Rhodri Jones was Chief Executive Officer of Thorndike Aerospace, a growing sub-contractor to the defence industry. He divided his time between his offices in Surrey and his four-storey house in Islington. He had rung from there; she had taken a taxi from Harley Street, clutching her scuffed medical bag with white knuckles, and hoping it was nothing serious.

The black cab pulled to the kerb of the Islington square. She handed the driver twenty pounds and told him to keep the change. She stabbed at the buzzer on the panel next to the glossy black door, but did not wait for a response; she unlocked the door with a key that Rhodri had given her long ago.

She met him in the foyer, the neck of his shirt unbuttoned, a tie hanging loosely around his neck. His freshly combed hair was still wet, as if he had recently emerged from the shower.

'Rhoddo, what's wrong?' she asked breathlessly.

'Oh, bit of a problem,' he mumbled, leading her into the ornately decorated flat. 'I just need a bit of assistance ...'

The sting of cigarette smoke assailed Sara's nostrils as she entered the room. Standing at the window, looking out onto the street through lace curtains, was a woman in her early twenties. Her cigarette dangled loosely from her lips, and she wore nothing but a black brassiere and a short leather shirt. One arm was cradled in a makeshift sling, fashioned from a hastily torn bed sheet.

A wave of nausea passed through Sara. 'Oh, God, Rhodri.'

The woman turned around, and looked at Sara with dull eyes. Tears had carved a trail through her make-up. The flesh-toned paint could not disguise the bruise that was forming on her right cheek. Registering the look of anger and pity on Sara's face, her expression hardened. Removing the cigarette from her lips, she spoke with flat sarcasm. 'I had a small mishap.'

'Looks like you did,' Sara replied, just as flatly.

Rhodri pretended not to hear, and wandered to the gilt-framed mirror above his mantle. He began to knot his tie, ignoring Sara's fiery gaze. Her stomach was tight with rage. Once, Sara had assumed that the blurring of sex and punishment was a perversion limited to a small group of ex-public schoolboys – a childhood of abuse, calcified into adult vice. Certainly, she had not imagined that her brother would ever engage in such practices. For that matter, nor had any of the defence ministers, sheikhs, or leaders of military juntas with whom he rubbed shoulders twigged his darker, more libertine tastes. He paid his professional victims well to keep his private pleasures private.

As her brother finished with his tie, Sara spoke in a low, barely controlled voice. 'Rhodri, we need to talk.'

Rhodri nodded and gently pulled his jacket from the sofa. He inclined his head towards the double doors that led to the dining room. Sara drew an unsteady breath and followed.

He closed the doors behind them and leaned for support on a rosewood chair. 'I know you're angry,' he began.

'Angry? Angry doesn't begin to describe my reaction to this.'

'I know. You're right. What happened here was inexcusable.'

Sara shook her head. 'That's too easy, Rhodri. You can't just say sorry and make it go away.'

'Sara,' he said, his tone imploring, 'it was a game, that's all … it got out of hand.'

'A game?' Sara gasped. 'You've hurt her!'

Rhodri nodded contritely, and Sara noticed he was trembling. She hoped, with righteous malice, that he was feeling genuine remorse, a sliver of pain that might stop him gliding over the upset he had caused.

He shook his head in self-recrimination. 'I've already asked her forgiveness, which she has granted me. She's more understanding than I have a right to expect, and so are you. I think she may have a broken arm. I was hoping you might –'

Abruptly, Sara cut him off. 'No, Rhodri. I will not bandage her.'

'Sara,' he whispered desperately, 'she needs attention!'

'I agree she does – but I won't be part of this, Rhodri. You've got to face up to what you've done. We'll take her to the Whittington's A&E.'

'No!' her brother barked. 'They'll call the police.'

His face registered genuine fear, and Sara could not help feeling a stab of guilt for refusing him. But she could not give in; this was for his own good. 'Then I suggest you ring your solicitor,' she said.

'Sara, please ...' he said, his voice wavering.

Suddenly, he choked on a sob, and tears welled in his eyes. His face contorted, and he began to weep fulsomely.

'Oh, Rhodri ... you need help.'

'I know.'

'You've got to talk to somebody. A professional.' She reached out and grasped his arm. 'I can arrange it,' she said firmly. 'I'm sure Dr Shapiro would see you.'

'Oh, Sara,' Rhodri sobbed, 'I ... I'm so sorry. I've got to go now.'

She stared at him blankly. 'What?'

'My driver's waiting outside. I have a meeting in thirty minutes, in Hampshire. I'm going to be late as it is.'

He wriggled into his cashmere jacket and tugged at the French cuffs of his shirt. Tears were still wet on his face. 'I'm so sorry,' he repeated, his voice husky.

Sara shook her head in bemusement as he dabbed at his eyes with a handkerchief and backed into the hallway. She listened to his shoes rap against the mosaic-tiled floor, and heard the door open and close behind him. She stood for a moment – frozen, blinking – and choked back tears of her own. Why had Rhodri called her to sort this out? Why had he thought she would be such a ready accessory to his crimes? Because her older brother knew he was all she had. Because their awful past had made each of them what they had become.

For twenty years, Sara Jones had been seeking answers, and was no closer to finding them than she had ever been. What had she done all this for? So that she could patch up Rhodri's playmates? Is this what fate had intended for her?

If it was, then fate could go to hell.

She composed herself, and strode dutifully back into the sitting room. The woman had lit another cigarette, and fresh tears glistened on her face.

'Are you okay?' she said gently.

'Yeah,' the woman whispered. 'He just got excited.' Her expression slackened. 'I'm getting out of this business anyway,' she added.

'You should,' Sara said, and opened her medical bag.

Sara placed the paint roller back in its tray and sat down on one of the kitchen chairs. She winced; recalling that final, decisive afternoon with Rhodri always caused bile to rise in her stomach. She remembered leaving Rhodri's house feeling so utterly complicit, and loathing herself as much as her brother. Rhodri always managed to weaken her resolve with his combination of contrition and naïveté.

It was his naïveté that affected her the most. Although a successful businessman, Rhodri was as innocent as a child. Her brother did not always understand the consequences of his actions. Even in their teenage years, it had been Sara, two years Rhodri's junior, who took the responsible decisions on their behalf, and cajoled her brother into doing what was best for him.

But was being childlike – or perhaps childish – an excuse? Did Rhodri's lack of awareness permit Sara to witness what he did and still love him? Or did her softness make her as guilty as he was? Sara had never come up with an answer, only a restless suspicion that the question itself indicated something wrong with her life.

After she had bandaged up Rhodri's victim, Sara had telephoned Ceri Lloyd. Although there was only eight years' difference in their ages – Sara was thirty-four, Ceri forty-two – her older friend had always been a surrogate mother. Unmarried, with no siblings and two healthy parents, Ceri had a wealth of concern to spare, which she lavished on her job, her passion for local politics, and Sara Jones.

'I'm just not happy here any more,' Sara had said. 'London is awful. My patients don't need me, the police work is unpleasant, and I don't know why I'm suffering through any of it.'

There was a few seconds silence, before Sara surprised herself by adding, 'In fact, I'm thinking of moving back home to Wales.'

'Sara – that's wonderful!' Ceri had cried, immediately adding, 'You'll come and live with me, of course.'

'What?' Sara gasped. She could not imagine living in a house filled with country music and stale cigarette smoke.

'You know I've more room than I need,' Ceri continued. 'You can have an entire side of the house to yourself …'

'Ceri, hang on a minute! I was just thinking out loud.'

Her friend pressed on, unstoppable now, 'You'd rather live on your own? Then I know a perfect farmhouse for you. I'm sure you could get it for a song – it's been on the market for a year …'

That night, Sara had not been able to sleep for thinking about the possibilities. If she couldn't change Rhodri, at least she could distance herself from him. If she couldn't close the emotional gap between herself and Jamie in the shadow of their mutual loss, at least she could widen it with physical separation.

Once she had convinced herself that a move was possible, the rest had been simple. She put her Pimlico flat on the market and sold it the same week. She bought this farmhouse for a fifth of the money she had received for her flat, and took the part-time mental health job Ceri had recommended her for.

And now, Sara thought, there was nothing left to do but decorate her new home and hope that Jamie Harding could soon bid her a fond goodbye. But for that to happen, she knew, Aberystwyth's killer would have to take his leave as well. And there was something about that symbol, about those handwritten names, that made such a scenario seem rather unlikely.

Mrs Davies' small house was in the centre of a terrace, on a cul-de-sac at the northern end of Aberystwyth. As she climbed the steps to her front door and removed her keys from her handbag, Eldon Carson moved around the terrace and eased along a path that ran behind it. A tall wooden fence crowned with barbed wire enclosed the back gardens, but Carson had visited before, and he knew that the gate to Mrs Davies' property was not bolted.

A half-moon was rising in the orange sky, and the garden was a patchwork of amber-hued shadows. Carson leapt noiselessly onto a low, flat-roofed tool shed beneath a willow, and sat cross-legged, watching the back of the house. Within seconds, the kitchen light had snapped on, and Mrs Davies appeared at the sink, filling a kettle. He studied her as she brewed a cup of tea.

Concentrated. What was she thinking of?

She was thinking about an upcoming train journey, to visit her daughter and two grandchildren in Northampton.

She was thinking about whether to record a favourite

old movie on television tonight, and when she'd get a chance to watch it if she did.

She was thinking of an old tune.

The kitchen returned to darkness; a moment later, the first-floor bathroom window cast light over the branches of the tree above his head. He stood and grasped one with both hands. By the time he was at eye level with her bedroom, Mrs Davies had switched on a portable television set at the foot of her bed, and was removing her clothes in the strobing, milky light.

She had decided to watch the movie. At least until she fell asleep.

Carson was no voyeur, but peering unseen through this old lady's bedroom window caused a tingle of illicit excitement. He smiled in spite of himself. Maybe being here was a risk, he thought … but this was his reward. Seeing Mrs Davies here, now, alive.

Besides, he thought, it had been an evening of risk.

He was committed to it now, danger was a path he had chosen, a wheel set in motion that he had no choice but to run with, ready or not.

Eldon Carson smiled fondly as he watched the old woman pull a lacy summer nightgown over her head, and take a small sip of camomile.

'You're safe now, Mrs Davies,' he whispered.

FIVE

The next morning, Sara was on duty at the Promenade Drop-In Centre. She gazed out of the large bay window at the stony beach before her. It was practically deserted, the tourists having read the newspapers and decided to holiday somewhere without a resident killer.

All summer, the familiar sights of Aberystwyth had summoned unbidden images from Sara's childhood. She could almost feel herself out there now, a young child running naked, wet and shivering, across the stones in rubber jellies. Mummy holding a beach towel, Daddy skimming stones with Rhoddo.

She could see the family driving to Cadair Idris, their special mountain, for a day's climb. Or visiting Aunt Issy in Machynlleth, and later poking through the craft shops on the high street. Mummy buying her some pretty Celtic jewellery. So many memories.

The drop-in centre was a service provided by Sara's mental health charity. Her job there was to co-ordinate volunteer counsellors to staff it during opening hours, three days a week; when no volunteer could be found, Sara was required to be on hand herself. On pleasant summer days, qualified volunteers were always thin on the ground, and she had found herself spending an increasing amount of time here. Since the murders, few people were willing to sit alone, greeting strangers with mental health concerns.

The Centre received a diverse range of clients, from depressed students to farmers trying to cope with financial crises. It also played host to a fair share of homeless visitors, passing through the town – although they were sometimes most interested in the free coffee.

Sara could never guess what kind of person would walk through the door: a few weeks previously, a male student in a state of maudlin drunkenness had stopped for a cry, and then turned nasty. Sara had been rescued by the arrival of his more sober mate. The safety of the volunteer counsellors was now a concern that weighed heavily on her mind. She found it hard to believe that the Centre was not equipped with something as simple as a panic button, and had intended to bring it up at the monthly meeting – before it was disrupted by a visit from her past.

In the short term, to ensure her own safety, Sara had started carrying a syringe in her medical bag, pre-loaded with 400mg of pentobarbital. The drug, a barbiturate, was once used to treat everything from anxiety to epilepsy, and was ideal for sedating patients. It was seldom used any more, because of its highly addictive nature, and the fact that overdoses could be fatal. However, it was much faster-acting than any modern alternative.

Sara had not told anybody about this powerful protection. Medically, using sedation as a form of restraint was a grey area at best – and even to consider barbiturates these days would be looked upon as a form of medical malpractice. Had she run it past the charity's solicitor, she knew what the answer would have been.

Sara, however, was not interested in legal opinions. If her life were ever in danger, the legal niceties of her solicitor would be of no help. And with a killer loose, she was unwilling to take chances.

Today, the Centre was empty. Sara returned to the

Pembroke Library

Items that you have checked out

Title: Already dead / Stephen Booth.
ID: DCPL0006682274
Due: 26/01/2022

Title: Dead in time / Terence Bailey
ID: DCPL10003687879
Due: 26/01/2022

Title: No place to die / Neil Broadfoot
ID: DCPL70003393392
Due: 26/01/2022

Title: The hound of death: and other stories /
Agatha Christie
ID: DCPL10002224876
Due: 26/01/2022

Title: The murder game / Rachel Abbott
ID: DCPL70003398803
Due: 26/01/2022

Total items: 5
Account balance: €0.00
Checked out: 8
Overdue: 0
Hold requests: 0
Ready for collection: 0
05/01/2022

Thank you for visiting us today

folding table she used as a desk, where she had laid out prints of several of the crime scene photographs Jamie had sent her. When she heard footsteps on the stairs, she looked up with a gasp, then chided herself for being so jittery. Deliberately, she gathered the photos into a pile, covered them with a pad of paper, and instinctively tugged her medical bag closer.

Ceri entered the room, and Sara sighed with relief.

'Passing through,' the detective said, helping herself to coffee. 'Have you been out recently? I've never seen Aber so empty at tourist season. Usually the Prom's packed with people. Now, our only visitors are reporters.'

Sara joined her old friend, who stared disconsolately through the window. On the Promenade, the bandstand was closed, its corrugated metal doors pulled shut and padlocked. The children's swimming pool overlooking the beach was empty, the clear water's surface flat and unwelcoming. Colourful flags were strung from poles along the length of the sea rail, but on this windless day they hung limp and lifeless. Ceri stared at them. 'Those bloody things should be flown at half-mast,' she said grimly.

Sara sighed. She retreated from the window and sank onto the sofa. 'Change the subject, will you?'

'Okay, then,' Ceri said, 'tell me what happened last night.'

Sara replied with a grin. 'He kept it professional.'

'I suppose that's admirable.' Ceri said grudgingly, She popped a cigarette in her mouth and lit it. A blast of blue smoke shot from her nostrils.

There was no point in reminding her of laws about smoking. 'Why don't you sit down?' Sara replied. 'You get agitated when you stand.'

Ceri pulled a plastic chair away from the table; its metal legs skidded against the floorboards with a shriek.

'You shouldn't worry so much about me and Jamie,' Sara said. 'We were never very serious.'

'Really?' Ceri's tone was sceptical.

Sara shrugged. 'It was the type of thing any co-workers could fall into.'

'So you slept with him for fun?' Ceri frowned and took a pull on her cigarette. 'That doesn't sound like you.'

Sara tugged her short auburn hair pensively. Ceri was right – it didn't sound like her. Fleetingly, she wondered if she was telling either of them the truth.

'I wouldn't call it fun,' she replied slowly. 'Comfort, maybe. You have to understand, the investigations were never pleasant.'

The inspector snorted a blast of smoke knowingly. 'Few are – and with occult crime, things are bound to get ugly.'

'Even when there turned out to be no occult connection,' Sara replied, 'the crimes themselves were always upsetting. I found that a lot of police officers shield their feelings by making morbid jokes about the victims –'

'Not around me,' Ceri interrupted. 'My officers know I don't like it.'

'Jamie was different. He empathised with victims – and others connected to the case, like me. He made us feel we were making the best of a bad situation, trying to heal wounds.'

Ceri drained her coffee and dropped the fag-end in the cup. Her silence sounded to Sara like an accusation.

'He's a decent person,' she stressed. 'When I got pregnant, he asked me if I intended to keep the baby. I told him I would never have an abortion without a good reason – and there simply wasn't one. I'm financially secure and emotionally stable; I was perfectly well-equipped to be a mother. He didn't put any pressure on me … instead, he proposed.'

'So?' Ceri said flatly.

'So, wouldn't you call that decent?'

'I suspect it was more than decency,' Ceri said wryly.

Sara closed her eyes and massaged her temples; the conversation was giving her a headache. 'What do you mean?' she asked.

'I mean,' Ceri said, 'that Jamie Harding is deeply in love with you.'

Jamie drove along the coastal road that linked the harbour town of Aberaeron with Aberystwyth. To his left, Cardigan Bay sparkled in the pure-white sunlight, sailboats cutting through the choppy waves that skimmed its turquoise water. It was unnerving to think that all this beauty – the placid serenity of this place – had been the scene of such horror in Sara's life.

Until he and Sara became lovers he had known nothing of what had happened to her parents. In a rare moment of intimacy, she had revealed her desperate and lifelong pain. Somehow his words of comfort had seemed so awkward and small.

In the days following her revelation, he had searched online newspaper archives, collecting the details of the day on which her childhood had been wrenched so violently from her. He hadn't told her about his research, but didn't think it intrusive. He had wanted to help: to understand her past, so that he could offer her a better future.

Then, a series of events took place so quickly that they still didn't seem real. Sara had become pregnant, Jamie had proposed, and she had lost the baby. That loss was also the death of their relationship, for reasons Sara had never explained. All he had managed to discover was that Sara had suffered an 'incomplete spontaneous abortion,' likely due to a genetic abnormality. That wasn't uncommon in older mothers, he had been assured ... as if thirty-four were old, and as if that fact would lessen his grief.

On the day she fled London, Sara had left a brief message on Jamie's mobile. He could still hear her words in his mind, thin and distant: Goodbye ... sorry ... please don't call.

At first he had obeyed. He tried to keep tabs through Facebook, but she stopped posting, then deleted her account. Finally, he lost patience and rang – more than once. She always let his call go to voicemail. Finally, she changed her number.

To his right, he took in the green and brown hills that rolled back for miles from the road. The only man-made thing he could see was a line of wind turbines stretching across the horizon. Their white blades, turning in a synchronised, graceful rotation, seemed as natural a part of the landscape as the hills on which they stood.

When Special Branch had received the email from Aberystwyth CID, Jamie studied the symbol, and recognised a possible occult link ... and a conflict-free path back to Sara Jones. He imagined it all: she would have no choice but to help; they would discuss the case; and slowly, their conversation would turn more personal. But he hadn't guessed Sara's ability to divide the personal and professional would be so firm. Last night, in the face of her uncompromising professionalism, he'd been stymied.

Now, he asked himself why he couldn't have simply shouted, 'Damn it, I love you!'

Jamie was snapped from his reverie by a low pulse of sound behind him, which turned into a ferocious shriek as a fighter jet passed. It was an incongruous feature of Mid-Wales: the sparsely populated, mountainous terrain made it ideal ground for RAF training manoeuvres. Visitors had to get used to military aircraft ripping the sky when they were least expected.

As if set off by the tremors overhead, Jamie's mobile began to vibrate.

After listening to the grim news with a sinking feeling in the pit of his stomach, he pressed down hard on the accelerator.

'Believe me,' Sara said with a dismissive shudder, 'Jamie Harding is not in love with me. That's why I couldn't face him after I lost the baby. I knew he'd try to be compassionate, but I wasn't interested in watching him cover up his relief.'

Absently, Ceri crushed her empty polystyrene cup and dropped its remains in the bin next to her. 'You were right to leave London,' she said. 'You know I never liked your involvement in forensic psychology – it's the last thing you should have mucked about with, considering what you went through as a teenager.'

'Do you blame Jamie for that?' Sara asked.

Ceri stared at her blankly. 'Of course I do.'

'Well, you're wrong to. I was involved with that kind of work before I ever met him.'

'Maybe peripherally – but that was all. When Harding started using you as his own special consultant, you got yourself sucked into a world you never deserved to be part of.'

A dishevelled man with a bedroll strapped to his back and a small cloth bag over one arm entered the room cautiously. Sara sat up and greeted him professionally: '*Bore da.*'

The man stared at Ceri, noted her police uniform warily, and helped himself silently to coffee. Sara shrugged and turned her attention back to her friend. She spoke in a low voice. 'I don't regret anything,' she said, an edge of petulance creeping into her tone. 'When you came to me, afterwards, you saw me at my worst. It's no wonder you hate Jamie.'

Ceri shook her head stubbornly. '"Hate" is the wrong word.'

The vagrant eyed her again, gripped his cup firmly and trudged down the stairs. They heard the street door swing open, and shut with a rattle.

'Maybe I don't know Harding from Adam,' Ceri said softly, 'but I do know the life he leads. Trust me, you wouldn't want to be married to his lifestyle.'

Reaching out, Ceri stroked her friend on the back of the hand. 'My advice: give Detective Inspector Harding whatever insights you've had, then tell him you never want to see him again. You deserve an easier time of it.'

Sara shook her hand away. 'I don't want an easier time,' she snapped. 'As for forensic psychology – I've been trying my whole life to understand what happened when I was fourteen. You should know that.'

Ceri sighed. 'The difference between us is that you still think there's something you can comprehend. I'm more cynical. Sometimes bad things happen, often because some people are plain wicked. There's no point in looking any farther.'

Sara's phone rang, and she picked it up with something like relief. Ceri watched her expression turn swiftly to despair. When Sara rang off, she ran to the bay window, straining to see the north end of the promenade. 'Oh my God,' she muttered, her jaws clenched tight.

'What's wrong?' Ceri asked, her voice hollow with trepidation.

'That was Jamie,' Sara replied. 'They've found another body, with the same MO.'

'Where?'

'Up there, on Constitution Hill.' She turned to Ceri, her face noticeably pale, even under her carefully applied make-up. 'Ceri, it's a teenage boy.'

At the top of Aberystwyth's Constitution Hill stood the world's largest Camera Obscura – a round building where tourists could watch events outside projected onto a circular screen. They were popular amusements in Victorian times, but this one was only thirty years old. To reach it, visitors had to climb a zigzagging path, or ride the Cliff Railway carved into the side of the rock.

On this bright, warm morning, the entire northern end of Victoria Terrace was sealed off with blue-and-white police tape. Sara and Ceri pressed through a small crowd of spectators and reporters. The reporters shouted questions and snapped photos with furious professionalism, while the locals watched silently, their expressions solemn, troubled.

Sara and Ceri ducked underneath the tape, and a constable escorted them to the railway car, where they were lifted slowly upwards. The observation area at the top was a wide lea of gravel and grass, with a restaurant surrounded by picnic tables. The Camera Obscura itself loomed over them, on a hillock to their right. Over at one picnic table sat a young woman staring blankly towards the restaurant. Sara guessed that she had discovered the body. Two forensic experts crawled about the area, as Jamie conferred with the CID detective inspector, his sergeant, and the local police surgeon.

Sara approached them, with Ceri following. 'Where's the boy?' she asked flatly.

'Round the side, near the back of the building,' Jamie replied. 'Found about ninety minutes ago.' Sara glanced at the young woman again, and noted that she was shivering, despite the heat of the morning. 'Although,' Jamie continued, 'ramblers must have passed by before then.'

They walked around to the side of the restaurant. Ceri scanned the path that ran up the nearby hillock. 'Unless someone actually looked down, the body would have been easy to miss.'

Hanging in the air, Sara caught her first, faint whiff of excrement; the boy had emptied his bowels as he died. He was dark-haired and around fourteen. A swarm of insects darted around him. Sara crouched down, and fanned them away from the boy's face. It had once been angelic.

'One of the constables identified him,' Jamie said. 'His name was Aled Morgan; he lived on a council estate in Penparcau.'

Sara noticed that Aled Morgan's cheeks, temples and forehead were dirty and torn, as if struck, but no blood had run from the wounds. On the right side of his throat was a single slash of about ten centimetres.

The police surgeon crouched next to Sara. 'An oblique wound,' he said, 'long and deep. I'm no expert in this type of thing, but I'm guessing it was made from behind.'

'It was,' Sara said dully. She forced herself to squint more closely at the slash. 'I'd say it passed through the external jugular vein, the internal jugular, and the common carotid artery. There are no hesitation marks on the neck; the offender managed it in a single stroke ... although the margins are slightly variegated.'

'Sorry?' asked Ceri.

'The edges of the wound are jagged,' Jamie explained grimly. 'His knife's dull.'

'How long would the boy have lived?' Ceri asked.

'Not long, thank God,' said Sara. 'He'd have lost consciousness immediately, then died of an air embolism to the heart.'

Jamie jerked his head towards the observation area. 'It happened over there, at that table near the fence.'

He led them back to a picnic table. It, and the gravel and grass under it, were coated in dried blood. To the left was a stunning panorama of Aberystwyth, its coastline curving in an arc towards the pier. Beyond that were the castle and harbour. The sun, Sara guessed, would have been setting to the boy's right.

'We know he was smoking cannabis,' Jamie said, 'possibly enough to miss his assailant's approach from behind. It seems that the offender pushed Aled's head into the table, pulled it back up by his hair, and then slashed his throat.'

'Have his parents been notified?' Ceri asked.

Jamie shook his head. 'The constable went to his mother's house – she isn't home. He's making enquiries as to her whereabouts.'

'Wouldn't she have noticed him missing last night?' Sara asked.

'You'd be surprised,' Ceri said. 'Some kids stay out late. Maybe the mother works shifts, leaves before he wakes up …'

Sara thought of the poor boy's mother, at work, maybe half a mile away, unaware that her child was sprawled at the top of Constitution Hill, dead. She walked back towards the café, and the crumpled body on its far side. 'What about the symbol? Is there one?'

Jamie tilted his head. 'Nothing visible, but we haven't moved the body. The pathologist is on his way up from Cardiff. I wouldn't be surprised if he found one drawn somewhere on his skin.'

Jamie looked back towards the rear of the pub. 'Did you notice his facial wounds?'

'Post-mortem,' Sara said with a nod.

'How do you know?' Ceri asked.

'They haven't bled,' Sara replied. 'Living people bleed, corpses don't – their blood isn't circulating.'

'It seems that he beat the boy after death,' Jamie said.

Overhead, the RAF fighter jet screamed by. Jamie waited until the aircraft's roar quelled to a dull rumble before adding, 'Sounds like another message, doesn't it?'

Eldon Carson stood, brooding, at the window of his room in the Bryn Y Môr Guest House. The imposing hotel, once a hall for nineteenth-century women students, sat at the end of Victoria Terrace, in the shadow of Constitution Hill. Having chosen it for its location, Carson had reserved his room by telephone a week ago, and was relieved its owner hadn't asked for a credit card number. He had been at the window since before dawn, distractedly ripping sheets of paper from a thick spiral notebook, cutting them into strips and colouring them with the few pencil crayons he carried, then folding the strips into shapes. Some were abstract structures, others remarkably competent origami animals: a swan, a giraffe, a cat. They littered every surface of the room.

Now, Carson gazed down at the rubberneckers standing next to the police tape, waiting for the body to be brought down the hill. How much did these people understand?

Watching the aftermath of yesterday's actions brought back all of its angst: the pounding blood in his neck, the hyper-alertness, the pensiveness, the nausea. Especially the nausea. Killing Aled Morgan had been the hardest thing Carson had been forced to do since embarking on this terrible, necessary course.

He didn't want to think about that poor kid; Carson's new responsibility sickened him. Still, he forced himself to watch its aftermath, from the moment the waitress rode the rail car up to work, to the police's response after she found the body, to Sara Jones arriving on the scene with the lady cop. Seeing her there, passing through the security cordon, had caused him to shudder in anticipation. Even through binoculars, Sara looked so cool, so well-crafted – like one of his origami swans. The immaculate makeup, the designer khakis, the expensive russet blouse ... all perfectly matched to the red-brown sheen of her short, spiky hair. Only a perfectionist could make hair look like that.

But even she misjudged him. They all assumed he was a psychopath, and that was infuriating. Carson burned with the desire for them to understand what he understood, to come to the same realisations that he had arrived at. To know he wasn't to blame.

Nonetheless, there was no point in telling them straight; it would sound like the ramblings of the insane. To win their forgiveness, maybe even their gratitude, he had to lead them along. The question had been, what hints, clues, and signs would guide them to the right conclusions? It had not taken Carson long to realise that burning Kapadia had been too subtle. When the radio said he'd been trying to destroy evidence, he'd felt physically sick, and knew he would have to give them more to work with.

Live and learn. Carson looked down to one of his paper sculptures, onto which he had drawn his special 'Eye in the Pyramid' design. Would they understand now? He hoped so. At least Sara Jones would – she would have to know the truth.

Because Sara Jones needed Eldon Carson.

When Aled Morgan's black-bagged body was loaded into the back of an ambulance in front of the Cliff Railway Station, Carson knew it was time to go. Soon, the cops would learn of the muscular young American who'd taken a room just before the murder, and left right after its discovery.

And after they learned that, he thought, sitting down at

the small desk across from the bed, they would receive this. Carson pulled his notepad towards him, and began to write a letter.

SIX

Over the next couple of days, Sara did her best to force from her mind the image of Aled Morgan's stained yellow T-shirt, and the lad's dark brown fringe tumbling over his slumped face – the face that had been beaten after death. Whenever she felt compelled to phone Jamie about the pathologist's findings, those pictures would form in her mind like spectres, and she would find a less upsetting diversion to occupy her time.

Sara had stopped taking her anti-depressants some time ago. She knew Dr Shapiro would not approve, but she had made other attempts to keep her feelings at bay. She had continued, compulsively, to decorate her kitchen – sanding, filling cracks, painting walls, making everything smooth, bright and uniform. This psychological ruse had been at least partly successful: it had filled Sara's spare hours, but now she found that the labour was not mentally challenging enough to keep her mind from wandering. Banishing images of Aled, Sara had only created a vacuum, which she filled by thoughts of Jamie Harding.

It was Thursday evening when Sara first realised she was missing him; they hadn't spoken for maybe twenty hours. She told herself she was mislabelling the emotion: Jamie's re-emergence was bound to stir up memories. It did not mean the hollowness she felt without him was significant.

Yet, just before drifting off to sleep in the wee hours of Friday morning, she had found herself wondering what it would be like if they became a couple once again.

Sara's job at the mental health charity was supposed to be part-time, and Friday was one of her days off. That morning, without the clock-radio to rouse her, she woke up late, with one certainty buzzing in her mind: if she and Jamie ever did get back together, she did not want the kind of relationship they'd had before. She was no longer willing to settle for a haphazard affair that meant nothing to either of them. And that understanding had allowed her thoughts of Jamie to fade through the morning, as if exhausted by so much wear and tear.

In the early afternoon, she entered her kitchen looking for lunch, and stopped to admire the progress she had made in the room. Every wall now glowed a pleasant golden yellow. The paintings which had once graced her Harley Street office hung on either side of the Welsh dresser, and an Aboriginal parrying shield was mounted next to the refrigerator. Encouraged by what she saw, she resolved to begin clearing the stable of boxes – perhaps that very afternoon. She needed indoor activities: a heavy fog had rolled in off the bay, and was snaking its tendrils around trees and through shrubs, hovering above the ground like wraiths. She certainly did not want to go out in weather like this.

She poured herself a glass of red wine and shuddered. This, she thought, was what it should have looked like on the day Aled Morgan was murdered. Instead, the pleasant weather had made a mockery of the dead boy. Gulping her wine, she tried to shake away those visions – the same ones she had been shutting out for two days. Stained T-shirt, tumbling fringe, and a lifeless, angelic face.

Shuddering once more, Sara pulled open the fridge and took stock of the contents. She needed distraction, and decided that making a bigger-than-usual lunch would keep her occupied.

She settled on linguini with a home-made sauce. Working her way through a second glass of red wine, Sara fried finely chopped mushrooms, leeks, and garlic in a large cast-iron skillet. In London, she had eaten most of her meals out, and had only begun to discover the pleasures of the kitchen after moving to Penweddig. And they *were* pleasures, she was learning. Making her own meals had become yet another form of therapy, a way to create something beautiful and beneficial to her life every day. She tossed a handful of chopped tomatoes into the frying pan, lowered the heat, and cocked her ear.

Outside, she heard the scraping of holly bushes against metal. Sara's three-bedroom cottage lay on the outskirts of Penweddig, set into a hillside. Visitors had to drive along a potholed dirt path, overgrown with weeds and holly on either side. The farmer who owned the path had agreed to clear the brush and repair the lane, but so far had done neither. The sides of Sara's BMW were already scratched, and any visitor's car faced a similar fate.

She looked out the window to see Jamie's Land Rover sweeping around her large driveway, and was surprised to feel her pulse speed up. She checked her appearance in the glass of a cabinet. Pulling open the kitchen door, she noticed that Jamie had small bags under his eyes.

He laid his briefcase on Sara's large pine table, and withdrew his handkerchief, mopping his forehead. Sara had not noticed how hot the hob had made the kitchen.

'That smells good,' he said.

She smiled, and took the frying pan off the heat. 'It's sauce for linguine. Almost ready.'

He slumped in a chair. She wondered if he was here on business, or had just stopped by for lunch. 'You look tired,' she said, putting a pot of water on to boil.

Jamie made a sound of agreement and Sara poured red wine into a goblet. 'Too tired for this? I've also got beer.'

He sat forwards, forcing himself into alertness. 'I'll settle for juice.'

'Ah ... of course,' Sara said, feeling disappointed. It was a business call. She filled a tumbler. 'So,' she said, handing him the glass and slipping quickly into role, 'what did the pathologist find?'

'There was a symbol, and one name, written on the boy's back.' Jamie took a quick gulp of juice, and hesitated. 'Our villain has an interest in your friend, Mrs Davies.'

Sara gasped. 'From the mental health charity? It was her name?'

Jamie nodded blankly. 'Don't worry,' he said, 'a detective constable has already spoken to her, and they've installed alarm mats and various other equipment at the premises.'

Sara sat, suddenly weakened by the peculiar sensation of finding herself linked in another, strange way to this case. 'I was with her when Aled Morgan was murdered,' she said. 'Did she have any connection to the boy?'

'It appears he worked for her. Odd jobs, gardening.'

'The poor woman,' Sara whispered. 'How is she taking the news of his death?'

'If she doesn't stop leaving us messages with more questions, everyone's going to go mad.'

Sara smiled in spite of herself. Mrs Davies had a habit of throwing herself into situations that didn't involve her at all – Sara could imagine what she must be like in a case where she was a central character.

'Naturally,' Jamie went on, 'she's wondering why the

killer might be concerned with her, and her relationship with the late Master Morgan. Frankly, so am I.' He popped open the clasps of his case. 'A lot has happened since we spoke.'

Sara nodded in agreement. 'It certainly has.'

'More than you know,' Jamie said. 'The offender has made contact.'

'What?'

He pulled out a rumpled piece of paper from his briefcase. 'This was received in the morning's post.'

Sara took the paper from Jamie's hands. It had been torn from a spiral notebook. As Jamie rose and filled his drained tumbler with water from the tap, she read the small, very neat handwriting:

"Please try to understand my motives. I know the truth of events before they have been revealed. I did not ask for this, but realize now I cannot run from the duty it brings. The Kapadia family, Miss Elliott & Mrs Davies are safe, & that is what matters. One of you will know the truth."

Under the words, as neatly rendered as it had been on flesh, the murderer had left his signature: the eye, the pyramid.

Sara stared at it, her eyes were blank with thought.

'First impressions?' Jamie asked.

Sara nodded slowly. 'I think I know what he's on about.'

He arched an eyebrow. 'You know?'

'Well, I have a hunch ...' Suddenly, a swell of certainty rose within her, and she blurted, 'Jamie, this guy thinks he's psychic.'

The inspector stared at her levelly, his expression implacable but his eyes thoughtful.

'I'm sure of it,' Sara added emphatically.

He sat silently and rubbed his tired eyes. 'The possibility had occurred to me, too,' he said.

Sara felt a prickle of defensiveness. 'Have you discounted it?' she asked.

'Not out of hand. He says he knows the truth of events before they have been revealed. That could refer to psychic powers, but it could also mean he's got inside information from some other source.'

'That's not likely when you consider his emblem,' Sara countered. 'My bet is that that eye represents him – or at least his psychic powers.'

Jamie leaned over her shoulder and looked again at the photocopied note. 'So he believes his supposed powers present him with a duty. A mission.'

'The mission to administer justice,' Sara agreed.

The more she articulated these thoughts, the surer she was that she was right. It was almost as if she was thinking with the killer's mind, understanding what he understood.

Sara stared at the symbol drawn on the bottom of the note. Suddenly, she had another flash of insight. 'It should have occurred to me before,' she said. 'I know what these semi-circles at the bottom of the pyramid are. They're scales – symbolic scales of justice.'

Jamie raised his eyebrows, then nodded thoughtfully. 'That's possible … but justice for whom?' he asked.

'For the Kapadias … Miss Elliott … Mrs Davies. He was never threatening them, Jamie, he was avenging them!' The pot on the hob boiled furiously and steam was filling the room. 'He believes he can look at people and see the wrongs that they've done – and who they've done them to. He feels that this special power gives him the responsibility to do something about it … so he kills them for their crimes.'

She opened the refrigerator door and drew out a packet

of fresh pasta.

Jamie frowned sceptically. 'What did little Aled Morgan do to Mrs Davies?'

Sara paused. 'I don't know,' she admitted, peeling the plastic packet open, 'but don't you think it's worth finding out?'

Jamie shook his head, bemused by the force of Sara's enthusiasm. 'Look,' he said patiently, 'even if we find out that Aled had wronged Mrs Davies, where does that leave Carol Elliott? All Dan Williams ever did was buy fags from her.'

Sara dropped pasta into the boiling water. 'That's what Carol Elliott claims. But who knows what their relationship really was? Maybe he did something she's afraid to admit.'

She looked into Jamie's green eyes. He was sceptical, but wanted to give her the benefit of the doubt. For reasons more complicated than she could articulate, she needed Jamie to be convinced. 'And we don't know how Mr Kapadia treated his family,' she said.

Jamie broke their gaze, and stared into the distance, blinking several times. 'To accept this premise,' he said finally, 'you'd have to believe the offender really is psychic.'

Sara shook her head. 'You don't have to believe that at all,' she said. 'It's possible there was no connection between Miss Elliott and Mr Williams, but the killer imagines there was. Or maybe they were acquainted, but he knows about it by some other means.'

She strode back to the table and dropped into her seat. 'Look, Jamie, I don't have all the answers. But based on this letter and that symbol, my gut says I'm on the right track.'

Jamie thought, then chuckled mirthlessly. 'A psychic vigilante multiple murderer. Jesus.'

They remained silent for a moment, listening to the light rain which had begun drumming on the kitchen's flat roof. Finally, Jamie broke their silence. 'What do you really believe about psychic phenomena?' he asked. 'Do you think they're real?'

Sara took a deep breath and exhaled slowly. 'You and I have both seen things we can't explain,' she said. 'But I've also found that most people who claim to have special powers are either deluded or lying for their own gain.'

'Most,' Jamie agreed. 'But it's hard to say that about all of them, isn't it?'

She chewed on her lower lip, but avoided answering his question. 'I need to talk to the people our killer claims to have avenged. Then, maybe I'll know more.'

Jamie nodded. 'I think it's a good idea.' He rubbed his eyes, still tired but visibly more relaxed. Sara smiled awkwardly, and stood again. She put the frying pan back on the heat.

'One of you will know the truth,' Jamie quoted. 'What do you think he means by that?'

Sara shook her head. 'I have no idea,' she said.

She did not voice her suspicion that she might yet learn.

All morning, Jamie's physical exhaustion had clashed with the adrenaline rush, and spirals of questions, that came in the wake of important new evidence. His conversation with Sara had offered the kind of insights he had so often relied on in the past. Her trenchant observations and furious certainty had always made her a valuable ally – and now he felt she might be his ally once again.

And yet, as they ate in near-silence, Jamie realised neither of them knew where to take the conversation next.

It was the first time they had shared a personal moment since the previous winter.

Without consciously intending to do so, Jamie found himself saying, 'Inspector Lloyd doesn't like me, does she?'

Sara looked up at him with surprise that gave way quickly to a look of wry amusement. She chewed her food slowly and swallowed before saying, 'She respects you as a detective inspector.'

Jamie smiled at her diplomacy. 'Do I threaten her?'

Sara wrinkled her nose. 'Why would you?'

'Well …' He shrugged. 'I thought she might see me as competition.'

'Really?' Sara asked dubiously. 'I can't imagine why; you two have nothing in common. You work in London, she works here. You're from Special Branch, and she runs a sub-station.' She took another mouthful of pasta, as if the issue had been resolved.

'I didn't mean professionally,' Jamie countered, and drew a deep breath before plunging ahead. 'I meant, she might see me as competition for you.'

Sara swallowed and furrowed her brow as she turned over the implications of Jamie's suggestion. Deliberately, she set down her fork. 'What do you mean?' she asked, an edge of suspicion creeping into her voice.

He shrugged awkwardly and wondered how he could put it without sounding like a lout. 'I mean, don't you think she's … well, perhaps a bit sweet on you?'

Sara stared at him blankly. '*Sweet on me*?'

'Bad choice of words,' he conceded, and groaned inwardly. He found himself wishing he could turn back time by about ninety seconds. 'I only mean,' he stammered, 'that I've noticed she –'

'Ceri cares about me, yes,' Sara bristled. 'And I care about her. She's like a mother to me.'

'A mother? She's only a few years older than you.'

'Eight,' Sara said crisply. 'She's forty-two. And back when she was twenty-two, she took care of Rhoddo and me. On the day our parents died.'

Jamie froze in shocked embarrassment. Ceri Lloyd had not been mentioned in any of the reports he had seen. He realised how superficial his knowledge of Sara's past had been.

'I'm sorry,' he whispered.

'She was only a young constable then,' Sara continued. 'She soothed us, comforted us as well as she could. Even after we'd moved in with our aunt, Ceri would visit, talk to our social worker, and take us out now and then.'

'It's nice that you had someone special like that,' Jamie said contritely, 'and that you're still close.'

He lowered his gaze and twirled strands of linguine onto his fork.

SEVEN

Mrs Davies' house was not what Sara had expected. She had imagined a cramped warren of eccentric mementoes, floral storage boxes, and piles of yellowing paper, befitting a widow who had developed a strange cluster of interests and habits. Instead, Irene Davies' living room was sparsely furnished in a tasteful blend of dusty blues and greens on cream. Delicate porcelain figurines were arranged neatly on glass shelves. A glass-topped coffee table held a bowl of porous stone fruit. The range of charities and causes to which the old woman devoted her time was represented by a series of labelled file boxes, in alphabetical order along a wall. Other than these, the room was uncluttered, and spotless.

This pleased Sara. Not only did it suggest that Mrs Davies had more sides to her than Sara had given her credit for, but also that some of them may have been closer to Sara's own tastes and personality than she might previously have assumed. Perhaps the old woman wasn't exactly a kindred spirit, but Sara felt badly for having stereotyped her, for caricaturing her in her thoughts.

'I was shocked,' Mrs Davies said, holding a large bone china cup and saucer on her knees, 'absolutely shocked. I mean, one couldn't have called Aled a sweet boy, not by any means – he was rather troubled in fact, and could be awfully sullen – but I was fond of him, deep down. When I heard about his …'

She shifted uncomfortably. 'When I heard what happened, I telephoned his mother, both to pass on my regrets – it was only courteous, I thought – and to suggest some counselling options I thought she might be in need of.'

She shuffled her velour-slippered feet on the rich wool carpet. A sleeping Chihuahua stretched. 'She was rather rude to me, as it happens. I put it down to grief.'

Sara nodded, and took a sip of her Earl Grey tea – the only tea Mrs Davies had that was not herbal. The woman was doing her best to appear composed, but Sara knew that these events had shaken her. 'What kind of work did Aled do for you, Mrs Davies?'

'Oh, gardening, cleaning, what-have-you.' She waved her free hand. 'I prefer to devote my time to causes, and I don't see why I should push the Dyson around when there are young people needing a pound or two.' She pursed her thin lips. 'I didn't like to hear about the cannabis – I don't want to think that was where my money was going. I often thought that Aled would benefit from an intensive course of counselling. I only regret now that I didn't suggest it to him.'

Mrs Davies fixed Sara with a sharp stare, and said, 'Now, Sara, I have answered several of your questions, perhaps you can answer one or two of mine. I suspect that your detective has not told me everything about the danger I am in. He refuses to return my telephone calls.'

'He's very busy,' Sara said.

'I don't imagine the police install alarm mats in a woman's home for no valid reason.' She plucked at the pleats in her skirt. 'Why was my name left on Aled's – well, his body?'

Although police had been keeping news of the killer's

strange forms of communication from the public, the detective heading the investigation had told Mrs Davies; there was no other way to explain their sudden interest in protecting her. She did not know about the eye in the pyramid symbol, only that her name had been found inscribed on Aled. She had been asked to keep that information quiet, and had done so.

Now, Sara decided it was safe to tell the woman as much of the truth as she could. 'We're working on the theory that he was trying to get revenge against Aled, on your behalf.'

'On *my* behalf?' Mrs Davies gasped. 'What in heaven's name for?'

'We're not sure,' Sara said. 'I was hoping you might have some idea.'

Mrs Davies drew in a hesitant breath, and set her teacup down on the carpet. As she did, her hands trembled slightly, and the bone china rattled. 'I can't imagine why anyone would kill Aled because of me,' she said.

'How was your relationship?' Sara asked. 'Had he done anything recently to annoy you?'

Mrs Davies remained silent for a time, rocking slightly in her chair. Finally, she spoke in a quiet voice. 'Well ... I did catch him stealing from me,' she admitted.

A surge of something like excitement pulsed through Sara, but she forced herself to remain nonchalant. 'Tell me about it.'

'There isn't much to say,' Mrs Davies said. 'I was relaxing in the garden, and came in to find him going through my handbag. He made some excuse and denied stealing anything – but ten pounds had disappeared. Knowing what I know now, I can only assume he took it for drugs.'

'Was this the first time you'd noticed anything missing?'

She clenched her frail jaw, and raised her eyebrows as if pondering whether to say any more. Sara had never known Irene Davies to resist that temptation. Finally, the woman said, 'As a matter of fact, I had lost small amounts before, but I'd never connected it to Aled.'

She paused, then added, 'Or, if I had, I didn't have enough proof to say anything. Of course, when I caught him at my handbag, I asked him about all of it. Perhaps I accused him outright, I can't remember – but, either way, he simply called me a filthy name and ran off. A few minutes later, I realised he still had a key to my house.'

'He kept a key?'

'It was more convenient that way. I'm often out.'

Sara sat very still, pondering the implications. Finally, she said, 'Mrs Davies, at the Mental Health meeting you were concerned about a prowler. Did you ever consider it might have been Aled?'

The woman stiffened, then nodded almost imperceptibly.

'You spoke to Inspector Lloyd that same night,' Sara continued. 'Why didn't you mention your suspicions to her?'

'I didn't want to get the boy in trouble,' Mrs Davies replied. 'I know you think of me as a busybody, Sara, but I don't enjoy seeing children in trouble with the police.'

'Then why did you report a prowler at all?'

'I wasn't certain it was Aled. And if it was, I hoped the occasional patrol car might frighten him away.'

'You also started calling his home,' Sara said, and Mrs Davies appeared startled that she possessed this intelligence. 'You left messages on his mother's answering machine.'

'Rather a few, I'm afraid,' the old woman admitted with a sigh. 'I wanted my key back. Wouldn't you have?'

Sara could imagine the tone of the messages, and was

not surprised that Aled's mother did not want her condolences now.

'What could I have done differently?' the old woman said plaintively, spreading her hands. 'Would Aled be alive today if I'd told Inspector Lloyd the truth? Or if I'd just let him steal my money?'

'I don't know, Mrs Davies,' Sara said. 'Either way, this is not your fault.'

Mrs Davies arched her eyebrows, as if she considered the jury still to be out on that issue. When she spoke again, her voice was melancholy. 'I've lived in this town a long time,' she said. 'I can remember the tragedy of your parents' deaths. When you applied for the job at the Task Force and someone told me who you were, I was surprised that you would want to come back here. Recently, I was even more shocked to find you'd got yourself involved in this murder investigation.'

She shook her head and looked at Sara with something like reproach. 'How can you stand it?' she asked.

'Mrs Davies,' Sara said briskly, 'at the moment, we don't know who the killer is ... but clearly, he knows you. It's possible the two of you have even met. Can you think of anyone – any unusual person – you have been in contact with recently?'

Irene Davies smiled thinly and swept a bony hand over the row of file boxes, each representing a charity or special interest group. 'Sara, look at what I do with my time,' she said. 'How can I help meeting strange people?'

Sara pulled away from the house, a knot of tension in her stomach. It was the way she always felt after dealing with Irene Davies. Her driving was less accomplished than usual in the stop-go Saturday traffic, starting with lurches and stopping with jerks. When her mobile rang, she punched the car's Bluetooth button so hard she nearly cracked the screen. 'Yes, hello,' she snapped.

'Let me guess,' Jamie chuckled. 'You've just interviewed Mrs Davies.'

'Oh, hi,' she said awkwardly. They had not spoken since yesterday's uncomfortable lunch. 'Mrs Davies isn't so bad.'

'Did it go well?'

'I found out some things,' Sara replied, taking strength from her official role of psychologist. 'Aled Morgan had been stealing from her. And he had a key to her house.'

'Interesting. Were you planning to talk to Carol Elliott today?'

Sara confirmed that she had an appointment at the Spar where Miss Elliott worked.

'Good,' Jamie replied briskly. 'Let's meet there in five minutes.'

'You want to come?'

'I need to. Your theories about her connection with Williams might just turn out to be more accurate than I thought.'

A prickle of anticipation did away with Sara's frustration. 'What have you learned?'

'Not over a mobile,' Jamie said. 'I'll see you outside the shop.'

When Sara got to the front of the shop, Jamie was waiting. She looked at him eagerly, and he smiled grimly. 'The late Mr Williams,' he said crisply, 'was a rapist.'

'What?'

He nodded and brushed a lock of copper hair from his eyes. 'Convicted in Wolverhampton, when he was sixteen, for sexually assaulting an ex-classmate. Four years later, he was questioned for two other assaults in Birmingham, but never prosecuted. Since then, he hasn't stayed in one location for long.'

Sara stared at him. 'Why didn't you know this before?'

'We didn't find any identification at the scene, so the only details we had were the ones he had supplied to his employers.'

'Why does that matter?'

'He had listed his year of birth as 1989, when actually, it was 1991.'

Sara blinked. 'And?'

'I suppose he was afraid the construction company would ask the police to run a check on him,' Jamie continued. 'Under the Rehabilitation of Offenders Act, his conviction would become spent after ten years, and they wouldn't have had to know about it – but his rehabilitation period still had two years to run.'

Sara shook her head in puzzlement. 'I'm sorry, I'm not following you. Obviously he didn't want to risk his employment, but what has the year he was born got to do with it?'

'Without fingerprints, a police search is conducted by name and birth date. With inaccurate data – and that could simply be the wrong year of birth – the search will turn up no convictions.'

'That's incredible!' Sara gasped.

Jamie raised his hands in helpless agreement. 'It wouldn't protect anyone from a major investigation – but even then, it might slow us down,' he said.

'So you're agreeing with what I said before? That Mr Williams may have raped Miss Elliott?'

'Or maybe tried to. We know he patronised this shop.'

Through the window, Sara could see Carol Elliott sitting at the till, laughing with a male customer.

'Let's go in,' Jamie said.

When Jamie and Sara entered the shop, the young customer skulked away, and began looking randomly at bags of flour and packs of Bisto. He was dressed in cut-off jeans, a cheap padded jacket, and a backwards cricket cap. Jamie introduced himself and Sara to Miss Elliott, then turned and flashed his badge at her only customer, asking him to make his purchases quickly and leave. The shop, he said, would be closing for a few minutes.

'Er – he's not a customer, actually,' Carol said. 'He's my boyfriend, Brett. I asked him to be here.'

The spotty young lad looked up, eyes dull with defiance.

'It would be better if we could talk alone,' Sara said quietly. 'Our questions might be a bit personal.'

'S'okay,' the lad called from the corner of the shop. 'S'not embarrassed 'round me.' He had a Mancunian accent.

Jamie turned to Carol and stared questioningly. She licked her lips nervously. 'I'd rather he stayed, please.'

Jamie shot a glance at Sara, his green eyes shining with annoyance. Sara shrugged.

'Okay,' he said at length. He withdrew a notebook and pen from his pocket and tore a sheet from the back. On it he wrote *Back in 15 Minutes*, and stuck it to the door. 'Can you lock this?' he asked.

The girl secured the door and led them out the back entrance, to a small paved area littered with boxes and wooden skips. They perched where they could, and Brett lit a cigarette.

'Do you remember when you last spoke to the detective constable? He showed you a picture of Mr Williams.' He held out the photograph. 'Please look at it again.'

Carol glanced at it, and Brett leaned over her shoulder to study it as well, smoke leaking from his slack lips.

'You told the constable that this man would come in occasionally for cigarettes, is that correct?'

She nodded nervously. 'Yeah.'

'And you don't recall ever seeing him outside this shop?'

'No.'

Jamie hesitated, and looked warily at both Carol and her boyfriend before saying, 'We have reasons to believe that this gentleman might have hurt women in the past ...'

He left the sentence dangling, hoping Carol might volunteer information, but she just stared at the concrete ground.

'Hang on,' interjected Brett, 'whatcha mean hurt?'

Jamie's eyes scanned the bowed brick walls that surrounded the patio. They were old, chipped, in bad need of re-pointing, and looked barely stable enough to support the loops of rusty barbed wire that topped them. As tactfully as he could, Jamie explained about Mr Williams' juvenile conviction for rape. As he spoke, Carol's eyes widened.

'Now, we're not suggesting that Mr Williams was responsible for any local crimes,' Jamie concluded reassuringly, 'but if he was – if he ever tried to hurt anyone around here – we need to know that.'

Carol nodded as if she understood, then said, 'What are you saying?'

Sara leaned towards her, feeling a wave of empathy for the girl. She was unused to police interrogations, and was probably embarrassed to be talking about these delicate matters in front of her boyfriend. It was obvious that Brett was not providing the comfort and reassurance she had been hoping for.

'Sometimes, Carol,' Sara said gently, 'people who've been harmed by men don't always want to tell the police about it –'

Suddenly, Carol gasped. 'You think he raped me!'

Brett jumped up. Instinctively, Jamie rose to his feet.

'Fuckin' hell!' Brett cried. 'Didja, Carol? I mean, did he? Were you ever …?'

'No!' Carol shouted at him, tears of embarrassment welling in her eyes. 'I sold him cigarettes, that's all!' She started to cry. 'I barely ever spoke to him!'

Sara moved to Carol, and put an arm around her, muttering calming words in her ear. 'Hey, it's okay, calm down …'

Brett tried to rush towards them, and Jamie shot out a restraining hand.

'Anyone done that, I'll fuckin' do him,' Brett spat, seemingly unaware that the man in question was already dead.

'You calm down, too,' Jamie muttered under his breath. 'Let's leave Carol alone for a moment, okay?'

'Shhh,' Sara went on, 'everything's all right …'

'I will, Carol,' Brett went on. 'I fuckin' will.'

Navid Kapadia and his family had lived in the town for nearly two years, yet their rented house – a semi-detached box with salmon-coloured brick cladding in the Waunfawr district above the university – looked as impersonal as the day they had moved in. The Kapadia family had been allowed back by police to gather their possessions, but they had little to pack. Other than a few decorations – a brass wall plaque of the Kaaba, an onyx tea-set, a rug – the furniture had come with the house, and had a cheap, makeshift quality that was no fit setting for Fatima Kapadia's beauty.

She was a young-looking woman with intelligent, mournful eyes. Her sombre brown-and-grey dress and matching head-scarf only accentuated her striking appearance. Fatima sat on the sofa blinking away tears, while her twelve-year-old daughter Jamila dutifully laid cakes and biscuits on the table next to Sara, and her eight-year-old son Yusuf sat quietly on the floor next to his mother.

'It is intolerable that they have only now released Navid's body,' Mrs Kapadia whispered with restrained bitterness. 'It is a duty for us to bury our dead quickly. I told the police as much – it has been impertinent of them to keep us waiting.'

This was the most awkward of Sara's three meetings, worse even than Carol Elliott's embarrassed hysteria and her boyfriend's Neanderthal ranting. She realised that, to Mrs Kapadia, the actions of the authorities must have been indistinguishable from cultural insensitivity. Today, as a representative of everyone who had inconvenienced the family since Navid Kapadia's horrible death, Sara had felt on the defensive from the time she entered the house. To find out what she needed to know, she was going to have to risk alienating Mrs Kapadia further.

'What will happen to your husband's body now, Mrs Kapadia?'

'We will accompany him from London to Karachi tomorrow evening. After burial, I am to return here, to put the last of our affairs in order.'

'You're moving back to Karachi?' Sara asked.

Fatima closed her eyes. 'Oh, yes.'

'Well, please be assured that the police are doing everything they can to find your husband's killer. As I'm sure you've heard, there is almost certainly a link between his death and those of the two most recent victims.' She hesitated, then plunged forward. 'In order to try to establish connections, we need to ask questions that probably aren't relevant, but need to be eliminated from our thinking.'

Mrs Kapadia's dark eyes stared at her. 'What do you mean?'

Sara's gaze fell to the floor, where Yusuf watched her

with wide eyes. Awkwardly, she said, 'Do you think perhaps the children …?'

'Go to your room,' Fatima snapped.

Jamila reached down to Yusuf and took his hand. They moved away silently.

'Forgive me for being personal,' Sara continued, 'but my colleagues and I have been wondering if everything was … well, all right between you and your husband?'

Fatima's eyes seemed to grow even darker. 'Everything was normal,' she said tightly.

'Then, your relationship was a good one? Your husband got along well with the children?'

Her voice began to waver with the beginnings of anger. 'As I have said.'

Sara nodded, trying to appear empathetic, but feeling as though she were committing an assault against this gentle, restrained woman. 'Did your husband have any friends or contacts at the university who showed an unusual interest in your welfare?'

'My welfare? What do you mean?'

Sara realised that she had been holding her breath. She released it slowly through her mouth. 'I'm not certain exactly. Someone who might have witnessed an exchange between you and Mr Kapadia, perhaps, and taken it the wrong way –'

Without warning, Fatima slammed her hand into the side of the sofa, and shouted, 'I have answered your question! There was no reason to show any interest in my welfare!' She caught her breath, and fought for dominance over her emotions. At the edge of the doorframe behind her, Jamila stood silently. When Fatima spoke again, her words were carefully controlled and precisely chosen.

'Navid met a lot of people, and I was not in the habit of socialising with them. He has been dead for two weeks, and the authorities have done nothing but hold his body against my wishes and ask me a series of intrusive questions. I am tired of it.'

In the hallway, Yusuf began to weep, more frightened by the new, deadly calm of his mother's tone than by her outburst. Jamila retreated deeper into the shadows to comfort him.

'Mrs Kapadia, I'm sorry if I've offended you –'

'I wish we had never come to the United Kingdom,' Fatima said quietly. 'There is nothing more I can tell you.' Her tone softened. 'I sincerely hope you capture the man who has done this ... but please understand, I have answered so many questions.'

'Of course,' Sara said, grateful for being allowed to conclude the conversation with dignity. 'I won't take up any more of your time.' She rose, but Fatima did not join her. Jamila emerged quickly from the hallway. 'I will see our guest to her car,' she told her mother, then nodded to Sara. Fatima followed their progress to the door with dark, hollow eyes.

Outside, Jamila walked with Sara down the line of paving stones that bisected the small, manicured lawn, to the smooth, new road on which she had parked her car. The killer's drawing had been washed from the pavement, but Sara wondered if she had chosen the exact spot where Mr Kapadia had been murdered. If that thought had occurred to the young girl, she masked it well.

When they reached the car, Jamila spoke quietly. 'Why did you ask my mother those questions?'

'I'm sorry,' Sara said. 'I didn't mean to upset her.'

'No ... I mean, why did you want to know about my parents' relationship?'

The girl's eyes were bright, burning with an intelligence and sophistication that Sara was not used to seeing in someone so young. She tried to give her a warm smile, to indicate that her previous questions had not been important. 'We're following up a few lines of enquiry, that's all.'

Jamila nodded and licked her lips nervously, as if waiting for Sara to ask her something. Sara did not know what Jamila expected to hear, and remained silent.

Finally, the girl hung her head. 'He used to hit her,' she whispered.

Sara blinked in surprise. 'He did?'

'Not all the time – sometimes, he would get frustrated.' She glanced nervously at the door to her house. 'Lately, it had been getting worse. My mother was never happy here; she wanted to return to Pakistan. They would argue when Yusuf and I were in bed. She threatened to take us home herself, to leave without him. Her family has become very important in Karachi, much more so than his. He said she was trying to humiliate him.'

Jamila bit her lip and choked back her sobs. Sara reached for her hand and made sounds of comfort. Such emotion seemed out of place in this sterile neighbourhood of white plastic fences and trellises still awaiting vines from the garden centre. Eventually, she asked, 'Did your father ever hurt you or your brother?'

'What?' gasped the girl. 'No, never!' She swallowed hard, trying to rein in her tears. Sara noted how much she looked like her mother.

'It's all right,' Sara said, 'you'll be home the day after tomorrow.' She looked towards the house, and saw Fatima staring out the window, watching them.

'You'd better go in,' she whispered. 'Your mother needs you.'

EIGHT

Sara and Ceri stood in the stable amidst cobwebs and cardboard boxes, trying to sort out some of Sara's possessions. The boxes were full of things that had been of no immediate use to Sara when she had first moved to Penweddig: books by the score; old files; and assorted bits and pieces from her office and flat in London. Now that the house was assuming a semblance of order, she felt freer to unpack, and find places for them. The moving company had done a fine job packing, but had failed to label anything. On this Saturday afternoon, after Sara had conducted her interviews, she and Ceri stood in the dank stable with a kitchen knife each, slitting open boxes and peering at their contents.

'I'm telling you,' Ceri said, pulling open a box filled with medical and psychology texts, 'this whole area is absolutely terrified. Every time someone hears a noise at night, they ring the police headquarters. The few tourists who still wander into town get suspicious looks from nearly everybody.'

Sara lowered a large box from the top of a stack onto the stable's uneven cement floor, and wiped a trickle of sweat from her forehead. 'Fewer people are visiting the Drop-In Centre, too,' she said breathlessly. 'We might as well close the place until this character is caught.'

Ceri nodded glumly and squinted through the small,

square panes of dirty glass in the stable's double doors. 'Have you ever watched the seafront on a foggy night?' she asked. 'The clouds of fog roll in from the bay and swamp absolutely everything, until you can't see clearly. That's what the fear in this town is like. It's rolling in huge clouds and blinding everyone.'

She frowned, removing the last few books from the cardboard box and flipping it over. 'Do you ever feel it? Alone out here?'

Sara shrugged. 'Only when I don't keep busy.'

Picking up a kitchen knife, Ceri slit the packing tape that held it together, and pressed the cardboard flat. 'What breaks my heart most is the kids,' she muttered. 'Since Aled Morgan's death, there just aren't any children on the streets. Have you noticed the playground next to the castle? It's deserted.'

She cut the tape from another box and pulled open its flaps. 'I'll tell you one thing: if that Morgan woman had only kept a better watch on her son, he would still be alive.'

Sara looked up with an expression of uncertainty mingled with distaste. 'Come on, Ceri,' she said, 'it's not really fair to blame Aled's mother.'

'Oh hell!' Ceri snorted, 'I think it's more than fair. What was that woman doing, letting him run all over town, stealing from people and getting high?'

'That woman worked hard to support the two of them,' Sara said. 'She couldn't always be around.'

'Face it, Sara,' Ceri huffed, 'Problems like these don't happen overnight. She created that kid's personality. She's got to take some responsibility.'

Sara shook her head obstinately. 'It's not always easy for parents to control a child who's determined to go his own way,' she said. 'I know. Think of what my parents went through with Rhoddo.'

Ceri looked up at her, her mask of self-righteous intolerance slipping.

'I know it was before you knew him,' Sara went on, 'but my father was about as stern with him as he could have been. It didn't help – if anything, it only made him worse.'

'Maybe you're right,' Ceri mumbled. She looked away, unwilling to challenge her friend on such a delicate topic. 'Now, what do you want to do with these books?'

When Rhodri Jones Junior was nine months old, he had caught meningitis and nearly died. Although doctors eventually pronounced the baby fully recovered, his mother, Kay, was never convinced. She had read up on the disease, and discovered that it could have troubling after-effects, often much later in life, including epilepsy and learning disabilities. Throughout Rhoddo's childhood, she had treated her first-born as if he'd been fashioned from porcelain.

Such over-protectiveness had always irritated Rhodri Jones Senior, who saw in his son a normal, healthy lad who could only be damaged by the clucking ministrations of his mother. This disagreement had simmered throughout Rhoddo's childhood, becoming particularly intense when there were other problems in the Joneses' marriage.

Despite being the cause, or excuse, for his parents' occasional battles, Rhodri had grown up to be a bright – some said brilliant – boy. By his mid-teens, he was surprising teachers at his local school with the complexity of his responses to their questions – on those occasions when he chose to answer them. More often, he had sat at his desk with darting eyes and tapping feet, observing a vital inner world that his classmates did not see and could never have imagined. Teachers left him to his own devices because his marks remained at the top of the class.

For his sixteenth birthday in the autumn of 1995, Rhodri had lobbied for a motor scooter from his parents. His father had been against it, but Kay Jones had always found it difficult to deny her boy anything. Rhoddo had received his scooter – a 100cc Yamaha – and things had changed. He started playing truant, preferring long rides through the hills to attending those classes that had always bored him. By early December, the school secretary had begun to ring home with unnerving regularity. Sara's father and Rhodri had begun to argue.

Sara could still vividly recall one evening at the end of the second week of that December. Sprawled across the living room carpet, she had been doing her homework by the blaze of the fire in the grate. Her mother had already bought the family Christmas tree, and Sara could remember its blinking fairy lights throwing a regular yellow flash across her papers. Mrs Jones had been in the kitchen baking cinnamon bread, and the house seemed to be warmed by its spicy aroma. It was a scent Sara would always identify with her mother.

Her father sat in his favourite chair, a hardback novel resting unread in his lap. Sara recalled his crimson cheeks, still flushed from the frigid, coal-black night. He had been outside looking for Rhodri. Sara was having trouble concentrating on her homework; she felt a trepidation that was very near dread. There had been a furious kind of concentration in his waiting, a smouldering rage that Sara had seen before, and knew could combust with little warning.

Outside, the burr of Rhodri's scooter rose and stopped, and the wooden front door pushed open with a squeak. Sara held her breath as her father closed his book quietly. In the kitchen, the oven fan switched off, and the house was silent.

Rhoddo entered the room, pulling off his gloves and sniffing from the cold. Rhodri Jones Senior did not look at his son as he spoke. 'Do you want to keep your birthday present?' he asked.

It took Rhoddo a second to register the question. 'Huh?'

Sara glanced at him from the corner of her eye. His expression was slightly glassy, his pupils dilated. *Please say whatever he wants, Rhoddo, just be nice to him.*

'I said, do you want to keep your birthday present?'

Rhoddo made a perplexed face. 'Yeah,' he said, 'of course I do.'

'Well, you won't,' he said. 'Not unless you start attending classes. Rhodri, this is getting absurd – your mother and I are now having conversations with your school every day.'

Her father's voice was developing a strained edge. Sara could sense – physically feel – the imminent escalation of the argument, a snowball about to become an avalanche. She forced herself to study the needles of the Christmas tree, to concentrate on the blinking lights.

'Your behaviour puzzles them,' her father continued. 'They know you're bright, and wonder why you can't seem to take the pace. People say you lack backbone.'

Rhoddo stared at his father disbelievingly. 'Who says that?' he asked. It was a trait of Rhodri Senior to spoil otherwise valid arguments by stretching the truth.

'Everybody,' his father replied sharply. 'It can't go on. You've got to start attending classes.'

Rhoddo shrugged. 'Okay,' he said, and shrugged off his jacket.

Her father stood. 'You're not being serious. You have no intention of changing your behaviour in any way.'

Rhodri draped his jacket over the arm of the sofa and

sighed long-sufferingly. 'There's nothing they can teach me,' he said. 'They're doing work I could have handled three years ago.'

Her father glared. Maybe Rhoddo had exaggerated, but there was truth in his point. When he was younger, he had skipped a year of school, and now he was the youngest boy in his class. His parents were hesitant to allow him to advance any faster, but he did often find his work simplistic.

'Don't you care about your future?' Mr Jones asked.

'Sure,' Rhoddo replied, 'but if you can't live life the way you want to, there's no point in living at all, right?'

Rhodri Jones Senior started at the boy, annoyance momentarily overshadowed by puzzlement. 'If you don't care about your own future,' he said, 'perhaps you might think of me. Do you know how it looks to have my son to behave in this way?'

Rhodri stared at him for a moment, his mouth open, his mind clearly whirring. Then he smiled cunningly. 'Ahhh!' he said, wagging his finger at his father as if the older man had confessed to a dirty secret. 'That's all you care about, isn't it? Not me, you.'

'Don't be ridiculous!'

Be quiet, Rhoddo, please be quiet.

Sara heard a rustling from the kitchen, then noticed her mother's shadow in the hall from the corner of her eye. It was still.

'It's true,' Rhoddo said, his voice now light with gleeful superiority. 'You know I don't need that school – but you need an obedient son, so everyone in Aber will admire you!'

'Rhodri,' his father barked, 'you're trying to make me angry now, aren't you?'

Rhodri snorted. 'Truth always makes hypocrites angry,' he taunted.

Before he could say anything else, his father's hand had flown up and struck him across the cheek. Sara, who had been pretending not to see the altercation, cried out. 'Daddy!' She felt helpless, wanting to protect Rhoddo from her father, but unable to do anything more than weep.

'You be quiet,' he snapped, and Sara bit down hard on her lip.

'You fucking bastard!' Rhoddo cried, tears in his eyes. He raised his hand to the side of his face, which was mottled scarlet.

Their mother leapt to the doorframe. 'Rod, that's enough!' she shouted at her husband. She held her arms out to her son, who ignored them.

Mr Jones was breathing heavily now, glaring at the boy. His face was redder than Rhoddo's, burning with shame. Hitting Rhodri had been out of character, a sign of growing loss of control over his son. 'Go to your room,' he rasped.

'Fuck you,' Rhoddo spat, sweeping up his jacket and pushing past his mother.

'Rhodri!' she cried.

The door squeaked open and slammed shut, and the motor of the motor scooter snarled in the cold night air.

Rhodri Jones Senior composed himself, and squeezed through the doorframe past his wife. With furious conviction, he slid shut the heavy steel bolt on the front door, and turned and moved towards the kitchen, to do the same to the side door.

'If he wants to stay out,' he muttered, 'then he can stay out all bloody night.'

For the better part of the last hour, Sara had listened to the muffled crescendos of her parents' argument down the hall. The recriminations had died slowly, as they lapsed into furious silences, then drifted into sullen sleep. Sara itched with the urge to run downstairs and unbolt the doors – but that was something not even her mother dared to do. Besides, she knew that Rhoddo had other ways to get into the house.

Sometime around midnight, she heard his motor scooter buzz up the lane, then grind to a halt on the stone driveway outside. Seconds later, dull thumps struck the house as her brother climbed onto the flat roof extension, then eased open his bedroom window.

After he had pulled off his boots and jacket, Rhoddo crept along the hall and nudged open her door. 'Sara?' he whispered.

'I'm awake,' she said.

She watched him enter the room, and slump onto the edge of her bed. She slid up the mattress until she was resting with her back on the padded headboard. 'You okay?' she asked.

Rhodri blew air between his lips dismissively. 'I'm not worried about him,' he said, tilting his head towards their parents' bedroom. 'He's like this whenever they're pissed off at each other. Did they fight when I left?'

'Once they thought I couldn't hear.'

Rhodri laughed, then winced in pain.

'How's your face?' Sara asked. She reached out her fingers tentatively, and stroked his cheek tenderly.

'Doesn't hurt,' he said, pulling away.

They sat silently until Sara noticed her brother's shoulders shaking. 'Hey,' she said, wrestling the covers off her legs, and crawled forward. Rhodri's face was streaked with wet trails that glimmered in the orange glow of the nightlight.

'It's okay,' she said, laying a hand on his shoulder. He half-turned to her, and they hugged until he could swallow thickly and draw in a deep, irregular breath.

'Where do you go?' Sara whispered. 'On your bike, I mean.'

Rhodri shrugged. 'Around. I drive on the lanes.'

'Isn't it cold?'

'Yeah. But it's better than being here. This place is so … cloying.' He ran his hand down Sara's arm until it rested on her wrist. He squeezed it gently. 'You feel it too, don't you?'

She nodded shallowly, frightened to make such an admission, even to Rhoddo.

'If you weren't here, I'd go crazy,' he whispered.

Sara felt her throat constrict, and feared she might cry if she answered. After a time, she drew a deep breath and grasped his hand.

'Don't you worry,' she said to her older brother. 'We're both going to be just fine.'

'Good God!' Ceri gasped. 'What the hell is this repulsive thing?'

Sara stepped over an obstacle course of boxes to see what Ceri had discovered. By the time she got to the other side of the stable, her friend had picked up a shrivelled papier mâché skeleton from the box. It had real human hair glued to its head, and a foul-smelling sachet tied around its neck with a frayed leather thong.

'A gift from a witch doctor,' Sara said.

Ceri glared at the object with increased distaste. 'A real witch doctor?'

Sara chuckled. 'Who's to say? He was a big help on an investigation, though, and he promised me that it would ward off evil spirits.'

'I'm not sure which I'd rather keep out of my house,' Ceri replied. 'Evil spirits or this thing.' She placed the wizened doll on the cement floor and rooted through the box. 'What else have you got?'

She pulled out a silver dagger, its handle topped with a horned devil, and inscribed with a combination of Hebrew lettering and magical sigils. 'Another souvenir of your other career?' she asked, her nose wrinkling.

'I'm afraid so,' Sara replied. 'They're not things I'd collect for fun.'

'I should hope not,' Ceri huffed.

'If you don't like them, don't dig any deeper. You haven't come to the voodoo dolls yet.'

Ceri shook her head and looked at the box with incredulity. 'Well, I suppose you can't stop the weirder bits of your life from resurfacing forever,' she said.

Sara chuckled and grabbed a tape gun. She imprisoned the bizarre objects in their box, and resealed it with thick, brown packing tape.

'Yes, I can,' she said.

That evening, Jamie sat with Sara in her living room. She had turned the overhead light off in favour of three candles, which glowed on the mantle. Spicy cinnamon wafted through the room. An Annie Ross track played softly from a Bluetooth speaker while Sara, curled on one side of the love-seat, sipped red wine. In a chair opposite, Jamie – officially off duty – nursed a tumbler of bourbon.

After they left the Spar shop earlier that day, Sara had invited him around for drinks in the evening. He had taken it as an act of forgiveness for overstepping the line at lunch the day before. Now he badly wanted to perceive the candlelight and soft music as permission from her to say what, until yesterday, had seemed unsayable.

There was a part of him that warned against trying, especially in the wake of that *faux pas*. The room's ambience, he knew, did not necessarily imply that Sara wanted to have a personal conversation: she simply preferred candles to artificial light, and enjoyed sultry jazz. Yet still, there had been moments since his arrival when Jamie imagined catching in his peripheral vision a fond glance, an intimate smile. Every time, they had seemed to fade like a mirage.

And Sara was talking about the case.

'Everything I learned today,' she said, 'suggests that my theory about the killer is plausible. You have to admit that.'

'Oh, yes,' Jamie said. 'I agree with you now. He might well have been trying to avenge those people.'

He could feel an inane grin frozen onto his face, and loathed himself for it. Perhaps he was being overly cautious, having slipped into his defensive posture of affability, his non-threatening willingness to keep to neutral topics.

'I have to admit, though,' Sara continued, 'there are some troubling questions. He's chosen a pretty strange collection of villains to target. Especially for a vigilante who thinks he's psychic. I can almost understand executing a rapist – but what about a man who hits his wife? That makes him a coward, sure, but he didn't deserve to die.'

Jamie nodded, wishing he could find a suitable way to change the topic.

'And what about Aled Morgan? I found nothing to explain why he would target a teenage petty thief.' She shook her head sadly. 'The poor boy. Ceri blames his mother for his death, but I don't think that's fair.'

Sara stopped short, as if by mentioning Ceri's name she had changed the rules of engagement. The silence seemed to challenge Jamie to fill it.

'Speaking of Ceri ...' Jamie began hesitantly, 'I'm sorry about what I said.'

'Never mind,' Sara said with a relieved smile. 'It's understandable.'

'Thank you.' He took a deep pull on his drink. 'Still, I have to admit, it's puzzling.'

'Oh?'

'The last few months, I mean. If it's not Ceri's influence, why haven't you been willing to speak to me?'

For a moment, Sara sat very still – then she raised her eyebrows. 'I wasn't ready to talk about it,' she said. 'It's been hard for me, Jamie, surely you know that?'

Jamie nodded. 'Times have been rough,' he said finally, 'but you can't bury your head in the sand forever.'

Sara straightened on the love-seat, placing her feet flatly on the floor. 'What are you saying?'

'I'm saying, at some point we need to talk about how things stand.'

Sara squeezed her eyes shut and threw her head back in frustration. 'Forgive me for finding that ironic, coming from you,' she snapped. 'Maybe you could tell me *how things stand*?'

'I don't know,' he said. 'Are we engaged or aren't we?'

Sara raised her head slowly from the back of the chair and stared at him in astonishment.

'I don't remember withdrawing my proposal,' he added.

He watched her expression soften, her lips part, her eyes widen helplessly.

'I had no idea you'd still want to,' she said, haltingly. 'Everything's changed so much.'

'Nothing has changed,' Jamie said firmly. 'I wouldn't have asked you to marry me if I didn't love you.'

Sara drew a long, apprehensive breath, and looked down at the floorboards. A breeze blew softly through a window and made the candle flames dance. The shadows shifted. 'I'm not sure what to say,' she whispered finally. 'I think I love you too.'

Jamie had been waiting months to hear Sara say those words, and now they had come so easily. He sat dumbfounded for the longest second of his life, then rose and moved slowly to the love-seat. He took her hands in his. 'Say that again,' he whispered.

'I love you,' she repeated.

'Then … you will marry me?'

She closed her eyes as if in pain. 'No,' she replied. 'Not now.'

She pulled her hands from between his, and squeezed his fingers. 'It's hard to explain. You told me I shouldn't bury my head in the sand … well, I'm worried that marrying you might be doing just that.'

His expression was pained. 'Because you'd be running away from your past?'

She nodded.

'Sara, you wouldn't be! For God's sake, *I'm* part of your past now! I'm so tied up in your history, you couldn't untangle me if you wanted to.' He reached a hand up to her chin, and angled her face towards his until they were eye to eye. 'Look,' he said, 'I know more about your parents than you think I do. When you told me about their deaths, I … well, I needed to know more, to understand you.'

Sara's eyes widened and she blinked slowly. 'What are you saying?'

'I searched online, the very day after you told me. I did everything I could to understand what you'd been through. I don't claim to know everything, but I want to help you resolve all those questions that are stopping you from enjoying your life.'

Sara licked her lips pensively and took a breath through her mouth, as if she wanted to speak but did not have the words. Jamie leaned towards her and kissed her softly on her open mouth; she pulled away slightly, her lips remaining slack, until he pressed more firmly and she relaxed into his embrace. She kissed him then with a desperate sort of passion, until finally her face slid down to his shoulder, her fresh tears soaking into his shirt.

Jamie's thoughts turned again to Ceri Lloyd, and for the first time he admitted to himself how competitive he had been feeling towards her. He envied how well she understood Sara Jones' life.

'You don't have to say you'll marry me,' he whispered, 'not now. Just promise me one more thing.'

Her head shifted; she looked up.

'I want you to take me to your old home.'

Her watery eyes widened, tears glistening in the candlelight. 'My old home?'

'Sara, the last thing in the world I want is to upset you, but I think you understand how important this might be, for both of us.'

He tightened his grip on her. 'I want to see where your parents were murdered.'

NINE

Murder, after all, was what had brought them together.

The school bully, stabbed by Paul Sullivan in Mill Hill, had died the day after Sara and Jamie met. Suddenly, the hunt for two troubled teens became a murder investigation. Nonetheless, that evening, Jamie Harding had taken time to honour his promise, and take Sara to dinner.

Their time together – in a restaurant in Fitzrovia – was strained. Yesterday, they had shared the frisson of initial attraction and small, revealing glimpses of each other's history. Today, their new relationship was hampered by the case, which stood between them like baffling. The reality of a dead student and two disturbed teens on the run made their chitchat sound hollow.

Then, before the main course had even arrived, Jamie's phone had rung. He did more listening than talking, but Sara could tell by his face, and his monosyllabic responses, that dinner was already over.

'I've got to go,' Jamie said dully. 'They've found her body.'

Sara's throat constricted, and her lungs froze mid-breath. 'Vivian? Where?'

'The basement of a construction site in the East End. She's been stabbed.'

Sara closed her eyes as a wave of nausea rolled

through her as she saw the impish face of that young girl, both as she was in Sara's office, and in the horror-show make-up of the photograph. 'I'll go with you,' she said as Jamie threw money onto the table and gathered up his things.

'There's no reason for you to,' he replied.

'I want to.' She stood. 'You'll need someone to talk to the Loxleys.'

He shook his head. 'They've been informed.'

'By a constable?'

'Of course.'

'Damn it,' she breathed, 'that's no way to tell parents their daughter has died. Jamie, I was their therapist – and I was with them only yesterday! I could have –'

'You would have been a better choice.' Jamie interrupted. He stuffed his wallet into his breast pocket. 'But what's done is done. Go home; I'll call you later.'

Before she could reply, he dashed from the restaurant, just as the waiter brought their food.

Like her office, Sara's Pimlico flat was a place of deliberate contrasts. Primitive paintings hung on the walls; boldly coloured, highly textured rugs covered the floor, and tribal art stood on every surface: a Shona headrest from South Africa, a Peruvian pot, a Maori wooden figure. She lay on her living room sofa, trembling, staring at it all. The effect was so different from the casual disarray of the Loxley residence that they might have existed on two separate worlds. Yet the wave of bitter emotions that undoubtedly was breaking in that house, just an hour's drive away, was affecting Sara, even in the calming familiarity of her own things, her own life.

Why did Vivian Loxley's tragedy resonate so strongly? Did the thought of a vulnerable teenage girl remind her of herself twenty years before? Did the girl's waywardness, the thrall in which someone else was able to hold her, hark back to her brother's problems at that same age? Was it simply that Sara identified with the circumstances: violent death striking a cosy family home?

Or was it that Sara felt a sense of personal failure? She had let that troubled girl slip away, eighteen months too early, and fall into the arms of an unstable loser named Paul.

Sara jumped when her landline rang. She reached for the receiver so quickly that she knocked it on the floor, and hand to fumble after it.

'Yes? Hello?'

'Hey – it's Jamie.' His voice sounded tired, and very far away. Hearing it caused an unexpected sting of petulance to spear Sara. *He should have taken me with him ... I should have told the Loxleys ... he should have needed me more...*

She closed her eyes and forced those unworthy emotions away. She braced herself. 'Okay – describe it. I want to know how she died.'

Jamie hesitated. 'Does it matter?'

'For goodness' sake, Inspector Harding, I am a doctor,' she snapped.

She heard him sigh. 'Miss Loxley died from a single stab wound to the chest. It was a deep blow, very forceful and without hesitation. She was lying down at the time, on the dirt floor, in the basement of a new office development. There are no signs of a struggle. Around her body are symbols, drawn into the dirt, almost certainly inscribed by Paul after her death. Nobody here knows whether he's made them up, or got them from somewhere.'

'Copy them,' she said. 'I'll let you know. You say she was lying down without a struggle – you mean she didn't try to defend herself?'

'Maybe she didn't know what was coming. Or maybe she was high on something – we'll learn that from the toxicology report.'

'Okay,' Sara said quietly. Although her mind was flooded with questions, she could think of none that Jamie Harding could answer.

The phone line hissed. Sara could hear the quiet voices of police officers in the background. 'Look,' Jamie said, 'I'll be in touch, all right?'

'Sure,' Sara said.

She was grappling with the urge to ask him when, when she realised the line had gone dead.

The next day rolled by like dull scenery from a car window. Andy Turner's session came and went, then Sara nodded sympathetically while not listening to a shopaholic who had to choose between her husband and another bracelet.

Near the end of the afternoon, Emma knocked once and poked her head through the door, interrupting the day's final session. Sara frowned; being interrupted during a client's time was almost unheard of. She excused herself, and moved into the reception room, where Jamie Harding stood, looking pale and uncomfortable.

Sara's lips parted in surprise.

'I'll stay with Mr Bergson,' Emma muttered, closing the door to Sara's office behind her.

'They found the boy,' he said. 'By the river, near the building site. Officers found him thrashing about; seems he'd taken an huge dose of painkillers, and washed it down with brandy.'

'Oh my God,' Sara murmured. People who tried to kill themselves that way assumed they would simply drift off to sleep forever. Often, the truth was more grisly: they slept for several hours, and then woke up in searing agony.

'He passed away on the drive to the hospital.' Jamie moved toward her and took her hand firmly in his. 'I was hoping you'd come with me. I'd like you to talk to Vivian Loxley's parents.'

Sara blinked. 'Why now? You didn't need me last night.'

He swallowed before continuing. 'Because they found a piece of paper in his pocket, with two suicide notes on it … his, and Vivian's.'

Sara heard herself gasp.

'That's why there was no sign of struggle,' Jamie Harding said. 'She allowed him to him kill her.'

He squeezed Sara's hand more tightly. 'Vivian Loxley wanted to die.'

Paul's suicide note had shown a fatalism common to those suffering fear and regret in the wake of a devastating mistake. Vivian's note had been more pathetic. She had not wanted to live without Paul.

At the parents' home, Sara had done her professional best, but after the numb shock and tears, there was little to be said. When they left the grieving couple, Jamie offered to take Sara home … unless she wanted to pick up some food and go back to his place in Brixton.

Jamie lived in a large one-bedroom flat in an old, converted house. The decor was Spartan: white walls without pictures; limed floorboards; a leather sofa suite; and a laptop on the small kitchen table. It was the place of a bachelor who spent little time at home.

They ate Thai food straight from the plastic containers. Jamie kept up a stream of small talk, but Sara answered on auto-pilot; she was not so easily distracted from Vivian Loxley's tragedy. What had Paul Sullivan said to her that made her willing to give up her life? What power had he had over her? And from what demon had he obtained it?

After Jamie had taken away the remains of their dinner, he sat down next to her and took her hand in his. 'You're still finding it hard, aren't you?'

She nodded.

'More than the other cases you've worked on?'

'Much more. I knew her. She trusted me to help her …' Sara's throat closed up and she choked on tears.

He pulled a tissue from a nearby box and held it gently to her face. 'You don't have to say any more,' he whispered.

'I want to.'

And she did want to. There was something about his concern, about the warmth of his gentle strength that sapped her dark, old emotions of some of their power. For the next several minutes, Sara told him the story of her parents' murder.

When she had finished, he said, 'I'm sorry. If I'd known how painful this would be for you, I never would have got you involved.'

'Then I'm lucky you didn't know.' She took his hand. 'I'm glad I met you.'

He sank back in the sofa. 'It would have been nice to have met under other circumstances.'

She smiled, and pulled his arm around her shoulder.

They sat in silence while the sky outside grew dark.

That was the first night they made love. Through the autumn and winter, into the New Year, their altered relationship had grown like a fragile new life – until the small death that brought it to a sad, silent end two months later.

TEN

Clarach was a small holiday community, located a couple of miles north of Aberystwyth. It boasted a beautiful stretch of beach, and stunning views up the coast, but the aesthetic was marred by clusters of caravans sitting haphazardly opposite the shoreline.

It would have been a long walk to follow the roads from Clarach to Aberystwyth; the swiftest path was over the cliffs that separated the two centres. In places it was narrow, and the danger of slipping, of plummeting over the edge, made such a journey inadvisable at night. Nonetheless, Eldon Carson hiked up the steep, twisting path to the cliff-top as the last glow of the sun was vanishing behind the calm sea.

Except for that red haze that clung to the horizon like a low cloud, the sky was a deep azure. Carson's heart beat rapidly. The pounding was not the same as the thudding he got just before a killing – that was caused by a sickly excitement, and it had lessened each time, as Carson grew more certain of the rightness of his actions. No – tonight his racing pulse was the result of something different. It came from a strong sense of connection to another human being; something he was feeling for the first time in his life.

Carson hiked along a flat ridge until he came to a patch of familiar ground: the path between Clarach and

Aberystwyth led to Constitution Hill. He surveyed the scene with an air of melancholy, and thought about how, throughout his life, he had found it near impossible to relate to those around him. It was not for want of trying; he had genuinely wanted to fit in – but there had been no one who could understand him. No one who saw things the way he did.

Carson had wandered far in order to find someone who could.

Before making his descent into the town, Carson stood atop the hill where he had killed the Morgan boy, and looked out at the lights, the cars, the occasional pedestrians strolling the promenade, preparing himself for contact. First, he would visit that old white house, just to see that everything was in place.

Then, he would wander through the town, and, at exactly the right moment, he would keep his appointment with Dr Sara Jones.

On Monday evenings, the Drop-In Centre stayed open until nine o'clock. It was the one night that Sara made sure to be on duty, in case anyone wanted to speak to her personally. She was becoming popular with local hypochondriacs and the elderly, both realising that she offered a two-for-one chance for them to detail their psychological problems and also obtain medical advice. Usually, she referred them to their GPs.

It had been a busy evening, and Sara had escorted the last of her visitors down the stairs and out the door just after 9.15. She was late for a dinner date, and had left her briefcase, medical bag, and a few other odds and ends in the Centre, intending to retrieve them before heading home.

Sara had met with her group of nurses and social workers at a tandoori restaurant on the pier, and they had questioned her about the murders. Although she had told no one of her involvement, Sara had been spotted by the press on the previous Wednesday, as she pushed through the crowd at the foot of Constitution Hill. Photos of her approaching the Cliff Railway, on her way to Aled Morgan's murder scene, had appeared in several of the national papers, leading to lurid speculation about an occult dimension to the case. The caption under one tabloid photo had read, "The Devil's Work? Welsh call Spook Shrink as body count grows."

Over dinner, she was preoccupied, not by the case but by thoughts of Jamie. It felt strange to have admitted she loved him. Until she said the words, she had not consciously realised her emotions stretched that far. Despite her feelings, she had been serious when she rejected the idea of marriage. She had felt that accepting Jamie's life would be denying her quest for her own. She felt she had betrayed her parents by not understanding their deaths, and had failed Rhodri by not preventing his descent into the savage life he kept hidden from the world.

Yet, Jamie had tried to reconcile her needs with their love. She wanted desperately to believe his claim that accepting him would be enlisting an ally. Sara was not convinced, only hopeful, and it was with hope that she had agreed to his desire to see the house where the murders had happened. Perhaps, she thought, by observing how they related at that most terrible of spots, she would know whether they might have a future together.

Such thoughts continued to swirl through Sara's mind as she joined her friends for drinks at a nearby pub. She hoped she was better company than she thought.

It was about 10.30 when she made her way, alone, down the promenade. The sky had dimmed to a deep indigo, and anything not illuminated by the streetlights was in silhouette. In the wake of the murders, most Aberystwyth women had stopped walking alone in the dark and, as she hurried along the pavement, Sara felt exposed, vulnerable.

Her mind was foggy with lager and gin. She shouldn't drive like this, she thought, and decided to make a cup of coffee and review paperwork at the Centre before heading on to Penweddig. That would give her time to sober up, and to get a grip on herself, and stop being frightened of shadows.

She unlocked the door, secured it again behind her, and pulled herself up the dark staircase. Inside the large room, she switched on the overhead fluorescent lights, which gave the old upholstered chair and sofa, the Formica tables and the orange plastic seats a harsh glow. The Centre was so quiet she could hear the lights buzzing, and she flicked on a radio for comfort. Ella Fitzgerald was singing 'The Starlit Hour'. Sara filled the kettle, and took her case notes out of her briefcase.

Several minutes later, she paused from her work, suddenly alert without knowing why. Taking a mental inventory, she cocked her head … it was a sound, barely audible under the music. She reached out and slowly switched off the radio.

Downstairs … the scratching of metal on metal. Someone was picking the lock.

She sucked in a trembling breath and rose so fast the plastic chair toppled to the floor with a clatter. She cried out, and rushed to the phone, fumbling the receiver, punching in the number of the police station.

'It's Dr Jones at the Drop-In Centre on Marine Terrace,' she gabbled, 'please send a patrol car immediately, there's an intruder –'

Downstairs, the door's cheap lock sprang open, and

Sara dropped the phone. Groping for her medical bag, she dashed to the light switch and plunged the room into darkness. Very softly, someone was climbing the stairs. She could not control the sound of her terrified panting.

She thought of the fire escape, outside the back window, but the footsteps were growing louder; there would never be time to struggle with the creaking wooden frame. Breathless, she hurried towards the lavatory at the back of the Centre. The rush of blood was loud in her ears, and the orange streetlight that filtered through the window threw an elongated shadow before her. She slipped into the small back room and rooted about in her medical bag for her syringe as the lights flickered on in the main room.

'Please come out of there,' called a voice. An American accent. Southern. 'You don't need to be frightened.'

Sara hesitated, her mind whirring. He knew where she was, and there was no escape from this small room. She would not let him trap her; she would have to face him. Keeping her hand concealed in the bag, she edged into the main room.

The man stood in the doorway. He was in his early-to-mid-twenties, with dark brown hair that looked as if it had once been short, but had grown without being trimmed. His complexion was dark, his expression brooding, and his eyes intelligent.

'The Centre is closed now,' she said, her voice tight. 'I have called the police.'

From nowhere, a warming calm took hold of her mind. It felt like a tranquilliser, pulsing down and dulling the adrenaline that had constricted her muscles. She did not understand her new emotions, but suddenly she felt safe. When the young man spoke again, his voice was soothing. 'I haven't come here to hurt you,' he said.

111

He inclined his head towards the centre of the room. 'May I come in?'

'I think you already have,' she answered slowly.

He took a few more paces into the room, and stood, straight but relaxed. 'Congratulations,' he said. 'You were almost right in so many of your assumptions. I want you to know the truth, Miss Sara. It's crucial that you do.'

Sara nodded calmly, hoping she could keep him talking until a constable arrived.

'Okay,' she said, 'what is the truth?'

He smiled, as if he had read her thoughts. 'Are you afraid?'

'A little.'

'Why?'

'I'd be stupid not to be.'

'You reckon?' He angled his head thoughtfully. 'Answer me this: if I was inclined to, could I kill you, right now?'

Sara pursed her lips, then said levelly, 'You could try.'

An abrupt guffaw. 'You know I could. But you understand I don't intend to, right?'

Sara's expression remained neutral, and she said, 'Okay.'

'And you're curious, too. I haven't come to hurt you, so you're puzzled about what I do want. You'd hate to play my game … but it's the only way you'll find out what's what.'

Stepping backwards, he added, ''Specially since I'm not hanging around 'til the cops come.'

Abruptly, he turned his back. 'Follow me,' he said, 'I got something to show you.'

Then he was gone, skipping swiftly down the stairs. As he did, Sara found herself able to think clearly once more.

This young man was the killer.

Her mind filled with the image of Aled Morgan's body

slumped next to the pub on Constitution Hill – he had done that! All talk of wanting to tell her the truth was laughable in the light of that single, pathetic image. A combination of panic and anger churned inside her.

She heard the door close downstairs as he left the building.

There was no time left to wait for the police. What he'd said was true: if she didn't follow, she'd lose him.

And he had to be caught. She flung herself after him, feeling no fear. She believed what he said. He did not want to harm her. He expected her to play some other role in his game.

Sara charged down the stairs two at a time, and wheeled out the door. Already, he was turning the corner, onto Terrace Road, leading away from the sea front.

Sara chased him past darkened shop fronts until he turned left onto Cambrian Street. Gasping for breath, she skidded to a halt at the corner several seconds later, and scanned the street. Her prey was nowhere to be seen. In the distance, a police siren wailed. A pack of students, part of the small band who remain in Aber through the summer, were stumbling past, en route from one pub to the next.

'Excuse me,' Sara blurted. 'I'm looking for a man – did you see a man?'

One of the group – a beefy boy cultivating an unsuccessful moustache – sensed her distress with malicious glee. 'Yes, indeed,' he cried, spreading his arms wide, 'I am the man you're looking for!'

'Yeah, in your dreams,' another chortled, and fixed Sara with a blurry stare. 'Actually, ma'am, he's right over there,' he said, pointing in several directions at once.

'No, wait!' chimed another, pointing up Terrace Road towards the train station. 'He's catching a train. I saw him.'

'A bus,' giggled a girl gamely. 'Try the buses!'

For a moment, Sara's mind blanked, refusing to recognise drunken bravado. Didn't these people realise there was a killer on the loose? In frustration she threw herself down Cambrian Street. Halfway along, the killer was waiting calmly down a side turning. As soon as she noticed him, he turned and continued on his way at a brisk pace. She dashed after him, sweat dribbling down her cheeks.

He led her into an affluent area not far from the hospital on the eastern fringe of town. Above them on Penglais Hill, the floodlit facade of the National Library glowed brightly. Everything around Sara seemed darker in contrast. At the front of a large gabled house, the killer stopped long enough to make eye contact. She saw him grin. He skipped around to the side of the house, and she followed, only to reach a dead-end patch of grass and an open bathroom window. There was nowhere else he could have gone. Without thinking, she jumped, and, balanced awkwardly on the sill, before landing a foot inside, on the toilet. The porcelain clanked and scraped as she lowered herself onto the ceramic-tiled floor.

Except for Sara's laboured breathing, the house was totally quiet – and very dark. She held her arms in front of her, and swam through shadows, poking her head into the silent living room, the large empty kitchen, and a child's untidy play room. The only sound was her own panting, and the blood pulsing in her ears. Cautiously, she climbed the creaking stairs to the first floor. One bedroom door was open, at the end of the hall. By the orange flicker of a nightlight, she could make out a single bed – and, inside it, the small shape of a child under blankets.

Her stomach churned. On the other side of the bed stood the killer.

Sara threw herself forward, and skidded to a halt at the

side of the bed. The killer did not move as she laid a hand on the child's straight blonde hair.

Her head was still warm.

'I told you not to be frightened,' whispered the killer. 'This little girl's okay.'

He stooped down and stroked her head. His fingers brushed against Sara's, and she flinched. 'Her name,' he added, 'is Rachel Poole.'

Sara withdrew her hand slowly from Rachel Poole's hair.

'I said you were nearly right in your assumptions ... but you hadn't yet arrived at the truth. If you had, you would feel nothing now but relief – relief and joy.'

The killer straightened, turned, and gently tugged at the curtains behind him. He gazed beyond the streetlamp that illuminated half his face – as if, from here, he could see the whole world.

'What you failed to realise, Miss Sara,' he continued, 'is that anyone who can see into the past, can also see the future.' He shook his head sadly. 'I didn't kill those people for anything they had done. I killed them for the horrible crimes they would have committed ... if I had allowed them to live.'

Sara felt her lips part in astonishment.

The killer stared at her and spoke with absolute conviction.

'Rachel Poole is alive for one reason only: because, a few hours ago, I killed the man who would have murdered her tonight.'

ELEVEN

The conference room in Aberystwyth's police station was a large space on the first floor. Its west-facing wall is dominated by a wide, floor-to-ceiling arc of glass bricks, which diffused daylight through the room. Two days after meeting the killer, Sara sat with her back to the east wall, blinking past the silhouettes of CID officers, into the bright glare that overwhelmed her vision. Above her was a portrait of the Queen, and next to her were three whiteboards, on which a number of sketches, papers, and photos had been Blu-Tacked. The collage featured a Photofit picture of the suspect, based on Sara's description. She had spent all yesterday in the forensics department at police headquarters in Carmarthen, helping to put the identification photograph together. Surrounding it were shots of each of the murderer's victims – including the fourth and most recent, whose body had been found only yesterday.

Edmond Haney, a retired headmaster from Solihull, had been executed in his holiday caravan in Clarach. He was known to have visited the caravan park alone for the past four summers, and was described by the other holidaymakers as a pleasant man who enjoyed sunbathing on the beach, and had kept largely to himself. A strip of bedsheet had been tied around his throat after death. His genitals had been removed and, in a new twist, inserted into his mouth. Unsurprisingly to Sara, little Rachel Poole's name had been inscribed under the symbol drawn on his skin.

Sara and Jamie sat side-by-side in red-upholstered office chairs, with Ceri at the end of the front row. The CID men before them had been convened at Jamie's request by Detective Chief Inspector Conroy, who was heading the investigation.

'The offender,' Sara said in deliberate tones, 'is a white male in his middle twenties, who speaks with a soft American accent – probably from one of the south-eastern States. Behind me, you can see a Photofit, based on my description. It is accurate.'

She gestured towards a blown-up photocopy of the Eye in the Pyramid next to her. 'You know about this symbol, and my theories regarding the offender's personal belief system. My encounter with him on Monday evening has proved those to be accurate: I am left with no doubt that he believes himself to be psychic. Furthermore, he is certain that, had he not killed his victims, they would have committed terrible crimes against the individuals whose names he recorded.'

A few of the detectives glanced at one other. One young man frowned sceptically.

'What has puzzled us are the ways in which he desecrated each of the bodies. We suspected they were messages of some sort, but couldn't crack the code. Based on everything else we know now, his messages have become clear.

'I am now convinced that the killer believes Navid Kapadia would have burned his children to death.'

The detective who had frowned made eye contact with Sara. He shook his head in what he no doubt hoped was amused disbelief, but it looked to Sara like confusion. He was out of his depth.

'We know that Mr Kapadia was experiencing considerable friction in his marriage,' Sara continued, speaking directly to the young detective, 'and that he had had intense arguments with his wife about whether to return to Pakistan. We also know he would occasionally strike her.'

She used the tip of a pen like a pointer, and tapped on the second victim's picture. 'Dan Williams was a convicted rapist, and after death the offender severed his genitals. At one point, we had suspected that Carol Elliott – the woman whose name was found on a scrap of paper inside Mr Williams' throat – had been raped by him. Now, we believe that the killer suspected she would have been, had he not prevented it.

'Similarly, Aled Morgan used to work for Mrs Irene Davies, and engaged in petty theft to support his drug habit. The killer beat his body after death – we suspect this was a message that Aled would have beaten Mrs Davies, perhaps in a failed burglary.'

'I'm sorry, Miss Jones,' the sceptical detective interjected, 'but, if you don't mind my saying, it sounds a little far-fetched.'

'I know,' Sara said. She understood that this was a town where any murder was a rarity, and until recently, multiple murder non-existent. It was likely that none of these detectives had ever worked a case like this. Then again, this case would be unique for most Scotland Yard detectives.

'Do you actually believe it?' he asked.

'Do I believe Aled would have beaten Mrs Davies to death? Who knows? Do I believe the offender thinks so? Definitely.'

She paused and sipped from a coffee cup filled with water. The CID men muttered to each other. 'Finally,' Sara continued, 'and most recently, we have Mr Haney. I know for a fact the killer thought he was about to murder five-year-old Rachel Poole, because he told me so. Mr Haney's genitals were severed, and inserted into his mouth.' She paused, and then added, 'I'll leave you to imagine why he might have done that.'

Detective Chief Inspector Conroy cleared his throat, and said, 'So you are not claiming that the offender is actually psychic?'

'No, sir. I am saying the killer believes himself to be psychic. Whether any of what I have just described would actually have occurred is irrelevant. The point is, he thinks that he is performing a service to your local community – and my guess is, he'll keep right on performing that service until you stop him.'

Everyone fell silent as they pondered Sara's words. From a cell downstairs, a single shout sounded.

'Thank you, Miss Jones,' said Conroy. 'Now, gentlemen, I'd like to call upon Inspector Harding from Special Branch to bring us up to date on the hunt for the offender.'

Jamie stood, and Sara wandered away from her chair, to the glass wall at the back of the room.

'The offender,' he said, 'was known to have stayed in the Bryn Y Môr Guest House next to Constitution Hill on the night that Aled Morgan was murdered. The house-to-house teams have been unable to trace his whereabouts since that night …'

Eldon Carson lay on a blue vinyl exercise mat, eyes closed, his breathing regular, like a man asleep. Part of his consciousness was there, feeling the uneven floorboards on his back through the thin mat, but another, less-definable part of him was in Aberystwyth, listening to Jamie Harding talk about him.

Since his night at the guest house, Carson had been

constantly on the move, drifting from fields to barns. He had seldom ventured into public; his likeness was now too widely circulated. Until recently, it had been easy to live in such a peripatetic way. He was young and fit, and carried few possessions: spare clothing; a toothbrush; a razor; and handwritten notes about his targets. But he was getting tired, and this lifestyle had begun to feel like a punishing regimen.

He had suspected that this day would come, and had taken steps to make it easier on himself – such as making the acquaintance of a loathsome form of life called Trevor Hughes. Hughes was a member of a so-called British Nationalist group known as Race Riot. This far-right fraternity, based in south-east London, had a very few die-hard followers in Mid-Wales – Trevor Hughes being one of the most fervent, and most stupid.

Carson had had no trouble convincing him that he was a member of a Georgia chapter of the Ku Klux Klan, on a White Power tour of Celtic Britain. After one beery evening discussing ludicrous racialist theories, Hughes had invited Carson to stay as his guest in his secluded bungalow, just off the road linking Clarach with Bow Street. For the last few nights, Carson had been sleeping on an exercise mat in Hughes's spare room, amidst a collection of free-weights, and surrounded by Aryan-power posters, right-wing flags, and stacks of racist literature.

Willing himself to view events as they happened was one of Eldon Carson's less reliable skills. His clearest psychic impressions always came to him unbidden – as if he'd just happened to find the right frequency.

This had occurred when he had first arrived in Aberystwyth, and observed Navid Kapadia buying a newspaper at WHSmith. That mundane moment had caused a rush of awe, like nausea, to swell in his belly and rise to his throat. His travels through Britain had been aimless, pointless, a journey through small towns, reading the petty angers of their inhabitants. Then, as he had approached Aberystwyth, he had felt a calming rightness about his direction. He had not understood why he was here until that moment in the newsagents. He was struck with a sickening force by an image of that man – the one so innocently buying a newspaper – dousing himself and his children in petrol, then waiting for his wife to open the door. That had been the moment his destiny had solidified.

Yet, he had been horrified. He was not a killer! It had taken hours of shadowing Navid Kapadia, and being struck by wave after wave of horror emanating from the man's future, for Carson to realise that everything he had instinctively believed about right and wrong, about justice itself, had been superseded by his dreadful gift.

Later, when he saw Sara Jones, Carson had felt her strikingly familiar abilities buried – nascent, inert – deep within her. It was then that he had known that his new realisation would be understood by another. Understood and justified.

Carson observed Sara now, gathering her things together as the meeting in Aberystwyth was officially wrapped up, and its participants dismissed. He shook himself awake, sat up on the mat, and rubbed his face with his hands. The room smelt of stale sweat. Without a warning knock, the door handle jerked downwards. Carson looked up sharply. On the back of the door was a poster, featuring a blocky drawing of an armoured knight on horseback, raising his sword into the air. Underneath, it read "*Aryans Arise!*"

Trevor Hughes shoved open the door open and grinned. 'Thought I heard you awake,' he said. 'Can I grab you a beer?'

'No, thanks,' Carson said.

'You're getting old, mate,' Hughes said, his round face smirking. He pulled the door shut as he retreated from the room.

A few minutes later, Carson emerged from the bedroom. Hughes stood in the small landing at his front door, talking in low tones through a narrow crack, held by a security chain. To Carson's surprise, the young man he spoke to was dark-skinned. He watched the man slip Trevor a folded wad of notes through the small gap in the door. Trevor accepted the money, and counted it carefully, twice. Then he reached into his jeans and withdraw a small clear bag of brown powder.

'Now,' he said, 'piss off before someone sees you.'

The man nodded nervously, and Trevor closed the door on him, and turned around. 'Oh, hi, mate,' he said to Carson. 'Didn't hear you back there.' He smiled shyly. 'Don't think too badly of me, doing business with wogs. Round here, you take what customers you can get.'

He gestured with the fist that clutched the banknotes. 'I always charge 'em more than a white lad, anyhow. That one there, he's really messed up.' Trevor laughed, an ugly chortle. 'Smack's done him no favours at all.'

He thrust the money into his pocket and picked up his tin of beer. 'Once a week I take a run up to Liverpool to pick up stock,' he volunteered conversationally. 'This isn't a big enough market for them to bring it down. But I know all the main dealers. Liverpool's best, then Manchester.' He narrowed his eyes speculatively. 'Birmingham, if I'm in a hurry.'

He smiled, and took a pull on his beer. Foam trickled down his chin.

Carson stared at Hughes, feeling nothing but mute fury. After several seconds in which Carson simply stared at him in astonishment, Hughes began to look uncomfortable.

'Hey … what's the matter, mate?'

Carson gestured at a poster that proclaimed "*White Pride Worldwide!*". 'How can you be proud of yourself?' he asked, his voice steady and quiet. 'How can you feel so superior, when you've let yourself sink to this?'

Hughes shook his head defensively. 'Mate, I don't take the stuff,' he said. 'I just sell it.'

Carson swallowed hard, and fought to control his temper. Trevor Hughes was looking at him with hurt surprise. He had almost lost the plot, Carson realised, in his disgust for this man. He took a deep breath. 'Yeah,' he said, his jaw aching from the effort to control his words. 'I guess so.'

Trevor Hughes' relief was visible as his muscles relaxed and his shoulders slumped forward. 'Atta boy,' he said. 'Now, are you going to have a beer or aren't you?'

Sara and Ceri used the station's back exit: past the cells, through the secure outdoor area, and into the car park.

'It doesn't matter what this villain thinks he's killing for,' Ceri said, 'it all comes down to the same thing. Bodies.'

She glanced up at the wall, behind which sat the conference room. 'I just hope some of them took what you had to say on board.'

'They weren't hostile,' Sara said, walking Ceri towards her car. 'Just perplexed. They're not sure what to try next. I'm sure Jamie will talk them through it.'

Sara wasn't sure if it was her imagination, or whether Ceri had bristled at the mention of Jamie's name.

'Can I take you somewhere?' Ceri asked.

'I'm parked next to the cinema,' Sara said. 'It's a nice day; I'll walk.'

Ceri nodded and unlocked her car, as Jamie appeared from around the front of the building. Beyond him, Constitution Hill could be seen in the distance. The white Camera Obscura gleamed in the noon sun, looking quaint and charming. 'There you are,' he said, approaching. 'Did you sleep well last night?'

Sara smiled. 'Like a baby, thanks.'

Yesterday, Jamie and Ceri had independently put pressure on the Detective Superintendent to authorise a constable to guard Sara's house at nights. Sara had protested that she didn't need such personal – and unwarranted – attention. Nonetheless, last evening, a young man in uniform had trudged up and down the muddy lane in the light rain, until Sara insisted that he come into the kitchen. She had shown him where the tea was, turned on the radio for him, and gone to bed.

She had to admit, she had felt better for his presence, even though she knew that the killer did not mean to harm her. Instead, he had wanted to use her, to lead her into drawing the conclusions she had now drawn.

'I was wondering when we could keep our date,' Jamie said pointedly.

Ceri raised her eyebrows slightly, but did not look at Sara. Sara knew that to explain what Jamie meant would do nothing except anger her, so she pretended not to notice. 'I'm not sure,' Sara said vaguely.

'Take care of yourself, Sara,' Ceri huffed, and got into her car. She did not acknowledge Jamie.

Together, they watched Ceri's panda car pull away.

When she had turned into the steady traffic that sped along the Boulevard Saint-Brieuc, Jamie stared into the distance, towards Constitution Hill.

'What's wrong with right now?' he asked.

The village of Gefail was one single street, running

through a valley, surrounded by hills dotted with sheep and fields full of cows. It branched away from the road that linked Aberystwyth with Machynlleth to the north-east. Two hundred years before, Gefail had been home to a few craftsmen, who had served local farmers and the nearby villages. Two blacksmiths had practised there, as had the area's largest manufacturer of coffins.

By the time Sara's family moved in, the village had grown to eleven houses. A few were the homes of farmers, the rest housed professionals who practised in Aberystwyth. Mr Rhodri Jones Senior had been a solicitor, and his family had lived in the largest, oldest house on the street. It had been built by the blacksmith who founded the village. Gefail meant 'forge.'

Sara stared out the window at the passing fields and houses, tingling with apprehension about this experiment. She realised, as perhaps Jamie did not, the unfair burden she was placing on him: he had to convince Sara that opening this emotional wound would unite them, yet she had no clear idea of what proof she required from him.

When they turned off the main road onto the narrow street, Sara was startled to see that her favourite trees had disappeared. When she was a girl, the first hundred yards had been lined with old oaks, which had given the impression that they were standing sentinel to protect the village. Now, they had been chopped away to make room for new, two-storey houses, each designed to be distinctive, and every one looking exactly the same.

They passed the new white boxes, and rolled slowly to the older end of the street. To Sara it was like travelling back in time. 'There, Jamie,' she said finally, in a subdued voice, 'that one.'

When they pulled up in front of the ivy-covered red brick house, Sara began to tremble. The sun was gleaming off the white portico, and the fields just behind the conservatory were a dazzling emerald green, but the sight of her old home filled her with grey, queasy dread.

And when they came back, it was in livid, excruciatingly painful, detail.

TWELVE

In its quiet way, Mid Wales accepts, or at least tolerates, a dizzying variety of alternate lifestyles. Anarchists, artists, Buddhists, druids, and pagans run to the Welsh hills, choose their rural patch of land, and go about their peripheral business undisturbed.

In 1995, a commune for casualties of the rave scene set up stakes to the north-east of Gefail, in the picturesque Artists Valley. The four men and three women shared a single, remote cottage hidden in a wood, around the presence of their leader, twenty-eight-year-old Duncan Kraig. In the late 1980s, Kraig had been a pioneer DJ in Manchester's clubs, at a time when acid house culture still relied on its namesake as drug of choice. Kraig never really fitted into the lovey-dovey scene that evolved with the craze for MDMA; his hues had always been darker, and were deepened by the handfuls of LSD he had continued to swallow.

In his sets, Kraig tended to deliver apocalyptic insights – a dark hodgepodge of watered-down Aleister Crowley with a pinch of Anton LaVey – as part of the sonic mix. The few who liked it liked it a lot; to the ordinary clubber it was a bit of a buzz-kill. Less than a decade after he had made his name, Kraig found it hard to get bookings. He told his few followers he didn't care: the best raves were like the best magic. They weren't found in cities, but in nature.

He led his people to a new promised land, where they indulged in an orgy of drugs, drink, food and sex, to the thump of psychedelic techno. It was into this tempting bacchanalia that a seventeen-year-old local boy named Glyn Thomas wandered.

Things might have been different if Sara's brother had not been a casual acquaintance of Glyn Thomas. At first meeting, they appeared to have little in common. Where Rhodri was known for his edgy intelligence, Glyn had a reputation for sullen rebellion: living off his father but refusing to help with the family farm, and occasionally being arrested for minor crimes. They were always committed incompetently, and usually while drunk. In the beginning, the two boys had simply killed time together, but their comradeship deepened when Glyn introduced Rhodri to Duncan Kraig. Suddenly, Rhodri discovered a bizarre new world that excited him and appealed to his desire for new sensations. In that cottage in the woods, he was initiated into the adult world of sex with a vigour and diversity that few adults ever experience. He also discovered the pleasures of mind-altering drugs, which took him to places he had never seen, but recognised nonetheless.

Rhodri Jones began to spend a lot of time in the Artists Valley.

Nobody on the outside knew about the excesses of the Kraig's loose acid cult; nevertheless, when Mr Jones discovered his son playing truant with a group of adults in the woods, it worried and infuriated him. He ordered Rhodri to cease going there immediately, and tried to pressure the Aberystwyth police into investigating the 'English hippies'.

Mr Jones blamed Glyn Thomas for his family's problems. Decrying the older boy's influence over

Rhodri, he insisted the two end their friendship. Glyn refused, and defiantly visited Gefail nearly every day, engaging in obscene shouting-matches with Rhodri's father. Sara remembered them well, witnessed from her vantage point at the living room window: Glyn, a small figure with a defiant stance, his chest puffed out, hands on hips, standing on the gravel driveway. Her father, always in a cardigan, crisp trousers and leather house slippers, glowering impotently at the door.

'I told you, he isn't home.'

'Rhoddo's old enough to decide what he does and who he does it with.'

'If you come to my house one more time, I'll have you arrested.'

'If you so much as try, I'll kill you! You understand me?'

Meanwhile, in the Artists Valley, Duncan Kraig cautioned calm, and advised everyone to ignore the outside world: if Rhoddo's old man wanted to give himself an aneurysm, that was his business.

Then everyone's life changed forever. Rhodri and Sara's parents were murdered. Glyn Thomas disappeared, and the police launched a manhunt, declaring him their chief suspect. And, after their first interrogation, Duncan Kraig and his followers hastily parted company and drifted their separate ways, some returning to the mundane life of the outside world, others looking for new ways to escape it.

'You found your father upstairs,' Jamie said, squinting clinically up at the loft window. 'In his study.'

'When I got home from school,' Sara said. Her head was buzzing; she was finding it difficult to stand. 'I found my mother first, right there – in the hallway.'

Her mother had been lying with her head towards the

door, her blood drying on the mosaic tiles. She had been to the greengrocer's: a split paper bag lay, absorbing blood, with fruit and vegetables spilling from it. Sara had not screamed – she had simply frozen. Her mind had started turning over like a machine, systematically registering the grim new data: her father's car was outside, and that most likely meant that he was upstairs. Her mother was clearly dead, so calling the police could wait …

Jamie hopped up the single step to the portico, and cupped his hands against the stained glass window of the front door. He peered in through one of the clear squares, treating the house with the sharp interest he displayed at any crime scene. Sara sat down on the concrete step.

In the days after the murder, the police would piece together what they thought had happened to Sara's parents. Mr and Mrs Jones had been killed with Mr Jones' own shotgun, which had sat undisturbed in an outlying building for years. The building, a sizeable brick structure behind the house, had once housed the original blacksmith's forge, and Sara's father had always kept it locked. The murderer would have had to enter the house through the unlocked conservatory, remove a cluster of keys from a hook in the kitchen, and retrieve the gun from the barn. Then he had climbed to the first floor, and stood at the bottom of the stairs leading to the loft study. Mr Jones had emerged from his study at the top of the stairs, and the killer had gunned him down. Police speculated that, as he tried to leave, he had been discovered by Mrs Jones, returning from the shops in Bow Street. He had shot her before fleeing the same way he had entered.

The killer would have had to have known where Mr Jones had kept the keys to the barn, and where his shotgun was stored. These were things that Glyn Thomas, a frequent visitor to the house, undoubtedly knew.

Once the police had secured the scene, Sara had sat with Constable Ceri Lloyd in the house across the road, trembling as the horrible reality sank in. She had been there for about an hour before she heard the whine of Rhodri's motor scooter approaching. She and Ceri had broken the news to him together, and he had turned deathly pale, and spent the next two hours in the neighbour's bathroom, with the door locked, refusing to speak.

'Did the police know about Rhodri's involvement with Glyn Thomas?' Jamie muttered, as he moved towards the conservatory.

'They knew about him and his group,' she replied, rising to follow him, 'because Daddy had complained.'

Jamie peered through the window of the conservatory, and Sara felt like grabbing him by the shoulder, spinning him round to look at her. 'They must have known about Glyn,' she continued, 'but I'm not sure whether they thought of him as a suspect just then –'

Suddenly, a woman's voice called out sharply from behind the conservatory. '*Helo! Allai'ch helpu chi?*'

Sara started, as a middle-aged woman with greying brown hair emerged from the back garden. She wore a canvas apron, and soiled gardening gloves.

'Err … *na*,' Sara replied, in her halting Welsh, '*'ni jyst yn edrych.*' They didn't need help, she said, they were just looking around.

The woman frowned, and looked them up and down. '*O, be chi'n 'neud?*' She wondered what they were doing on her property.

Jamie, who spoke no Welsh, caught the gist of the conversation and extended his hand.

'Hello, madam,' he said. 'Lovely day. Perhaps you could help us? My wife and I saw a house in an estate agent's window in town, and we're trying to find it.'

Sara looked at Jamie sharply and he suppressed a grin. The woman removed a glove, and accepted Jamie's hand. 'A house?' the homeowner said, switching language in deference to the Englishman. 'For sale in Gefail? No, I don't think anyone is selling a house. Unless it's one of the new ones down the end.'

She gazed down the road with undisguised contempt. 'Newcomers,' she added.

Making their apologies, Sara and Jamie returned to the car. As they drove, the only sound was a jazz radio station that Jamie had chosen out of deference to his passenger. When they passed through Bow Street, Sara searched for the greengrocer's, the last place her mother had ever gone. It was now a fish and chip shop.

'Jamie,' she mumbled, her eyes fixed on the passing buildings, 'this isn't right.'

'What do you mean?'

'What we just went through, back there. It didn't help.' She pulled her eyes away from the passing scenery and bit her lip.

Jamie tapped his fingers against the leather cover of the steering wheel and then said, 'We were interrupted. The mood was wrong.'

'No,' Sara interjected, 'that's not it.' She shifted in her seat, and looked at him for the first time since she had got in the car. Her eyes were red. 'I don't think I can marry you,' she said quietly.

Jamie remained silent for several moments, then slowly switched off the radio and waited.

She sighed. 'I know you mean well, but I have to be honest. Your concern has become a bit ... cloying.'

Jamie's mouth twitched, as if for a moment he was tempted to fall back on his defensive grin. Either he decided against it, or was unable to summon it. 'Cloying?' he repeated.

She nodded softly.

He shook his head, as if trying to assimilate a foreign thought that would not fit. 'That simply is not true,' he said.

The firm simplicity of his challenge made Sara's skin prickle. 'How can you say whether it's true or not?' she snapped. 'I'm the one feeling smothered.'

He raised his eyebrows speculatively. 'Then your feelings are wrong. I am trying to help you.'

She let her head fall against the headrest and sighed. They had now passed through Bow Street, and farmers' fields stretched to either side of the road. The air smelt thick with chemical fertiliser. Sara straightened her posture and snapped the radio back on, and this small act caused Jamie's calm facade to crumble. He struck one hand forcefully against the steering wheel. 'God damn it.'

They passed under a railway bridge as a train vibrated overhead. The car trembled.

'You can't see it, can you?' he continued. 'How self-obsessed you've been. If you're feeling smothered, Sara, it's because you've penned yourself so tightly into your own little world that any other presence seems like an intrusion. You told me that you love me –'

'I do!'

'Then you've got to open up some space in your life.'

Sara snorted with sad irony, and Jamie's veneer of anger crumbled away. 'Is it because …?'

He faltered. Sara eyed him warily. 'Is it because we lost our baby?' he whispered.

For a moment, Sara sat quietly. Finally, she said, 'I've been thinking about retiring as a consultant psychiatrist.'

Jamie sighed and brushed a strand of hair from his eyes.

'More than that, actually. I've already decided. I'm willing to take the stand in this case, Jamie, but I'd rather you didn't rely on me again.'

He nodded slowly. 'Please don't make any hasty decisions. You've been upset by this visit to Gefail.'

Sara grimaced. 'Gefail has nothing to do with it. But since you brought it up, I would also appreciate it if you'd forget about my parents' murder.'

Jamie stared at the road ahead. 'Of course,' he said finally, his words clipped.

'And it might be a good idea if we didn't speak about our past relationship, either. Not the baby, not anything.'

Sara glanced at his reflection in the rear-view mirror as Jamie's studied calm dissolved into shock and confusion. 'What do you mean?' he asked. 'Forever?'

She sighed. 'I don't know what I mean. For now, anyway.'

THIRTEEN

A vicious wind dashed volleys of summer hail against the Centre's windows; they crackled like pebbles flung into the sea. Sara looked through the streaked window as she rinsed the cafetière, preparing for an early closure. Outside, the bay was bilious green: waves of spume crashed against the sea-walls, flinging spray that dashed onto the prom. Inside, the fluorescent lights gave the Centre a harsh glare. Since her encounter with the killer, Sara felt uncomfortable being in this room alone but predictably, it had become near-impossible to find volunteers brave enough to keep her company.

There was no reason not to go home, Sara reflected. On a day like this, all her regulars would be hiding behind the lace curtains of their warm homes. The less rational parts of their minds told them that if they were to meet a killer, it would happen on a day like this.

Suddenly, the door downstairs banged, and Sara gasped, nearly dropping the wet cafetière. She heard footsteps slosh up the stairs, and an unkempt man appeared at the door. His clothes were so shiny and soiled that they looked like worn leather. He wore a drenched bedroll on his back, and carried a small bag at his side. Sara struggled to place him – he had visited the Centre on the day Aled Morgan had been murdered, but left when he saw Ceri in uniform.

Today, his eyes were wild with fear.

'*Bore da*,' Sara said hesitantly. 'Come in and take off those wet things. We'll dry them off next to the fire.'

She moved to the old electric fire and switched it on. It sparked and hummed, and the smell of burning dust rose.

'No, no,' the man said, his voice wavering. 'I just want to tell you something.'

'Oh?' Sara said.

'I want to make a deal with you.' he continued with pathetic earnestness.

Sara nodded neutrally, and the man took a grave, trembling breath.

'I am willing to go away,' he announced. 'Far away … if he promises to leave me alone.'

'Who is it you want to leave you alone?' Sara asked.

The man stiffened, as if he suspected her of mockery.

She tried a different tack. 'You say you want him to leave you alone. Why wouldn't he?'

'Because I know,' he replied.

'You know?'

'About the killings.'

'I see,' Sara said.

'How much do you know?'

'About the killings?'

'Yes, about the killings! What else?'

He began to pace the room like a cage fighter, as if Sara's questions were part of an attack. He choked on frightened sobs. 'I just don't want to die!'

Sara edged towards her medical bag.

'You might wonder, why not?' the man railed. 'Seeing what I've become. But I hate being this.'

He turned, and looked at Sara imploringly. 'That's the only reason I went to him. I was desperate … surely you understand that.'

With a spasmodic jerk, he flung himself towards her. 'I

didn't mean what I said! Please, tell him that!'

Instinctively, Sara recoiled, wrenched open her bag, and grasped the pre-loaded syringe of pentobarbital. The bag dropped with a thud, and she waved the needle at him like a stiletto. He stopped, eyes widening in terror.

'You're on his side, aren't you?'

'Calm down,' Sara commanded. 'Stay there.'

She advanced towards him. The man shrieked, 'Don't hurt me! I didn't mean it!'

He stumbled for the door.

'Tell him I won't say a word,' he shouted, thudding down the stairs. 'Not a word to anyone!'

By late afternoon, the rain had swept from Wales down to the south-east. On the streets of London, it was a persistent drizzle. To avoid a soaking, Jamie had parked directly in front of Rhodri Jones' house, with two wheels on the pavement and his badge displayed on the dashboard.

He was no longer willing to rely on Sara's mood swings, and was tired of waiting passively for her. He knew the emphasis she placed on understanding her life; if he wanted to be part of it, he would have to understand it too. For that, he needed someone else to talk to. Ceri Lloyd might have helped, but asking her in defiance of Sara's wishes would only push his goal farther away. There was only one other choice, and so Jamie had told the Welsh police he had business in London.

It took several knocks before the casually dressed businessman answered his front door and invited Jamie in. Jamie could smell Rhodri's freshly applied aftershave. In the house itself, however, there were no homely smells, like the cinnamon candles that Sara burned constantly. It smelt little-used, and Jamie wondered whether Rhodri kept a flat somewhere, possibly near the Hampshire air base where his company did much of its business.

As he welcomed Jamie, Rhodri displayed the same well-known bonhomie with which he graced boardrooms and television interviews, but there was a narrowness to his eyes that revealed suspicion and unease. 'I wasn't aware that they'd reopened my parents' case, Inspector Harding,' he said, as he led Jamie into the sitting room. 'I'm rather surprised that they forgot to tell me.'

'There's no need to reopen it,' Jamie replied, taking in every detail of the room's ornate decor. Professionally decorated, he guessed. 'The case was never closed.'

'Ah.' Rhodri selected a bottle of Canadian rye from the small liquor cabinet, concealed in a large antique globe. He held up a crystal tumbler towards Jamie, who smiled in refusal.

The businessman mixed a drink for himself and said, 'You've been assigned to work on the case, now, have you?' His Welsh accent was stronger than usual, and Jamie wondered whether this was an affectation like the false bonhomie, or a reaction to unwelcome situations.

'Not officially, no,' Jamie replied. 'It's still under the jurisdiction of the Dyfed-Powys Police.'

'I see …' Rhodri paused and furrowed his brow, as if confused. 'Perhaps this is a daft question,' he said haltingly, 'but if you are not assigned to the case, why did you request this meeting?'

Jamie smiled with self-deprecation. He did not know Rhodri well, and had no idea how the man had reacted to his relationship with Sara. He understood that the two siblings were close; if Rhodri viewed Jamie as no more than a prying outsider, his suspicion was understandable.

'I'm here because I care about your sister,' Jamie said.

'Really?' Rhodri asked pointedly. 'So do I.'

Jamie allowed his silence to confirm that he

understood. The businessman invited him to sit, and he chose a wing-chair next to the bay window. He said, 'Mr Jones, I don't know how much Sara has spoken to you about your parents' deaths –'

'Recently?' Rhodri interrupted. 'Not at all.'

'Well, it's been troubling her more than usual. I'm trying to help her make sense of it.'

Rhodri sat opposite Jamie, and furrowed his brow in concern. 'Why has it been bothering her so much?' he asked.

'I suppose it's the effect of the murder investigation she's helping with.'

'That's it,' Rhodri agreed. 'The investigation you got her involved in.' He peered at Jamie and spoke in a low, accusatory voice: 'Do you think that was wise?'

'It was necessary,' Jamie said. 'Sara has a special gift.'

Rhodri grunted unhappily. They continued to discuss Sara in vague terms, encircling each other with words. After several minutes, during which they agreed once again a common concern for Sara's well-being, Jamie said, 'Would you mind if I asked you a few questions about your past?'

Rhodri, who had downed half his tumbler of rye and soda, had relaxed noticeably. 'Go on, then,' he replied breezily.

Jamie withdrew a notebook from his jacket pocket.

'Do you believe Glyn Thomas murdered your parents?'

Rhodri raised an eyebrow at the notebook, and puckered his face into a concentrated frown. 'The police are almost certain of it.'

Jamie nodded slowly and scribbled a note. 'On the day your parents died, you told police you'd been riding your motor scooter ...'

'I did that quite often,' Rhodri replied.

'Where did you ride to? Were you with Glyn at any time?'

Rhodri shook his head.

'What about Artists Valley? Did you go there?'

'Of course not!' Rhodri snapped. 'I had very little interest in those people, to be honest. Glyn was rather smitten with them, that's true, and he did take me there on occasion. But frankly, I found Duncan Kraig rather unsettling. Ravers were never my cup of tea.'

'I'm surprised,' Jamie said, 'that the papers didn't make anything of your involvement with that group, however small it was.'

Rhodri shrugged, and rose to pour himself a second drink. This time, he omitted the soda. 'They didn't know. My social workers shielded me from press intrusion. My acquaintance with Glyn Thomas was kept quiet by all concerned, and for that I am grateful.'

He sank back into his seat, and took a large gulp of straight rye, wiping his mouth with the rolled cuff of his shirt. He gazed into the middle distance of the room, and his voice quietened: 'To this day, I am suffused with guilt over the whole horrible thing. Had I not befriended Glyn, none of this would ever have happened.' He smiled sadly. 'Still, that terrible time could have left Sara and me two of life's emotional casualties ... but I'd say it strengthened us.'

The faraway look in his eyes vanished. 'Once the shock was over, we threw ourselves into schoolwork. Eventually, Sara studied Medicine and I read Economics. It's odd to think that was because of Glyn Thomas and Duncan Kraig.'

Rhodri stared at Jamie. 'What do you plan to do with this information, Inspector?' he asked. Before Jamie could reply, he went on, 'I wouldn't want to read this in a newspaper, or even a police report. Sara mustn't have her past opened to scrutiny again.'

Jamie inclined his head deferentially. 'Of course not.'

Rhodri nodded guardedly. 'Just so long as we understand that.' His gaze grew more intense. 'I will do anything necessary to protect my sister,' he said gravely.

Jamie glanced at him impassively. Was the man threatening him?

Rhodri looked at his watch. 'My car is picking me up in forty minutes, I'm afraid. I was hoping to manage a shower before then.'

'Ah,' Jamie said, standing. 'Certainly.'

'Anyway,' Rhodri said, his voice lightening, 'there's little more I can offer, except advice. Sara is headstrong. She gets ideas and won't let them go, even when they do her harm. I believe her obsession with our past is doing her harm. If you want to help her, concentrate on your job and encourage Sara to get on with life.'

He led Jamie into the foyer, where Jamie noticed a decoration he had missed before: an antique umbrella stand, holding several riding crops. Rhodri turned the deadbolt, and pulled open the door.

'After twenty years,' Rhodri added, 'I think it's time we allowed some scar tissue to form over these old wounds, don't you?'

As she drove home through the storm, the street person's anguished words had rung in her mind: *I didn't mean what I said. I don't want to die. You're on his side. I'll never tell anyone.* Clearly, the poor man thought Sara had some leverage with the killer. But why did he need that leverage – and how did he know she had met him?

She hadn't been home long before Rhoddo rang her mobile.

'Your boyfriend's rather obsessed with your history, isn't he?' he drawled.

'My boyfriend?' Sara replied. 'You mean Jamie?'

'I can't think of anyone else with the temerity to demand a meeting so he can grill me about our parents' murder.'

A hollow cavity swelled in Sara's chest. 'My God,' she said. 'He interviewed you?'

'You didn't know?' asked Rhodri, mock-surprised.

She didn't need this – not after the kind of day she'd had. 'What did you tell him?' Sara asked.

She did not imagine Rhoddo would have opened up to Jamie Harding. Even to Sara, he spoke little about their childhood. He did not reminisce about their father's impotent rage, or their mother's tight-lipped silences. And certainly not about the violence that brought both to an end.

'I told him to leave you alone,' Rhodri said.

Sara remained silent for a time. 'Thank you,' she said finally. 'Why did he come?' she asked finally. 'Did he give you a reason why he wanted to know so much?'

'Nothing that rang true,' Rhoddo replied archly. 'He said he cared about you.'

Sara sighed. Jamie's way of trying to show concern was infuriating. It was simply not on to delve ghoulishly into her past to demonstrate his compassion.

But Sara's fury wasn't easy to sustain. During their drive back from Gefail, it had seemed only proper, even necessary, to order Jamie out of her personal life … but now, the world seemed a chillier place for having done so.

'Sara?' Rhoddo said. 'Are you still there?'

'Oh … yes. Let's talk about something else.'

Rhoddo seemed to sense her mood, and distracted her with questions about the case. She told him about her unsettling visit from the street person at the Drop-In Centre. He showed genuine concern, and asked a number of questions about the man – his actions, his appearance, the things he said. He warned her against any further contact. 'He sounds dangerous.'

Sara promised to protect herself. Rhoddo was two very different people – one of them so caring and sweet, the other so tormented by horrors that it drew him into brutality to expiate his pain.

They spoke for several minutes more, mostly of inconsequential things, before saying goodnight. Sara set down her phone with sadness. She thought about all the turns their lives had taken, and what she might do to make her brother whole.

In their first summer at Aunt Issy's house, Rhodri had tried to kill himself. After their parents' burial, and the dying down of media interest in Duncan Kraig, life in their new home in Machynlleth had settled into something like normality. They finished the academic year at a grammar school in their new town, but neither of them made any close friends. They were too notorious, their stories too whispered-about. Rhodri settled down to work, and surprised everyone with remarkable GCSE results ... but still, he had remained quiet, withdrawn. He had kept to his bedroom, avoiding the guests that flowed in and out of the two remaining bedrooms at Aunt Issy's B&B.

Then one day, Sara had arrived home to find the house quiet; the guests were out and Aunt Issy was at the nursing home where she worked part-time. Nothing had seemed unusual as Sara made her way through the large entranceway, with its payphone and tourist brochures. Sara had climbed the two flights of stairs to her bedroom, enjoying the smell of fresh flowers and rose-scented pot pourri. As she neared the top of the stairs, she felt the skin on her arms prickle and she slowed, cocking an ear. There was a muffled rubbing from the door of

Rhodri's bedroom.

'Rhoddo?' she called. The rubbing stopped. 'Rhoddo?' she repeated. Suddenly, there was a thud against the door, and, a second later, feet kicking wildly against the wooden floor.

'Rhodri!' Sara screamed, and dashed the remaining few stairs, throwing herself against the bedroom door and twisting the knob frantically. She had had to shove with all her weight to push the door part-open, as if something had been piled against the other side.

Gasping with effort and terror, she squeezed through the narrow gap and screamed: Rhodri was half-slumped on the floor. The terrycloth tie to his dressing gown was bound to his neck with a slip knot, its other end secured to the large brass hook on the back of his door. Rhodri's face was mottled red, his eyes bulging and his chest heaving with rasping attempts to suck in air.

For a second she stood, paralysed. A succession of anguished feelings, much too rapid to solidify into thoughts, flickered through her mind. Images of her parents, dead and bloody, terror that Rhodri was dying, fear that she would be alone, the sense that she was unprepared for this.

Rhodri's lips moved, but the only sound to emerge was a series of horrible gurgles. Sara fell forward, wedging her hands under Rhodri's armpits and heaving up with all her strength. By leaning into her brother, she managed to push him against the door, and then work two violently shaking fingers under the cotton tie, loosening the slip knot and tugging it over Rhodri's head.

'Help me,' he said in choking whisper. 'I don't want to die.'

'You won't,' she said, tears streaming down her face, her body trembling. His neck was scarred with livid welts, which were oozing clear fluid. 'The rope is off now,' she said, choking on tears. 'I'm going to leave you for a moment.'

'Don't call anyone,' Rhodri gasped. His neck was starting to swell.

'Rhodri, you need to see a doctor,' she screamed, her voice cracking hysterically.

'No,' he said, but Sara fled the room, dashing for the telephone.

Sara rode with Rhodri in the ambulance. On the way to Aberystwyth, the attendants checked his breathing and heart rate, and took his blood pressure. Sara sat pressed into a corner, trembling and sniffling, her eyes aching sharply from wiping away so many tears. At Bronglais Hospital, the triage nurse checked Rhodri over again, and swabbed the marks around his neck. By now, Rhodri was more embarrassed than distressed, having to admit his suicide attempt to every nurse and doctor he came across as they took his medical history, did an electrocardiogram, and arranged for him to chat with a staff member from the psychiatry department.

Aunt Issy was located, and – once the nurses had learned about the death of Rhodri and Sara's parents – their social workers were alerted. From then on, both Rhodri and Sara began regular visits to a psychiatrist.

Sara never blamed Rhodri for what he had done. Even at the age of fourteen, she knew that it had been a panicked cry for help. Afterwards, she felt closer to her older brother, and more protective of him than ever.

FOURTEEN

Being around Trevor Hughes was difficult for Eldon Carson. He had shared many hours of conversation with the man, and found him to be stupid, unprincipled, randomly violent, and filled with hatred for all the wrong things. It was a rage that would one day erupt if not stopped. Still, for the moment, Carson needed Trevor Hughes.

That didn't mean he had to stay up all night talking garbage with him. He had excused himself early, and managed to drift into a light, fitful sleep. Suddenly, Carson was hit by an impression close enough in time and proximity, and fierce enough in intensity, to connect with a blinding force. Straight from a fevered dream, he found himself plummeting through a barrier of brilliant light. Even in his surest moments of knowing, of seeing the past or future, the journey had never been this violent. As he dropped, he fought against the near-paralysing sense of disorientation, and managed at last to find his centre, controlling the last few moments of his psychic fall.

He found that he had dropped into a maelstrom of carnage: the sounds of terror, contorted faces, bodies falling, blood spattering and seeping. Never had the emotions he experienced been as intense, or the vision so clear. Carson was terrified.

Where was he? When was he?

He pulled back, and willed himself to rise into the air. Don't panic, he said to himself. Freeze the moment – freeze it here.

He surveyed the still scene: red brick buildings, a monument, a castle, an abbey. *This isn't Aberystwyth ... but it's not too far away. Further north ... north and east. England.* Carson remembered travelling through this place on his way to Wales – he was in Shrewsbury. He drifted down over the frozen bloodbath below, until he located the storm's calm centre ... the blankness that was a man named Frank Linden Dundas.

He is going to do this. And he's going to do it soon ... Oh, sweet Jesus Lord, this is very, very soon.

Carson struggled to blot away the sensation and sat up on the mat, his head thumping violently. He burrowed through his satchel for a pad of paper, and began making notes and sketches. He knew that, if it was the last thing he did, he had to stop Frank Linden Dundas.

After feverishly working the plan through on paper, Carson was able to quiet his racing mind. He told himself this job would be no different than anything else he'd done – even easier in a way, because he had seen it so clearly. The only real problem was that it demanded he leave Aberystwyth for a time.

And that was a problem, because it meant abandoning Sara Jones.

A surge of anger pulsed through him. This new responsibility would take him away from his most important charge. That was bad. He had primed Sara; she was waiting. He knew she was in an emotionally vulnerable state. She needed him.

And, if he were to be honest with himself, contacting her was not totally unselfish; he had never found another person like Sara Jones, and coming to know her, to help her, was almost a holy quest.

Carson weighed it all up, and made a decision. He had just enough time. He would see Sara Jones, and then leave for Shrewsbury. He put away the hastily scribbled notes and stood unsteadily.

In the tawdry living room, Trevor Hughes drank beer and watched television. When Carson entered, Hughes looked up with his usual vapid grin.

'I need to borrow your car,' Carson told him.

Sara sat upstairs, in the second-largest bedroom, which she used as her office. She was drafting a letter to the Welsh Language Board, inquiring about grants. Today, the torrential rain – which had fallen for days in thick angular sheets – had finally blown away. It had left behind a pleasant, cool Sunday evening, disturbed only by the shrill roar of military jets on manoeuvres overhead. Through her office window, Sara could see sheep grazing on the wet hill behind her house, their wool reflecting the dim orange glow of the dying sun.

The letter was something she had been putting off since the end of last week. After Thursday morning's visitor, Sara had been unable to devote her mind to paperwork. She had told the police about the vagrant's visit, but so far nobody had managed to locate him.

By the time Sara finished the letter, the sky outside was a patchwork of dark blue shades, and the trees and bushes were uniformly black. Aside from the occasional bleating of a sheep, the night was still and quiet. The first vague indication that something was not right came as a distant sensation, light as a feather brushing against her forehead. She stopped and her eyes defocused; she groped to get a better sense of why her subconscious had pricked her into this still wariness. Had she remembered something else about the distressed man who had visited the Centre?

No, that isn't it.

Was it a sound? There was a muffled something downstairs. A creaking floorboard, a small thud. She told herself it must be Gareth, the constable on duty, but rose as quietly as she could. Gareth should be patrolling the lane outside.

'Gareth?' she called, warily.

There was no reply. She heard rustling – a body settling into a chair – and frowned.

'Hello,' she called, 'who is it?'

There was now nothing but silence on the ground floor below. She scanned the room for something to use as a weapon – her medical bag was downstairs. She settled upon a well-sharpened pencil that sat in a cup next to her computer. She grasped it like a stiletto and, tentatively, crossed the groaning floorboards. The light from the bedroom threw her long shadow down the blackened stairs. She peered down, into the dimness of her long, narrow sitting room.

In the sky above Penweddig, a fighter jet ripped through the air with a deafening shriek.

Sara winced, hesitated a moment, then descended slowly, with one hand skimming the stone wall for support. At the bottom, she thumbed the light switch. The fluorescent tube in the ceiling had been dying slowly for the past few days, and now it burned at the edges only, casting a feeble, milky glow through the room. As the dim half-light popped and flickered into life, Sara gasped. A man was sitting in the chair in the corner. She could not make out his face.

'Gareth!' she screamed, praying her guardian was nearby.

'Shhhh,' the man whispered. 'You're not in danger, I promise you.'

Sara flinched with startled recognition.

'We've met once before, Miss Sara,' her visitor said politely, 'though I don't think we've been properly introduced.'

He rose from the chair with the grace of an athlete, and extended his hand towards the shadows where Sara stood.

'My name is Eldon Carson.'

Sara remained where she stood, refusing to accept the killer's proffered hand. Eldon Carson shrugged and stretched out both his hands in a gesture of defencelessness.

'I'm not armed,' he said. 'I won't hurt you. Could you please drop the pencil?'

Sara looked down at her makeshift weapon, which was clenched tightly in her left hand. She let go, and it clattered on the floorboards. Sara glanced past the killer, to the window looking over her driveway.

'I know there's a policeman outside,' Carson continued. 'Right now, he's at the end of the lane. He didn't hear you shout. If you call him again, or run, or try to get his attention in any way, I might have to hurt him. Nobody wants that ... especially not Gareth. So please – just for the moment – hear what I've got to say.'

Sara drew a wavering breath, and clenched her muscles, forcing them still. 'Go on then, say it.'

Carson balled his fists and drummed them against his thighs. 'There's so much to tell you. I need to leave this place for a while, but I wanted to see you again before I did.' He lowered his voice to a quiet, sincere monotone. 'That's how important you are to me.'

Sara raised her eyebrows. 'You've seen me. Now what?'

'I just want you to listen.' He held out his hands, in a gesture of supplication. 'I need you to understand.'

Sara scanned the dimly lit room, and finally sat down

on a love-seat. 'Talk away,' she said.

She had selected the seat because it was within easy reach of her medical bag. From the corner of her eye, she noted its exact position, and found herself wondering just how psychic Eldon Carson really was.

Jamie's flat was in a gentrified house next to a council estate off Brixton Hill. On this Sunday evening, his television blared highlights of an England test match in South Africa. Jamie listened to it while glancing out of the window at the street life before him. In the aftermath of the day's drizzle, it was a muggy night, and the heat had brought his neighbours drifting onto the pavement to chat, laugh, smoke and drink. At around ten o'clock, a hollow pang reminded Jamie that he had not eaten since breakfast – and the only things left in his fridge were several jars of condiments, two tins of beer, and a plastic tub of cherry tomatoes that were turning white with mould. He switched off the television, slipped on a pair of trainers, and joined the throng on his street.

There was a bar nearby that he visited every now and then. Each time, its name, decor, and the nationality of its serving staff had changed. Jamie headed towards it now, breezing past the Hare Krishnas dancing in front of Pizza Hut, and the man in white robes selling incense from a folding table. Pungent smoke curled through the hot evening air.

At the bar – an Italian place now – Jamie chose a table near the window, and ordered imported beer and something on a ciabatta. He watched the late-night record shop across the street and thought pensively. Tomorrow, he would make the five-hour drive back to Aberystwyth. That afternoon's conversation with Rhodri had left him unsettled; he had hoped the meeting would produce a reason to ignore Sara's discouragement, and continue delving into the deaths of her parents. Instead, Rhodri had repeated Sara's request to let the matter drop.

By the time his food arrived on an enormous metal slab, Jamie had decided to take Sara's request at face value. The more he pushed, the stronger the reaction against him. Tomorrow, he would drive straight to Penweddig and promise to stay out of Sara's business – and her life – as long as she wanted.

Maybe time alone could change things. In the meantime, his responsibility would be to continue to be of use in Aberystwyth, so that his Chief Officer would allow him to remain, and the Dyfed-Powys Police would continue to pay for him to do so. More than ever, he needed to stay in Aberystwyth, in the hope that Sara's turbulent emotions would swing in his favour again soon.

'Let me start by saying how well you do your job,' Eldon Carson stated. He stood only a couple of feet from Sara, towering over her as she sat on the love-seat. 'Everything you thought about me is right. What I did to Kapadia, Williams, the Morgan boy, and that pervert in Clarach. They were all messages.'

'Messages to whom?'

'At the start, to everybody.' He inclined his head. 'Later on, the messages were to you.'

'To me,' Sara repeated flatly.

Carson smiled and held out his arms in a symbolic embrace. 'And you figured it out! The way you detailed it to those CID men at the police station was incredible.'

'How do you know what I told them?' Sara asked.

Eldon Carson chuckled. 'Because I'm psychic,' he said. Suddenly, his tone grew earnest. 'You see, Miss Sara, that's the thing. That's what I've had to deal with: looking at a stranger on the street, say, and knowing he was going to burn himself and his children to death in his car, with his wife watching. Seeing some guy and knowing he'll rape and kill a young woman. How do you think I felt?'

Sara stared at him levelly. 'I suppose, pretty confused,' she said.

'Why's that?' he asked, surprised.

'Well, for one thing, you must've wondered why all these killers had descended on Aberystwyth. You see, Mr Carson, that's a problem I'm having with your story. Why are so many bad people here, of all places?'

Eldon Carson nodded appreciatively. 'A decent question,' he said. 'It's not that Aberystwyth is especially bad, Miss Sara. It's just like everywhere else. There's not a small town anywhere without three or four people who will, in time, do awful things. Trouble up to now's been, nobody knew who they were.' In the half-light, Sara could see him smile as he added, 'But I do.'

He stared beyond her, out the window at the darkening field of sheep beyond. 'That's what I have to face every day of my life. Let them call me a serial killer if they want to, I've got to do what's right.'

Sara took advantage of his distraction to edge closer to her medical bag. She knew her only hope to use the weapon inside was to keep him talking.

'You have to understand,' she said soothingly, dropping a hand towards the bag, 'it's not easy for someone like me to accept all this. I told CID you think you're psychic, not that I do.'

Carson turned to her, and she drew her hand sharply away from the bag. 'You've always been afraid of dogs,' he said, 'because you were bitten by one when you were three. You didn't remember that till now.'

Sara paused, startled. She did have vague memories of a dog ... snarling, leaping up, thick cords of saliva foaming as it barked.

'At your eleventh birthday party, the boys laughed when you said you were going to marry Gary Barlow. Until you were five, you had a stuffed panda named Charlie Chan.' Carson paused, concentrated, and then added, 'You always thought you lost it, but actually your brother burned it on a Guy Fawkes fire.'

Sara gasped at the thought of her favourite bedtime toy going up in flames. Suddenly, in her memories, she was five again, and Rhodri was a devilish seven-year-old.

'That is absolute proof I'm psychic,' Carson said with a smirk, 'because, until a few seconds ago, I didn't know what a Guy Fawkes fire was. And I'm still not sure about Gary Barlow.'

Calm down, Sara told herself, *and keep him talking. Wait for him to relax.*

'All right,' she said, 'even if I do accept you're psychic, how can you possibly see the future when it hasn't happened yet? The future's an open book. Isn't it true that anything might happen?'

The American hesitated, groping for the right words. 'About ten years ago, I tried to understand what I was feeling,' he said, 'so I started hanging around psychic fairs, Spiritualist churches, anywhere I might find a kindred spirit.' He grinned whimsically. 'I never did. But I did hear a lot of theories about psychic phenomena. The future may not be fixed, but that doesn't mean that *anything* can happen. Think of it as a series of probabilities, with some more likely than others.'

'Like what?'

'Well, as a medical doctor, you'd be more likely to take a job in a hospital than become a bus driver.'

'Of course.' Sara looked up at Eldon Carson's burning eyes, the concentration on his face. This was no randomly violent killer, but an intelligent and thoughtful young man.

'With some people, you might find several probabilities of equal strength. Then, the future is hard to predict.'

She nodded, encouraging him to continue.

'In other cases, there's only one likely probability, because all parts of a person's life flow in the same direction. Then, the future's near-written in stone.'

'So with Mr Kapadia …'

'Everything pre-disposed him to an act that would kill his children before the end of this summer.'

He spread his hands in a gesture of inevitability. 'A random element had to be introduced to stop it … and that had to be me.'

'But why did you kill him?' Sara asked. 'Couldn't you have just broken his leg or something?'

Carson turned his gaze once more to the window. 'Maybe I'm not a good enough psychic to know if that would have worked …'

His voice trailed away, and he gazed far into the distance, as if re-experiencing the grisly steps he had taken.

'To be absolutely sure,' he added in a quiet, faraway voice, 'Navid Kapadia had to die, before he took his kids with him.'

Seeing her chance, Sara jerked open the bag and groped for the syringe. She clutched it in her left hand like a dagger, and threw herself forward.

At the same moment, Carson made a graceful leap to the side, and twisted like a natural athlete, his hand shooting out for the syringe.

Shit! Sara thought. *He knew!*

She tumbled forward – but Carson, in mid-turn, had not yet steadied himself. Sara's right shoulder shoved against the back of his left calf as she fell, and he stumbled, lost balance, and toppled over her with a cry. She huffed as the weight of his muscular body crashed down on her, pinning her to the floor.

'You never asked me the most important question,' he gasped, winded. 'Why you? ' Before he had settled on her, she managed to twist her shoulders. 'You need me,' he cried. 'I can help you understand your life ...'

In a fluid motion, she pulled in her stomach muscles, shoved her left hand underneath her body, and brought the syringe down like a dagger, driving the needle deeply into Eldon Carson's right buttock. She pushed down the plunger and injected the tube's entire 400mg – four times the normal dosage. He bellowed as the solution burned through his muscles, and rolled off her, thrashing as powerful sedative began to course through his bloodstream.

On his hands and knees, he looked at her wildly, his expression one of surprise and fear, his skin draining of colour. 'No!' he cried.

Unsteadily, he stumbled to his feet, blanching as though he might vomit, and thrust an unsteady hand at the wall. To have so much of the drug injected so quickly was a form of torture. Sara was astonished that Carson was not howling in agony.

'Don't do this! You need me,' he repeated, his speech thickening. 'You're psychic too!'

He began to sway, and fell against the stone wall, grazing his bare arms and leaving streaks of blood. 'Think about it!' he gasped imploringly. 'You need to ... to understand.'

Carson's knees buckled, and he sank again to the wooden floorboards. Within seconds, he was moaning like a wounded animal, and slurring incoherently. Sara peered out the window, fearful that the constable might hear, but she could not locate him. She grabbed a thick linen napkin from the kitchen, and wedged it into his mouth.

Carson's body twitched; he was not yet unconscious, but uncoordinated like a drunk. From her medical bag, she withdrew a roll of gauze and wrapped it several times around his head, fastening it with fabric tape, securing the napkin in his mouth. Sara managed to roll him over and bind his wrists together with more gauze. When the roll ran out, she used the fabric tape, wrapping it around his wrists, and using it to immobilise his legs.

By the time she had secured him, Carson had slipped into deep unconsciousness. A shiver ran down Sara's spine as his final words resonated in her mind. She looked into his glazed, unfocused eyes.

'Now,' she said out loud, 'what am I supposed to do with you?'

FIFTEEN

Alone, on a dark night, in the quiet of a house surrounded by fields and trees, the boundaries between logic and intuition, right and wrong, are indistinct. Darkness promotes uncertainty; we rely on more primitive senses than logic to guide us. Sometimes they take us places we would not otherwise go.

Sara had sedated and restrained the murderer, Eldon Carson ... but she had not called the police.

Instead, she had dragged her drugged captive to the small stable attached to the living room – the one she and Ceri had cleared of boxes only recently – and, in the dark, tied him prone to a large wooden workbench. As soon as she had bound him securely, she collapsed into a fit of trembling and hyperventilation.

She fought the spasms in her limbs, forced herself to tear rectangles from an empty cardboard box and fit them over the stable's two small windows. Then she walked unsteadily to her kitchen, where she brewed coffee with great deliberation.

I need to think rationally, she repeated to herself.

I need to think.

She carried her mug of coffee up to her room, the hot ceramic burning her knuckles. He might be lying, she thought with desperate concentration, but what if he's telling the truth? After all, he had known things that nobody outside Sara's family knew, things she herself had half forgotten. It was possible that he had obtained the information from someone; perhaps he had met Rhoddo and learned about her stuffed panda, Charlie Chan. But what about the Gary Barlow story? Had Rhodri even been at her eleventh birthday party? Would he have remembered the Gary Barlow story?

Maybe an old friend heard these stories a long time ago, and told them to the killer.

Those would all be rational explanations … yet, on this dark night, they seemed less plausible than the irrational one: that Eldon Carson was psychic. And if he was, then maybe he *did* know who was going to commit crimes.

Sara would not act when the case had not been proven; the stakes were far too high.

What if he actually could stop the worst individuals from committing their evil acts? What then? Would I have the right to stop him? And how many innocent people would die if I did?

She pulled her covers chest-high. Eldon Carson's presence in her house was palpable, and Sara felt as though she were his prisoner, not he hers. She found herself wishing desperately that Jamie were at her side.

After nearly an hour had passed, Sara rose, and descended the wooden steps to the stable door. The roll of tape had settled in the corner. The contents of her medical bag were still scattered across the floor. She pushed the handle, and stepped down onto the cold, cement floor. The drug she had administered to Carson would, in normal doses, have sedated him for no more than a few hours. The amount she had given him would keep him under all night.

Carson lay across the grimy wooden workbench, ropes of bright yellow nylon fastened at his chest and pelvis.

His bound legs and feet dangled off the edge of the bench, and Sara, having run out of rope, had secured them to the workbench's legs with thick gardening wire. She knew that her captive would be very stiff when she finally released him – but he would feel so bad from the pentobarbital, he'd be unlikely to notice.

Sweating, yet chilled, Sara stood a silent vigil next to the bulk of his body, replaying their previous night's conversation. What had the young man meant when he shouted that she was psychic too? Had it simply been a ploy to unnerve her?

Then it had worked, she thought. She longed to be able to shake him awake, to ask him – but he would not regain consciousness for hours. She certainly was not psychic, Sara told herself, that was self-evident … but, standing alone in the fertile dark, troubling question grew in her mind.

If, twenty years ago, she could have prevented Glyn Thomas from murdering her parents by allowing his death, would she have done it?

The answer was obvious, and terrifying.

Sara had left and returned to the stable several more times that night, growing more and more exhausted, emotionally and physically. She waited with agitation for the moment her captive would wake, yet still he slumbered on. Sometime after dawn, she fell into a deep but uneasy slumber, from which she woke with a start just after nine in the morning.

When she stepped down onto the cold concrete floor, the sharp odour of urine made her retch. Carson's eyes were glazed but open. 'Oh, dear,' she said, fighting to sound calm, 'I did leave you rather a long time, didn't I?'

From the kitchen, she fetched a washing-up bowl of soapy water and a J-cloth. On her way through the living room, she picked up her medical bag, and set everything next to the old, wooden workbench. Through the corner of her eye, she could see Carson's pleading expression, but refused to make eye contact. Methodically, she donned surgical gloves, and selected scissors from her bag. Deciding against dulling them, she removed a pair of gardening shears from a peg on the stone wall, and made precise incisions up both legs of Carson's jeans. She pulled the soaking fabric away, removed his pants, and began to wash his clammy legs. 'Don't be embarrassed,' she muttered, 'I'm a doctor.'

Eldon Carson made muffled pleas through his gag. He did not know that she was as desperate to talk to him as he was to her. When she finished washing his legs, she slowly removed an empty syringe from her bag. Holding it in his line of vision, she stuck the needle into a glass ampoule, drawing the clear liquid upwards.

'This,' she said, her voice trembling, 'is haloperidol – a drug used to sedate psychopaths. If you think what I gave you last night was strong, you don't want to try this.'

She held the needle next to his thigh, allowing him to feel its pinprick. 'I am going to remove your gag now, and if you do anything more unsettling than whisper, I'm sending you back to sleep … understand?'

Eldon Carson nodded with uncoordinated vigour.

She snipped away the gauze, and tugged the napkin from his mouth. He gasped and worked his jaws awkwardly. His eyelids flickered and closed tightly, as if he were trying to control his mental faculties as well. Sara assumed he had one hell of a hangover.

Finally, in a hoarse voice, he said, 'Please … you must let me go. It's essential.'

Sara studied him with dispassionate eyes. 'So you can go and kill someone else?'

'Yes,' he said, slurring his speech, and fighting to

concentrate on his words.

'We don't need another murder in Aberystwyth,' Sara said.

'It won't be in Aberystwyth,' he replied. 'Not even in Wales. It's … something special. I hadn't planned it, but I've got to respond. Please.'

The man was babbling. Sara placed a finger against her lips and said 'Shhhh.'

She dragged a cobweb-covered wooden stool from the corner. She wiped it with the crumpled napkin that had been Carson's gag, and sat, returning the point of the syringe to his leg. 'We have things to discuss,' she said.

Carson drew in a wheezing breath, and spoke in a forced rasp. 'If I answer your questions, will you let me go?'

Sara allowed the needle to press more firmly against his skin. 'I didn't say that.'

'Please.'

She smiled maliciously. 'You've got very little choice but to humour me.'

Carson sighed and nodded mournfully. 'What do you want to know?' he asked.

'Everything,' Sara replied. 'Just tell me about yourself. Have you always been psychic?'

'It's become stronger as I've gotten older,' he whispered, then cleared his throat and spoke as clearly as he could. 'Even as a kid, I could sometimes see what someone had been through – or what someone else would one day put others through – as if I were watching television.' He looked at her with intensity, and spoke as if words alone could convince her to bend to his will. 'That's why you've got to let me go!'

She pressed the needle into him again. Carson grimaced, but continued. 'In my early teens, I realised how different I was. That was when I went looking for others like me. I met a lot of folks who claimed to be psychic but weren't ... but there were a few. I learned a lot from them.'

'Like what?'

'How to refine my abilities. Not stuff they teach you in high school. One guy – a stage hypnotist – showed me ways to control people's thoughts. He had more abilities than his audiences ever guessed.'

Carson shook his head reflectively. 'Despite the people I talked to, though, I never met anyone quite like me. Every psychic has certain gifts – things he can do better than others. I've always been sensitive to pain and violence. I can spot people who've suffered – and those who might cause suffering.'

The monologue had made him breathless, and he paused, squeezing his eyes shut and re-opening them slowly, as if to control a rush of nausea.

'How did you support yourself, once you'd left school?' Sara asked.

'My father had died by then, and he left me some money,' Carson replied. He hesitated before adding, 'And I sold some art.'

'Art?'

He nodded weakly. 'I'm a sculptor.'

Sara blinked. 'You're kidding.'

'Metal, wood, paper – I can use anything.' He grimaced and a released a small chuckle that came out as a series of wheezes. 'Funny, huh? The killer's really an artist!'

Sara smiled at the irony. 'So then, tell me – how did a sensitive artist end up killing people?'

He snorted. 'In my late teens, I moved down to Atlanta. It's a big city, and every day on the streets, I couldn't help seeing who the dangerous people were. Then one day I saw a guy, and I knew he was about to kill someone. I even knew the name of the man he was going to kill. About a month later, it happened again – and this time, I saw the murder, as if I were watching it as it occurred.'

'Did you kill the guys who were going to do it?'

Carson shook his head.

'You ran away,' Sara said.

Carson nodded. 'I decided to get right out of America. I flipped a coin between England and Australia, then bought a ticket to Heathrow with the last of my inheritance.'

Raising his head slightly off the bench, he looked into her eyes. 'Have I told you enough yet?' he asked.

'I know you're concerned,' Sara said, 'but we've got all the time in the world.'

'No, we haven't!' Carson wailed. 'If you don't release me, something very bad is going to happen.'

'Look, Mr Carson,' Sara said sharply, 'the fact that you're not in a cell right now means that I don't know what to make of you. By all rights I should just turn you over to the police and be done with it.'

She hesitated before adding, 'Yet something is holding me back.'

'I know,' he replied mildly. 'You won't turn me in.'

'Neither will I release you,' she said, 'unless I'm convinced that it's the right thing to do. And for that, I need to know more.'

'You need to know much more,' Carson agreed. 'Much more than I can tell you now. Let me go, and I promise, I'll come back as soon as I can.'

Sara shook her head decisively. 'You ended up in Aberystwyth,' she said in a firm voice. 'Tell me how.'

He closed his eyes and drew in a wavering breath. 'I avoided the big cities,' he said. 'I figured, the fewer the people I was around, the less the chance I'd experience what I'd felt in Atlanta. So I drifted. And the closer I got to here, the more I felt I was heading towards something important.'

Sara looked at him implacably. 'You mean murdering people.'

'No,' he countered. 'I mean you. I am destined to change your life.'

She closed her eyes wearily.

'You are psychic,' Carson insisted, 'You just haven't realised it. Miss Sara, I know exactly what you need, and I'm certain I can give it to you. Now think before you scorn this offer – think about everything you've ever wanted to know. I'm probably the only person in the world who can show you these things.'

Sara shrugged. 'Okay … so show me.'

'Believe me, I will. But now, you've got to let me go.'

'No,' Sara said flatly.

Suddenly, Carson sighed and closed his eyes. He grew very still, and Sara felt a wave of narcotic calm break through her body. Her thoughts became unclear, and the space just beneath her skull felt warm and fuzzy.

'What are you doing to me?' she gasped.

'Let me go now,' he said. 'Release the ties.'

Sara's body began to twitch, as if a current of electricity was passing through her skin. 'Stop it!' she commanded. 'Whatever you're doing, stop!'

Carson ignored her cry. He clenched his jaw and tightened his eyes, and Sara could feel energy washing from her body. Swiftly, she snatched up the syringe, caught her diminishing breath, and plunged the needle deep into his thigh. He went rigid, and lashed out with his bound legs – then his body relaxed, and his breathing became very shallow.

Sara grasped the workbench for support, and looked into Carson's slack features. She checked his eyes – they were rolled upwards, towards his forehead.

'Oculogyric crisis,' she murmured.

She imagined that his blood pressure had also sunk dangerously low. She injected him with an ampoule of benzatropine to counteract these side-effects, and knew that he would require another injection when he woke up, which would be in a day or so.

She noticed that she was trembling with shock, and breathing hard.

'I didn't want to knock you out again,' she panted, 'but if you wanted a test, here it is. Did you say that something bad was going to happen? Well, okay then, let's see if it does.'

Usually, good driving conditions were enough to put Jamie in a cheerful mood, but today, he felt sombre and listless. He wasn't certain why he had hurried to make it here, to Penweddig. His only plan was to admit defeat, apologise to Sara, and promise to stay out of her life. He felt like a man, wrongly convicted, rushing into the arms of his gaolers.

How would she react? Coldly, probably – but he knew that Sara would not intend it as an affront. She stifled her emotions whenever they were overwhelmed; it was the only way she could control them. To an outsider, this could make her seem far more composed than she actually was. He had learned this the hard way, during the awful culmination of last winter's romance. Her tendency to freeze was a trait Jamie unwittingly made worse. When he grew weary of being understanding, he would swing to the other extreme and press the issue.

A thought made him smile grimly: if he understood this so well, then why was he driving to Sara's house right now? Why visit her to promise to stay out of her life? Why not just stay out of her life?

Because it would have felt wrong. And Jamie Harding was entitled to the odd personality quirk too. He pulled into Sara's lane, and the holly bushes scraped against his Range Rover's dark blue paintwork. Jamie sighed and felt a wave of regret that he had ever volunteered for this assignment.

Sara heard the scrape of bushes against metal somewhere down the lane, and felt a shudder of dread. She dashed from the kitchen through the living room, skidding on a small Indian rug that lay in front of the stable door. She fumbled with the door's skeleton key, twisting it, securing the lock with a smooth click, and hiding the key between two books on the shelf. Gasping for breath, she paused to inspect herself in the mirror. Her face was deathly pale, her eyes had swollen into slits, and her clothes were rumpled as if she had slept in them – which of course she had.

If it's Ceri, I'll tell her I'm ill. If it's anyone else, it's none of their Goddamned business, anyway.

Sara forced herself to walk back into the kitchen calmly, as she heard the thud of a car door closing. Parting the curtains, she peered through the window.

Jamie Harding looked up and smiled hesitantly.

For a brief moment, she stared, stunned. Then she felt a cooling flood of relief.

Jamie tapped twice on the kitchen door, and shoved it open. Sara watched his eyes glint as he took in her dishevelled appearance – other than that, he made no outward sign that anything about her was unusual.

'Hello,' he said tentatively.

'Hi,' she replied with false cheeriness. 'Coffee?'

'That would be nice.'

As he sat down at the table, Sara ground beans and put them in the cafetière.

'How have you been?' he asked.

'Fine,' she said with a wavering smile. Self-consciously, she smoothed her rumpled chambray shirt. 'You caught me before I've had a chance to shower. These are yesterday's clothes … I just threw them on when I woke up.'

Suddenly, she squeezed her eyes shut, and clenched her jaw. Unwelcome tears rolled from under her eyelids. She wiped at the savagely, and opened her eye to see Jamie's expression of feigned normalcy disintegrating. He stood uncertainly.

'Actually, I've been a bit miserable,' she said, with a choked attempt at a laugh. He moved towards her, and she responded immediately by throwing her arms around him. Her face nuzzled into his chest, and she sobbed. 'I'm so sorry. I've been hopeless without you.'

He returned her embrace, but held very still, as if trying to sense what was troubling her. As he held her, he made soothing sounds. 'It's okay,' he murmured. 'Relax, I'm with you now.'

'Just forget what I said,' she sobbed, 'forget everything I've done to you. I need you.'

'Everything's all right,' he whispered.

She pulled away from him, and grasped his hand. It wasn't until that smaller contact that she became aware of her own trembling. 'Can you stay?'

Sara pulled him through the kitchen, into the narrow living room. She removed his jacket, tossed it on a chair, and manoeuvred him into the love seat. She joined him, saying nothing, and laid her warm head on his shoulder.

They sat silently for a long moment, and Jamie listened as her breathing returned to a calm, steady rhythm. In a low voice, he said, 'What's happened?'

Her moist eyes met his, and she bit her lip. Finally, she sighed and said, 'I've regretted the way you left.'

'I regret a lot of things,' Jamie replied softly.

She swallowed. A bitter taste burned in her mouth. 'For the last few days I've felt more alone than I have in a long time,' she said. 'Every time I feel that way, I know thing that's missing is you.'

Jamie opened his mouth but did not speak. Instead, he huffed in wonder and shook his head.

'What?'

'I came here to agree to your terms. To say I'll leave you alone from now on.'

Sara held his arm tightly and tried to smile. 'If you agree to my terms, I'll kill you.'

He laughed. She rolled off the love-seat, grasped his hand and pulled him to his feet. 'You go upstairs,' she said. 'I'm just going to grab that shower.'

SIXTEEN

Frank Linden Dundas knelt at the side of his bed like a man at prayer, although prayer was the farthest thing from his mind.

Frank had never asked much of life and, until recently, life had allowed him to go about his days untroubled. He had always enjoyed simple things, like morning tea, Marmite on crumpets, and televised sport – especially snooker. Frank had always been law-abiding. He believed in obeying rules, even when he did not agree with them. In his younger days, he had enjoyed target shooting, but after the handgun ban he had surrendered three weapons: a .357 Smith & Wesson 686-Plus; a 9mm Sig Sauer P226, and a .22 Hämmerli 208.

Now, as he slid a long, dusty case from under his bed, he regretted that: his one remaining weapon was this shotgun ... and even though the model had a folding stock, it was going to be hard to conceal.

He steadied his free hand on the mattress and pushed himself up. His other hand was shaking as it dropped the shotgun onto the bed. He unzipped the black vinyl case, and thought about the immensity of what he would do this afternoon.

As the first and last criminal offence that he would ever commit, Frank Linden Dundas had decided to kill Ian Carpenter, a father of two who worked at his local Jobcentre.

'And why not?' he mumbled to himself as he placed a satchel of three-inch shells next to the gun. He had lost the only person he had ever loved, he was so broke he couldn't meet this month's bills, and now he was in trouble with the law. Frank knew that life as he had known it was over – and if he was going down, Ian Carpenter was going go with him.

Yesterday, while he was waiting for his solicitor, the custody officer had taken his belt and shoelaces. He had had to do it by force; Frank would never co-operate with such an indignity. They had locked him in a cell: grey walls, blue lino floor, thick steel door, metal toilet with no seat. He had been upset; he'd had to take a shit. The bastards had looked at him.

He denied everything, of course.

'We have the testimony of Mr Carpenter's neighbour, who saw you do it,' they had said.

'It wasn't me,' he replied.

'She recognised your car down the street.'

'I always park there.'

'Mr Dundas, we are arresting you for criminal damage, and offences under the Protection Against Harassment Act. You must turn up at the Magistrates' Court at two p.m. on September fifteenth. Failure to do so will result in a fine or imprisonment, or both. The conditions of your bail are as follows ...'

Frank snorted sardonically. One of the conditions of his bail was that he not interfere in any way with Mr Ian Carpenter.

He tugged the shotgun from its vinyl case.

Sorry, Sergeant, but I'm going to have to violate that particular condition.

Frank had once worked as an electrician, for a small firm

of cable engineers that sub-contracted work from a larger communications company. He had installed telephone lines and cable television, and in some weeks he had worked up to seventy hours. During other weeks, he had not worked at all; Frank worked on a zero hours contract. The weekly uncertainty had been nerve-wracking, but he had earned enough to help support himself and his mother, in whose home, at the age of forty-two, he still lived.

Frank had never been good at making friends, and relied on his mother for company and support. When she first developed low-grade lymphoma – a cancer that attacks the lymph glands – he had almost welcomed it, as a chance to grow even closer to her, in her need for his compassion. He had not feared that he might lose her any time soon – the specialists said she might live for another fifteen years.

Sadly, they had not described the decline she could expect in her quality of life. After four years of chemotherapy, she developed shingles, a rash of tiny blisters on her scalp. On bad days, it caused waves of intense agony to surge through her head. Frank turned down work to care for her. Slowly, he watched her personality change with the decreasing health and increasing pain, and felt as if his most prized possession were being stripped away before his eyes.

In its sixth year, the cancer became more truculent, and his mother declined rapidly. As her life began to slip away, it grew increasingly hard for Frank to work, and he turned down every job that came his way. When she died, Frank went to the crematorium alone, and watched the curtain draw closed on electric pulleys, hiding the casket from view before its final journey to the furnace.

Until that moment, Frank had not had time to feel much emotion, dealing as he had with the administrative minutiae of her quiet death. Once his mother's ashes had been committed to the earth, he felt as if an injustice had been done him for which there was no hope of redress.

Eleanor Dundas left behind the small bungalow she had shared with her son, and a little over five thousand pounds in savings. Frank spent most of the money paying off his debts, and knew that he needed to return to work.

He called his old supervisor, but was told he would not be welcomed back. In the company's eyes, he had violated his contract by refusing to work. Frank spent the next few days scouting for another job, and even when nobody was interested in hiring him, he refused to worry.

Then he went to his Jobcentre to sign on. A nineteen-year-old girl told him that he wasn't qualified for any allowance at all – he had left his job voluntarily. He was not covered by National Insurance because his work had not been regular.

Frank demanded to see her supervisor, and was introduced to Ian Carpenter – a thin, balding man in his middle thirties, nattily dressed in an oddly coloured jacket and tortoiseshell glasses. Mr Carpenter had simpered at Frank, agreeing that he had 'slipped through the net.' He made a lot of unhelpful suggestions, none of which involved his department allowing Frank to have any money. Frank shook his head in bewilderment – this man did not care if he could afford to eat, and he had stared into those gleaming tortoiseshell glasses with growing anger. Frank hated Ian Carpenter then – and hated himself even more, for begging. And he did beg. He pleaded with the man to help him out, to accept his claim … but Carpenter had only smirked sadly, and said there was nothing that he could do.

Frank's inheritance money ran out over the next fortnight, when he had to pay both an overdue electricity bill and a gas bill. He put his mother's house on the market, but it was a small ex-council property, and the estate agent said they weren't selling especially well just now. The one adjoining Frank's on the left had been on sale for months. He began to devote the days to searching job sites, but there was simply no work to be had. For the first time, he started to feel desperate, and felt that some lateral thinking was needed to solve his problems.

Late one afternoon, he loitered outside the brick benefits office, and waited for Ian Carpenter to come out. He felt a chance meeting might yield better results, and planned to apologise for the intensity of his emotions two weeks ago, and ask the man to reconsider allowing him benefits.

Frank shadowed his prey for several blocks, along the High Street, past the Darwin Shopping Centre, to the tarmac playground of a primary school. He watched as Carpenter went into a portable classroom. When the man came out with a boy of about seven – tall and thin, just like his father – Frank hurried towards him with a warm smile, and familiar greeting.

'Frank Dundas,' he said. 'You spoke to me at the Benefits Office two weeks ago, remember?'

The man's eyes glazed, trying to recall, then he flinched with recognition. Frank chatted with false bonhomie, and Carpenter tried to shuffle away. Frank kept pace with him as he walked, detailing how he had spent the last of his money, and had resorted to putting everything on credit cards which were nearing their limit. 'So,' he said finally, 'won't you reconsider?'

Carpenter drew a long-suffering breath and sighed. 'Mr Dundas,' he said, 'I've told you before – you have to call the Benefits Centre.'

'I did! They won't listen.'

'Then there's nothing I can do for you.'

'You could intervene,' Frank cried. 'You don't realise

how much has been taken from me.'

'That,' the bureaucrat bristled, 'is none of my business.'

Several times that night, Frank fantasised about killing Ian Carpenter. First, he strangled him slowly, until his eyes popped out of their sockets and pinged against the glass of his Calvin Klein glasses. Then, he shot him with every one of his long-confiscated pistols – the .357 put the most satisfying hole in his sternum, but the .22 took longer to finish him, causing more suffering.

For the next week, Frank shadowed the man every day. Sometimes he would arrange himself so that Carpenter would turn the corner, and see him loitering menacingly on the opposite side of the street. Other times he would walk several paces behind him, neither gaining nor retreating. As each day passed, he could see Carpenter growing more and more edgy.

Finally, one day, his quarry snapped, and wheeled upon Frank on the way to his kid's After-School Club. 'Why are you doing this to me?' he shrieked. 'Can't you see that I can't help you?'

They were on a narrow, pedestrianised street, and several shoppers paused to watch their altercation.

'Leave me alone,' Carpenter shouted, 'or I will call the police! I'll have you sent to prison!'

Frank smiled and walked away calmly. That evening, he gathered up his electrician's tools, and disconnected the electricity, telephone, broadband and cable television at the Carpenter household.

Nearly two weeks later, the police invited him to the station for a chat. By the time they released him, returning his belt and shoe-laces, he had been given a date to appear in court, and left with no doubt that the evidence weighed heavily against him.

Now, with a small hacksaw, he sawed away at the barrel of his shotgun, knowing that his life was truly over. Whether he could actually be sent to prison for what he had done, he didn't know – but even if he couldn't, how would he continue to live? In days, his phone and Internet would be disconnected for non-payment – and the utilities would not be far behind. His career prospects were hopeless, and he was better off dead.

And at least there would be the satisfaction of seeing Ian Carpenter go first.

Carpenter usually picked up his boy at half-past five, always passing an oak tree next to a low brick wall on a lane a few hundred yards from the school. At a quarter-past five, Frank stood there with his shotgun wrapped in an old beige overcoat. The satchel of shells hung at his side. His plan was simple – when Carpenter passed, he would remove his gun from the coat, unfold the stock, walk towards him, place the muzzle as close to the back of Carpenter's head as possible, and pull the trigger. When Carpenter fell, he would squeeze a round into his back, just to make sure he was dead. By then, Frank assumed, onlookers might have been attracted to the scene, but they were unlikely to approach an armed man. There would still be time to sit on the wall under the tree, reload, and quietly end his life. He had sawn off the barrel of the gun specifically so that he would be able to reach the trigger with the muzzle in his mouth.

Things did not go according to plan.

Frank waited under his tree until well past the usual time. A few people passed – mostly women, heading to the After-School Club's mobile classroom – but there was no sign of Ian Carpenter. At five forty-five, Frank began to get nervous, and wondered whether he should go home and try again another day. The thought angered him – he had psychologically prepared for this, for his own death, and especially for Ian Carpenter's. He did not want to lose momentum. He did not trust himself to return.

Walking hurriedly towards the school, Frank scanned the avenue that paralleled its forecourt. Down near Welsh Bridge, he saw a gangly thin lad round the corner and disappear onto Bridge Street. Even at this distance, the boy's similarity to Carpenter was unmistakable.

Frank gasped. How could he have missed him? He began to hyperventilate. *He's come another way*, he thought, and began to trot down Quarry Avenue. *I'll have to kill him in front of the kid*. He yanked his overcoat off the gun and dropped it on the pavement, fumbling to bring the stock to its full size, and then clutched the gun with both hands. He quickened to a sprint; a woman rounding the corner from Claremont Bank yelped in shock. Frank ignored her, and continued to run. Several other pedestrians looked at him with dim surprise, but nobody tried to stop the man running with the shotgun. Finally, Frank emerged on a small shopping street. Immediately, he spied the boy loitering outside a butcher's shop and stumbled ungracefully. He caught himself, and walked resolutely onwards.

The butcher's shop's door opened with the sharp ding of a bell, and a thin woman emerged carrying a white plastic bag. With her free hand, she reached out for her son. Frank stopped, and time seemed to freeze. He stared at the woman, as she grasped the young boy's hand and began to pull him away.

Shit! he thought. It's the kid's mother … Carpenter sent his fucking wife!

He bellowed after the woman in rage.

As if in slow motion, he saw her turn and notice him.

She began to scream. Frank realised he was exposed in a busy street with a shotgun in his hands – and his intended victim was nowhere near. He would have to make the best of a bad situation. He could not kill Ian Carpenter ... but he could ruin his life.

Frank dashed the remaining few yards towards the woman. When he was within two feet of her, he squeezed the shotgun's trigger and discharged its shell squarely into her chest. The recoil bruised his shoulder and jarred him back. Mrs Carpenter tried to scream as she fell, but the sound was replaced quickly by a choking gurgle. She was still clutching her young son's hand, and the momentum of her fall swung the boy in an arc towards her. Frank pumped the fore-end, and his second shot caught the boy as he wheeled around, squarely between the shoulder blades. He was dead before he hit the ground.

At a nearby intersection, two cars collided. Pedestrians shrieked and scattered.

Frank paused for a moment and blinked, reaching into his satchel and pushing two more shells into the magazine. He focused on the mother and child, who sprawled together in a bloody puddle. The sight was awful, and caused his mind to blank. He could not remember what he had intended to do next, where he had intended to go.

The door to the butcher's shop pushed open behind Frank with a ding and he whirled towards it. An overweight man in a stained apron leaned out, and Frank discharged another shell. Because of the distance and the sawn-off barrel, the pellets flew wildly and sprayed him in the side. He stumbled, and crumpled into a foetal position on the pavement. His body heaved and gasped, and Frank – propelled now by the very hopelessness of his situation – stepped over the shaking form, and crossed to the High Street.

He pumped the gun and, at random, fired at the first person he saw – a young fellow in a shell suit, whistling as he unlocked the door of his illegally stopped Vauxhall Corsa. The blast caught him in the side of the head, and threw him down.

Fuck, Frank thought dully, *that kid's never done anything to me.*

He began to run again, making for St. John's Hill. In the distance, a police siren wailed. Frank ended up in the Quarry Park, where he reloaded, and ended the life of an elderly woman who had been walking her Labrador. The dog yelped wildly and cowered next to the body of its mistress. On a bench nearby, a young woman jiggling a pram looked up and screamed. Like clockwork, Frank jerked his gun towards her and squeezed the trigger. With the blast ringing in his ears, he noticed that the mother's arm was bloody, but the bulk of the pellets had ripped through the vinyl of the carriage. The mother was wailing as Frank stumbled closer to her.

He groped in his satchel. One shell left. The woman twitched with terror. Frank tried to smile at her. 'Don't cry,' he said hoarsely. 'I – I'm really sorry.'

He felt the urge to explain to her what had happened, to gain her understanding ... but he didn't try. He wasn't that crazy.

Frank Linden Dundas glanced away from the mortified woman, down at his shotgun. It was shaking now.

'I won't kill you,' he mumbled, as he felt his knees buckle. Frank allowed his body to sink down until he was crouching on the grass next to the mother and the bloody baby carriage.

He knew he could not kill this poor, whimpering woman. He needed that one, final shell for himself.

SEVENTEEN

On the seventh day of August, five people – including a seven-year-old boy and a nine-week-old infant girl – were murdered by forty-two year old Frank Linden Dundas in Shrewsbury town centre of Shrewsbury, Shropshire. Two other adult victims, including the dead baby's mother, were wounded, and the killer ended his own life immediately after the outrage.

As in the aftermath of similar shootings, the press and public engaged in a fierce debate of the issues raised by such a tragedy. Several of the papers called for an outright ban on all rifles and shotguns, while others took the line that there was no adequate legislation against the behaviour of madmen. Still others advised a tightening of the rules allowing shotgun ownership. The Home Office moved quickly to set up a public enquiry.

The tragedy pulled press attention away from the Aberystwyth case, for there had been no new killings for over a week, a week in which the killer appeared no closer to being caught.

Sara and Eldon Carson sat in her living room. The roller blinds had been pulled, casting a weak, blue-grey haze of light across their still forms. Today, news of the 'Midlands Massacre' was on every news source, and on everyone's lips.

'A baby,' Sara said faintly, 'he killed a baby.'

Carson sat brooding, but his eyes were dark with unspoken emotion.

'I could have stopped it,' she repeated for the fifth time. 'You could have stopped it. I could have let you.'

In the pit of Sara's stomach churned bilious dread.

Every random thought led back to the horror in Shrewsbury, and every thought of the dead people – the dead baby – caused pangs of something like illness to stab inside her. 'I doubted you,' she said, 'and you were telling the truth.'

'Yes,' he agreed. They both understood what she was guilty of; there was nothing more to add.

Sara swallowed, but her mouth was dry and her parched throat knotted at the effort. 'You can leave now,' she said in a cracked voice. 'I won't say anything.'

Carson appraised her with a calculating gaze. 'No,' he said finally.

'I'll be fine,' Sara said insistently.

'I'm sure you will. But I came here for a reason.'

'I don't want anything more to do with you.'

For the first time since she had released him, Eldon Carson moved from the chair. He stood, stretched, and joined her on the love-seat. 'That's not true,' he said, 'you just haven't thought it through yet.'

She bit gently on her bottom lip.

'Miss Sara, you need me more than anyone else you know. I know about your past – and what's more, I know how you feel about it. Do you think your boyfriend's going to give you more than I can?'

Sara started at Carson's allusion to Jamie.

'Just because you slept with him again, don't imagine anything has changed. He represents all the same things he did before – safety, security, and ignorance. I'm offering you knowledge. Don't make decisions about your life by default.'

Sara shook her head, but remained silent.

'I want you to think about who I am, and what I can do. With training, you could do it too. If you'd only let me, I could help you to understand your life.'

She stared at this killer. His voice was so earnest, his expression so open … he looked like any decent, conscientious young man.

'What do you get out of it?' she asked.

He sighed and smiled. 'Something nearly every creature on earth has a right to expect,' he replied. 'The chance to spend some time with my own kind.'

Sara looked at him bitterly. '*I'm* your kind?'

'You are. You'll come to realise that soon enough.'

She closed her eyes and gently rubbed them. 'You could make me do whatever you wanted to anyway, couldn't you?' she said. 'You could reach into my mind, and deaden my resistance, just like you did when …'

She stopped. Here was another tangent that led straight to thoughts of the dead, of a murdered baby.

'I couldn't,' he said firmly. 'My skills in that area are slight, Miss Sara, and, believe it or not, you would learn to control it pretty fast. You could probably have stopped me last time, even without using that syringe …'

He let his voice trail away.

And the events in Shrewsbury may never have happened.

Sara lowered her gaze, but did not reply.

'You are psychic,' he said insistently. 'We are kindred spirits, and that is rare. You need me.' Eldon Carson stared at her intensely until she raised her eyes and met his stare.

'Don't agree to anything,' he said. 'But if you're curious, at least let me try to prove what I'm saying.'

Sara looked up. 'How?'

His voice grew persuasive, even insistent. 'With one small experiment.'

Jamie sat at a wood-grain laminate desk, alone in the Incident Room of the Aberystwyth Police Station. Like the rest of the building, the room's decor was tastefully neutral. The carpet was grey, the upholstered office chairs red, the walls eggshell white. Pin boards were covered with maps, photos, and crime pattern analyses. Jamie felt sure that these things would not to help locate the offender. If he were to stay in Aberystwyth, he needed to pursue other leads, areas of investigation that drew on his unique skills.

The door creaked and Ceri Lloyd peered in. 'I'm told you want to see me,' she said neutrally.

'If it's not too much ...'

'Business?' Ceri said with a sardonic grin, 'Or pleasure?'

He smiled. 'Let's get some tea.'

They moved down the hall, to the station's large recreation room. Two officers, playing pool, nodded as they entered.

Ceri eyed him over her black coffee. 'To what do I owe the honour?'

Jamie smiled. 'I want to ask for your help.'

She sucked in her cheeks and studied him appraisingly. 'Do you now?'

'This investigation's stalling,' Jamie said. 'We have guys on the streets, but you and I both know that nothing's going to happen unless he gives us some fresh clues. I don't want to wait that long.'

'So Jamie Harding is going to single-handedly crack the case?' Ceri said with thin amusement.

'No,' Jamie replied. 'We are. I'm going to need your local knowledge, your advice.'

Ceri Lloyd eyed him shrewdly. 'You need to look busy,' she said, 'or you'll be on your way home.' She took a slow sip of coffee, adding, 'And you wouldn't want that, would you?'

She was sharp, he admitted to himself. 'Sara and I talk about you sometimes,' he said.

'I'll bet you do,' she replied.

'She thinks you'd like me if you only got to know me.'

Ceri arched an eyebrow. 'Sara sees the best in people.'

'I know you want what's best for her,' Jamie continued. 'So do I. For whatever reason, Sara has decided to spend time with me again …'

He stopped short, and made an expression of distaste at his own caution. 'Not for whatever reason,' he said bluntly. 'Because she loves me. And if she wants to be with me, she won't let you stop her.'

'I could just bide my time and wait for the force to send you packing.'

Jamie shrugged and lowered his gaze.

'But I don't think I will,' Ceri said, 'because Sara would be unhappy.'

He eyed her appraisingly. 'So you'll help me with the case?'

'Suppose it's a way to keep an eye on you,' she said.

Ceri dug her cigarettes from her handbag and eyed the door. Before standing, she added, 'I'm not going to let you hurt Sara again.'

At Sara's request, the superintendent had withdrawn her private constable; she would have lost him soon anyway. With the policeman gone, Sara no longer felt it necessary to draw curtains and blinds when Eldon Carson visited.

Sara felt apprehensive about the experiment they were about to try. For the past thirty minutes, she had been stretched on the living room rug, eyes closed, allowing

Carson to lead her through basic relaxation exercises. He said it was to put her in the right frame of mind.

Now, she sat on the love-seat with a pad of paper resting in her lap and a pencil in her hand. Carson was cross-legged on the floor facing her, with a white envelope in his hand and an air about him that was both playful and deadly serious. In the rectangle of sunshine that beamed through the front window, thousands of dust specks sparkled, as if they were electric.

'It has been suggested,' Carson was saying, 'that people whose lives have been touched by some sort of tragedy or misfortune are often extremely good psychics.'

Sara rocked slightly on the love-seat. This was the way she used to feel in school, just before an exam.

'Empathy is a useful trait for psychics – and that's a talent you display every day in your work. Another is the ability to look at things from unusual angles. Your education, both in medicine and occult studies has prepared you to think in unusual ways.'

He placed the envelope on the table next to her. Sara knew that inside was a photograph, which he had torn from an old magazine. Her task would be to visualise it in her mind's eye, sketch what she saw, and describe it to Carson.

'What I'm trying to make you understand is, you've already got the skills you need for this little demonstration.'

He tapped the envelope and grinned. 'So, relax.'

It was an odd exam, she thought. More like a game she might have played as a child. But the events of the past few days – and the chilling occupation of the man who sat across from her – made this a game of life and death.

'The way I see it,' Jamie said to Ceri, 'somebody must be sheltering this guy. There must be some individual he's gained the confidence of. That person may or may not know of his guilt.'

'That's obvious,' Ceri agreed. 'The trickier part is finding out who.'

Jamie nodded. 'That's what we need to ask. Who'd take in a strange American who doesn't want to be seen in public?'

Ceri pinched her lips together and frowned. 'It's got to be someone he shares an interest with,' she muttered thoughtfully. 'And I'll bet this guy doesn't have many hobbies. What he seems most interested in is killing people.'

'So he may be exploiting someone's passion for violence?'

'Subversives,' Ceri said. 'Anarchists, military fanatics, or extreme right-wingers.'

'That's possible,' Jamie said. 'We might also want to look at the psychic angle. He could be ingratiating himself with local psychic groups – maybe occultists, practitioners of ritual magic.'

Ceri inclined her head in agreement.

'Presumably,' Jamie continued, 'you keep files on these people.'

Ceri nodded, her enthusiasm growing. 'We have local intelligence files in Penweddig that cover some of the local freaks …'

Jamie smiled. He imagined that Ceri Lloyd had a broad definition of what constituted a 'freak'.

'… but the information about the really dangerous ones is kept by Special Branch in Carmarthen.'

'It may be that one of those individuals is harbouring our man – or else they'll know who is. How many subjects does Carmarthen have on file? I doubt we'd be able to visit them all.'

'You and me alone?' Ceri smirked. 'It depends on how

much of a career we want to make this.'

'That's why we'll need to rely on your local knowledge,' Jamie said. 'Within the parameters we've outlined, who would be likely to shelter someone like our offender?'

Ceri drained her coffee and crumpled the cup. 'Let's find out,' she said. 'We'll stop off at Penweddig, then head down south to headquarters.'

It had taken Daffy much of yesterday to amble from Aberystwyth to Penweddig, but he'd had nothing better to do. Last Thursday, he had promised Sara Jones that he'd go away and never come back ... but where else did he have to go? And even if he could think of a place, how could he get there? She had frightened him on that rainy day in Aberystwyth. When she pulled that weapon on him, he'd thought she was going to hurt him. Afterwards, as he played and replayed their confrontation in his mind, he had become confused. She was a smart woman – would she have pretended to be that naïve if she were not genuinely ignorant of the facts? How much had he told her? What kind of a person was Dr Sara Jones?

The day after, he had sat on the pavement on the opposite side of the street from the Drop-In Centre, obscured from view by the snack bar on the promenade. He had intended to follow her – to see where she went, who she met, what she was like. Although he had waited there for hours, she had not shown up; someone else was on duty that day.

On Monday the Centre was closed. So yesterday, not knowing what else to do, he had walked to Penweddig. He had tramped through the village several times, searching for her bright red car, and was almost ready to lie down in despair when he noticed a path breaking away from a housing estate, with the groove of tyre tracks worn into the mud. He had followed the path to a white pebble-dashed farmhouse, and his heart leapt when he spied her BMW parked on the gravel outside. He had tried to spy inside, but all the blinds and curtains were drawn, so he had spent the rest of the day on the pebble beach, thinking about his life, and cursing his fate. When the tide came in, he had crawled up the hill, and slept in the bracken.

Now, he cut down from a street on to the beach, and followed it to a path that led up to Dr Jones' lane. He hoped the curtains would be open today.

'This is an exercise I learned from a US Army psychic,' Eldon Carson said. Sara looked at him quizzically.

'Oh yes, the army uses psychics,' he continued. 'Why wouldn't they? In fact, the CIA's got paranormal instruction down to a fine art. What you'll be learning here is a tried-and-tested formula. I am going to assign a set of coordinates to the location pictured in the photograph. They are arbitrary – they do not relate to any map, or other system of measurement. Their purpose is simply to give you something to focus on, as you try to visualise the location. Understood?'

Sara nodded.

Carson shifted his position on the floor, then held still. 'Here are your coordinates: seven, one, three, zero, four, six, eight, two, five.'

Sara wrote the random numbers at the top of her paper, and waited. She was not certain exactly what she was supposed to feel. 'Nothing's happening,' she said.

'Yes, it is,' he insisted. 'There are impressions flowing through your mind at this moment – you are simply shutting them out.'

Sara tried to concentrate. 'I'm not sure,' she said. 'I can see a lot of things.'

'Tell me about them.'

'They're shapes – just shapes.' She frowned and shook her head. Any imaginative person was liable to invent shapes if asked to.

'Don't doubt yourself,' Carson commanded, as if he had read her thoughts. 'Go with what you see.'

Sara took a calming breath and looked inward. Now that she had permission to take the impressions she was receiving seriously, there was no doubt – she was seeing distinct shapes. Small ones in front, a large one, like a slab, in back.

'Tell me about it, Miss Sara,' Eldon Carson said. 'Describe what you see.'

'It's a large rectangle,' she said.

'That's fine,' he encouraged her. 'Draw it now.'

Her hand began to move uncertainly, outlining a rectangular shape which stretched the width of the page, then adding smaller rectangles inside. At first, it looked no different than the doodles she would sketch absently when she was bored – but as she watched the picture take form, she recognised it what it might be.

'I think it's the wall of a building,' she said. 'It's light in colour … beige? Grey? It could be stone, or concrete – I can't tell.'

'Go on,' Carson murmured.

At the bottom of her picture, she quickly added the other shapes, smaller ones that she saw in front of the wall. 'They're cars,' she said in wonder. 'It's a car park, in front of the building.' She hesitated, then added, 'Judging from the perspective, that building is huge.'

She paused, holding herself very still. The impression she was receiving were more detailed now.

'There's also another line of shapes, between the cars and the wall. They look like …'

A solid round base, branching off into many lines at the top. Branching. She focused more intently. 'They're trees – right here.' Her hand began to fly across the paper, as she sketched in the trees. 'They've got no leaves,' she muttered. 'It could be autumn, or early winter.'

As she said this, she began to feel a chill. It hung in a breezeless air. 'It's definitely cold here,' she said, 'but not enough to snow. And ...' She looked upwards at the massive wall, and noticed a staircase, leading to an entrance. 'I see an American flag hanging over a door.'

'Tell me what it feels like,' Carson ordered.

'What what feels like?'

'Try to get a sense of the building's personality, the mood of the people inside.'

Sara held still and focused on the image in her mind. Subtly, her mood began to shift, to fall into synch with that of the building. She was pricked by a sensation of calm competence, peppered by small eruptions of anxiety.

'A lot of people are in there, and they're very busy,' she said. 'Administration, routine things ... but also pockets of important activity.'

'Describe it.'

'I don't know if I can. There are decisions being made.' Sara furrowed her brow, bit her lip. She felt light-headed, and closed her eyes.

Several tense seconds passed before Carson said, 'All right, Miss Sara, you've done very well. I'd like you to do just one more thing for me. I want you to rise up into the air, and look at the building from above.'

'Rise up?'

'See it as a bird might.'

'How am I supposed to do that?'

'Don't think about it, just do it.'

Sara tried to clear her mind of doubts, and found her perspective shifting. She imagined herself floating up from the car park, until she was level with the flat roof. She urged herself higher, until she could look down on the entire massive shape. The building was a five-sided ring.

'It's the Pentagon!' she gasped.

As Daffy approached the house from the path, he exhaled hoarsely in relief. Not only was Sara Jones' car parked outside, but her curtains and blinds were open!

He stopped next to a large willow, and took in all the windows at once, nervously, hoping the doctor was not gazing out. He couldn't see her; the house was still.

Daffy approached the house quickly, wincing at the loud crunching noise his old boots made against the gravel. He edged around a corner of the house. The first windows he came to were frosted. 'The bathroom,' he muttered. The next set belonged to the kitchen, and from the very edge of the window, he peered in.

When he saw that the room was empty, he shuffled through a weedy bed of plants until he had a full view. It was a standard farmhouse kitchen, the kind Daffy remembered from his youth: slate floors; cobwebs hanging limply in the corners. The doctor had painted it bright yellow, and hung colourful oil paintings on the walls.

Daffy eased himself out of the plant bed, and rounded to the front of the house. There was a large shrub under the window of Dr Jones' living room. He squeezed behind it and crouched down between the shrub and the window.

He could hear low voices through the single thin pane of glass. Slowly, he raised his head past the peeling wooden frame, until he was peering into the room from the corner of the window.

In the bright light of several candles, he saw Dr Jones, eyes unfocused, engaged in an animated conversation with someone sitting next to the window. As she spoke, she sketched furiously on a sheet of paper.

Daffy watched her for several seconds. In his life on

the road, he had met a wide array of characters. Some had been good, several more unpleasant, and many insane; as a result, he thought of himself as a pretty fair judge of people. To Daffy's trained eye, this woman did not appear to be a bad person. In fact, she seemed rather sweet. Could it be true that she didn't know anything about the killings after all? That she was as innocent as … well, as Daffy himself?

Daffy could not make out who her companion was, but he noticed a smaller window on the far side of the room, next to the back door. Slowly, silently, Daffy disentangled himself from the shrub, and backed out onto the stone driveway. He tiptoed around the right of the house, past the stable, to the other side of the living room. When he was next to the small window, he paused and listened.

Their low voices drifted through the thin, single pane of glass. Daffy held his breath, and risked a glance. On the floor sat a man with shaggy hair and a black T-shirt. Daffy caught a good glimpse of his face, before pulling himself back, and quietly creeping back around the house towards the lane.

Daffy had never seen that man before. He wondered who he was.

Sara opened her eyes, and tiny flashes of light shimmered and swirled before her. Patches of sweat on her back and chest clung wetly to her blouse. It was an odd sensation, to emerge into a warm summer's day, when seconds before she had been shivering in an American winter.

Carson was grinning like a boy sharing a secret. He tore open the envelope, and tossed a photo torn from Newsweek magazine: one wall of the Pentagon in Washington DC, taken from the enormous car park.

'Convinced?' Carson asked.

Sara stared at the picture. She felt as though she could

have taken it herself. 'I don't know what to think,' she breathed.

'Yes, you do,' Carson replied firmly. 'You know exactly what this means.'

Sara closed her eyes. She had to resist the urge to believe everything Carson claimed on the basis of this evidence.

'You did this,' Carson said. 'You alone. I was only the facilitator.'

What, Sara wondered, if she could learn to do the things Eldon Carson could do? What if she could read not only hidden elements of the present, but of the past and the future as well? What might she, finally, understand? Sara began to feel the prick of something she had seldom felt before: greed.

'Okay,' she said warily. 'I'll admit I'm curious. That was weird enough to unsettle me, and I'd like to try it again.' Instinctively, she glanced out the window. 'But there are some obvious problems.'

'Such as?' he asked innocently.

'For one, you're a wanted killer. Every police officer in Mid Wales is looking for you.'

Carson smiled wryly.

'That's a bit of a problem, don't you think?'

He nodded. 'But it will be a problem whether I teach you or not.'

Sara furrowed her brow. 'If you don't teach me, you could run away.'

He fixed her with a mocking, wide-eyed stare. 'Where? Somewhere people don't inflict violence on others? A place I'd never need to kill another living soul?' He stood. 'No matter where I went, I'd have the same problems. The only difference would be, I wouldn't have you.'

He picked up his bag from the floor, peered quickly

out the window, and moved towards the kitchen.

'Where are you going?' she asked.

He turned. 'I won't endanger you by staying longer than I have to. I'll come again soon.'

'Where will you go?' Sara asked.

A smile. *Leave that to me.* He headed towards the door.

'How do you know you can trust me?' Sara called after him. 'How do you know I won't ring the police, and have them waiting next time you come?'

Carson stared at her as if shocked by the suggestion, then released a throaty chuckle. 'Because,' he replied, 'I can see the future.'

EIGHTEEN

In its Carmarthen headquarters, the Dyfed-Powys Police Authority kept files on any individual or organisation who might have presented a danger to the public. They were filed by category – extreme animal rights activists in one, religious fundamentalists in another – although some of the more misanthropic individuals managed to get themselves cross-referenced. Each file contained as much detail about the subject as the police had been able to collect, including background, habits, and associates, as well as any specific reasons that they had for wanting to keep tabs on the person.

Jamie and Ceri arrived in Carmarthen after visiting Ceri's own sub-station in Penweddig. There, she had shown Jamie the local intelligence files – her own special rogues' gallery. 'Here's a fellow in Lampeter who runs a group called Celtic Dawn,' she said. 'Far as I know, every member is English. I doubt even one of the silly buggers is Celtic.'

She pulled another file and said, 'Now, here's a group of real Celts: druids in Aberporth.' She shrugged. 'Mostly middle-aged men who wear robes and get pissed. Our villain wouldn't get much joy out of them, unless he likes real ale and poetry.'

In their brief time in Penweddig, Jamie had found himself warming to his new, unofficial, partner. He had wanted Ceri to like him – mainly so she would not cause trouble between him and Sara – but he had never bothered to wonder whether he could like her. He admired her sly, subtle wit, and her fierce loyalty to anything she gave time to.

They requested the necessary files and were offered a small meeting room to work in. Now, papers covered the table before them. Ceri pulled a file at random. 'Where do we begin?' she asked. 'This lad's a lefty-anarchist type, while these ones,' – she spread a few files before her – 'are neo-Nazis.'

One document caught her eye. 'We've got this guy on file in Penweddig, too,' she noted. 'A real charmer – a neo-Nazi and drug-dealer.'

Jamie caught a brief glimpse of Trevor Hughes' photo before Ceri slipped it back in the pile.

It was just after noon when Carson pulled onto the weed-covered tarmac outside Trevor Hughes' bungalow. He entered through the side door, and climbed the three stairs into the mildew-smelling kitchen. As he gulped a glass of water, he sensed Hughes struggling awake in his bedroom. Carson lightly touched his mind, and felt consciousness returning sluggishly, followed by a flash of anger.

Hughes stomped out of his bedroom, still naked and sweaty from sleep. Rolls of tattooed flesh jiggled as he bounded towards Carson. He had an Iron Cross tattooed above his groin. 'Where you been with my motor?' he shouted.

Carson finished his water, and placed the tumbler gently on the cracked Formica counter.

'I can't believe you,' Hughes continued. 'I invite you into my house, feed you, and what do you do? Piss off with my motor for fucking days!'

Carson winced at the shrill voice. His nerves twitched from the poison Sara Jones had shot into him. 'I apologise,' he said quietly. 'I had business.'

Hughes sidled up to Carson until he was only a few inches away; this oaf badly needed a shower. 'Not good enough, mate. You can buy a mobile phone for ten quid.' He grasped Carson roughly by the shoulder. 'I needed my car! I had business too!'

Carson took a deep breath, and fought to control his temper.

'I missed my connection in Liverpool because of you,' Hughes spat. 'If you weren't an Aryan brother, I'd crack your skull with a spanner.'

Without a second of warning, Carson pistoned his stiffened palm into Hughes' face, sending him reeling into the plastic garden furniture he used as a kitchen suite. Before Hughes could right himself, Carson was over him, his knife jerked from his boot and pressed into Hughes' meaty throat. Hughes goggled at the American, his nose streaming crimson.

'I told you – I had business, too,' Carson said. 'And there were complications. Okay?'

The neo-Nazi nodded rapidly.

Carson relaxed the pressure, but only slightly. 'Please don't shout or touch me again. It irritates me.'

He stepped back, allowing the larger man to stand.

'Yeah, mate … all right,' Hughes said, scouting the room for a napkin. 'I can go to Liverpool tomorrow, like.'

Carson turned away, looked through the rotting window frame. Patchy grass dotted with beer tins and takeaway containers. Strewn tyres.

'I've had times when things turned to shit, too,' Hughes went on. 'Once in Cardiff, me and some mates had words with these Pakis. They got their whole family out, swinging these metal pipes. We spent three hours in the cellar of an off-license.' He brayed with laughter. 'They weren't so brave later on that night, let me tell you.'

Carson squeezed the excess water from a tattered dishcloth and handed it to him. Hughes dabbed at his nose and scratched his groin.

'So tell me about your business problems.'

Carson stared at him blankly. 'Why don't you get dressed?'

The next day, Sara had lunch alone at a small whole food café on Pier Street, idly reading the cards and posters tacked to the walls. She was always amazed by the eclectic spectrum of life that congregated in such an isolated place as Mid Wales. Photocopied flyers pointed to Buddhist meditation classes, Reiki training, aromatherapists, women's healing circles, and a seemingly endless variety of other esoteric pursuits.

She returned her plate and bowl to the counter, and thanked the proprietor. He looked up from his iPad and smiled, but his reaction seemed sad. Sara sensed there was a piece to his life that was missing – something he had come to Aberystwyth long ago to find, but was still looking for. It was as if yesterday's experiment had left her with a heightened sense of awareness. All morning, she had felt able to look at strangers and sense their hidden emotions. She wondered if all psychiatrists should be made to undergo some form of psychic training.

Sara stepped outside, and turned towards Marine Terrace. It was a dull day, and fog was rolling off the sea, thinning as it drifted across the pavement. Sara wondered if she would ever be able to read Eldon Carson himself. She had no idea why he wanted to train her, or what he expected to get from it. Nonetheless, he offered something she wanted: the truth about her past, and a sense of direction for her future.

She crossed the street at an angle, heading towards the concrete steps leading to the door of the Drop-In Centre. Suddenly, Sara felt certain she was being watched, indeed, studied. She could feel the heightened state of someone observing her with intense concentration.

Slowing her pace, Sara tried to get a fix on its exact location.

It came from over her right shoulder. She braced herself and spun around. Half-obscured by a parked car stood a bearded man in filthy clothing – the same person who had accosted her in the Centre. He twitched nervously, torn between running and approaching.

'Please,' she said, edging closer. 'I'm not going to hurt you.'

'I've been watching you,' he said, his speech rapid.

'Do you want to talk to me?'

His head bobbed.

'What's your name?'

'Daffy.'

'Come upstairs, Daffy,' she said. 'We'll have a biscuit.'

Sara moved away, willing him to follow, but he remained secure behind his barricade. She stopped and held out her hand.

'Come on.'

Tentatively, he edged around the car, and offered her his shaking, dirty hand. She took it firmly, and he allowed her to lead him up the stairs.

Daffy sat in a plastic chair, cradling a cup of coffee and rocking back and forth rhythmically. Once Sara had calmed him, he spoke in disjointed monologues. He admitted spying on her, describing his several-mile walk between Penweddig and Aberystwyth. Finally, he related the events of their first meeting from his point of view. Sara saw herself through his eyes, strong and powerful.

'Why'd you try to stab me with that thing?' he asked.

'I'm sorry,' Sara said gently. 'I didn't know you then. I thought you were going to hurt me.'

His gleaming eyes widened. This surprised him.

'Why have you been watching me?' Sara asked as she reached out mentally, trying to feel his thoughts.

'I wanted to see what kind of person you were,' he said. 'Where you go, who you see.' He looked at her with puzzling irony. 'You can tell a lot about a person by the company she keeps.'

Sara nodded without understanding. 'And what did you see?' she asked. The emotion she felt in him wasn't fear; it was the jittery recklessness of a man who believed his cause had already been lost.

'A man,' he whispered, 'in your window.'

'Was it the police officer?' she asked with some trepidation. 'The one without a uniform? Inspector Harding?'

'He wasn't police,' Daffy replied with certainty. 'His hair was too shaggy.'

Trepidation gave way to dread. 'Did you recognise him?' she asked. She recalled her first encounter with Daffy, when he had said, *I know about the killings*.

Daffy frowned. 'Should I have?' he asked.

This startled Sara, but there was no duplicity in his thoughts. 'No,' she said.

Daffy set the coffee cup on the floorboards next to him, and rose stiffly. 'I won't spy on you any more,' he said with a sigh. 'You can't help me.'

Sara stood quickly. 'I can help, if you'll let me,' she replied.

He shook his head sadly. 'I see it now. Nobody can really help anyone.'

Daffy looked as if he were swallowing bitter medicine, or equally bitter words. 'I should never have come back here,' he said finally, and made for the door.

Years of life on the streets had taught Daffy that the homeless were as diverse a group as any other. Many had mental health problems and could be dangerously unpredictable, but the range of their likes and dislikes was as broad as anyone's. Some preferred to be alone, others looked for agreeable company. Daffy had learned to be wary, but not to reject the advances of a potential friend.

He was leaning against steel sea rails on a stretch of road beyond Aberystwyth's South Beach. He stared at the faint line where the dark sea met the black sky, wondering where to go now. The tide was in; he enjoyed the soothing sounds the water made as it lapped against the wall below.

He heard he crunching of footsteps over pebbles on the pavement, and a man in a loose overcoat stood next to him.

'It's my birthday,' the man said, 'and I'm celebrating.'

'Happy birthday,' Daffy said. The man smelt like he'd washed his face in strong liquor.

From his overcoat, the man pulled a bottle of expensive cognac. It was a quarter full. He handed it to Daffy. 'Toast me,' he said.

Daffy accepted the bottle, and swallowed. 'Here's to you,' he said.

Together, they finished the bottle. The stranger cradled it in his arm, and whispered, 'I've got another one hidden.'

'Have you?' Daffy asked.

'Over there, by the harbour,' he said, gesturing to the end of the jetty. 'Do you see where the railing's broken?'

Daffy looked down South Marine Terrace, past the Lifeboat Station. One section of railing was missing, right at the end of the pavement. It was blocked off with metal barriers and orange tape.

'There's a hole in the pavement,' he whispered, and winked conspiratorially. 'That's where it is.' He tugged at Daffy's jacket. 'Let's go get it.'

Daffy hesitated. For no reason he could put his finger on, he was suddenly wary of this man's insistence that he drink with him, out there, in the empty harbour, in the dark.

'Come on,' the man said insistently. 'It's my birthday.'

With a growing feeling of unease, Daffy surrendered to the man's pleas, and allowed himself to be tugged towards the broken sea-rails.

At the broken rail, the man separated the orange tape from one of the metal barriers.

'It's down there,' he said. 'See that crack?'

'Where?' Daffy asked.

'You're not close enough. You've got to move in.' He reached over and tugged on Daffy's jacket.

'Hey! Careful,' said Daffy, drawing back.

'Go on, get it for me,' the man said.

'Why can't you?'

'Cause it's my birthday.'

'I can't see it,' Daffy stammered. 'I don't know where it is.' His words were now racing as quickly as his pulse. 'Maybe you should get it. You put it there, after all ...'

The man slipped behind Daffy, and shoved him towards the break in the rail. Daffy could hear the tide smacking against the sea wall far below. He leaned backwards, into the man's hands, and the man thrust with force. Suddenly, Daffy felt his legs kicked out from under him. His knees impacted with the pavement in a nauseating pop.

Daffy cried out.

'Shut up!' the man snarled, and swung the empty cognac bottle at the back of Daffy's skull. Daffy jerked forward as blinding sparkles exploded before his eyes. The man wheeled Daffy around and pushed him down. With the second blow, the bottle shattered against Daffy's forehead. He wailed. Blood streamed into his eyes.

Daffy felt a sharp stab as the neck of the broken bottle pressed firmly into the spongy flesh under his right ear.

Before the bottle-thrust seared red pain through his neck, before one thudding kick sent him plummeting over the edge, Daffy heard the man's breathless voice from far away.

'Sorry, mate. This isn't personal.'

NINETEEN

The grounds of Ceri's sloping garden were large and well-manicured; several beds of beautifully arranged plants and flowers framed a pond stocked with koi carp. Sara sat with Ceri and Jamie at a picnic table positioned at the garden's highest point. Although it was only eight-something on this midweek evening, the sun had already started to set over the bay. It burnished the roof of Ceri's modern house, and made the grass turn the colour of rust. Sara drained her third glass of Chardonnay and wondered where the carp went over the winter.

'There was one guy,' Jamie said with a chuckle, 'who looked as nervous as I've ever seen anyone look.'

'That skinny kid who sends hate mail to the National Assembly?' Ceri chortled.

'I'm sure he was about to confess to something ... until he found out why we were there. When I mentioned the murders, he relaxed.'

Maybe the fish just stayed in the pond whatever the weather, Sara thought. Ceri might have to cover it, though, so they wouldn't freeze.

'He's the only lad I've ever met who finds murder reassuring,' Ceri said, then laughed while trying to swallow smoked salmon. She began to cough, and eased her throat with a swallow of bourbon. Sara helped herself to a fourth glass of wine and made a mental note to Google koi carp.

Ceri wiped a tear from her eye. 'Whatever the bugger's really done, we'll catch him,' she said. 'It's only a damned shame that none of this has brought us any closer to the bastard we're actually chasing.'

Sara found it odd that her friends had formed this unexpected alliance. For the past two weeks, they had interviewed an assortment of occultists, witches, ritual magicians, psychics, anarchists, and left- and right-wingers. When necessary – but only then – they had shown a reproduction of the killer's symbol, at least to those who had some grounding in reality. None of these efforts had advanced their investigation, but the experience had done wonders for their friendship.

Sara took another large swallow of Chardonnay. She had to admit, she was relieved that Jamie and Ceri had come no closer to their prey; as they travelled the length and breadth of Wales, chatting with fantasists, the man they were trying to catch had been visiting Sara nearly every day. Eldon Carson served as an unsettling reminder of Sara's culpability for the Shrewsbury deaths ... but time spent with him was also tremendously exciting. Eldon would choose a photo from a magazine, and quite often Sara was able to describe it. When the images came, they appeared as a series of shapes – a flat plane here, a right angle there – and then in greater detail, including sounds, textures, and feelings. Sara had grown increasingly excited about what she might be capable of doing, and anxious to learn more.

'It's ridiculous,' Ceri was saying, her tone growing indignant. 'You wonder what goes through some people's minds ...'

Sara would not have predicted it, but she was finding Eldon himself fascinating. When leading Sara through her psychic exercises, Eldon spoke with authority. At other times he seemed eager to absorb all the knowledge she could give him. He was especially curious about art. As a sculptor, he found the objects that filled Sara's house a source of constant wonder, and demanded impromptu courses in Primitive Art history.

'What's this one?' he would ask, picking up a thin stick, carved with figures perched one on top of another.

'It's called an Ifa Divination bell. It was carved by the Yoruba tribe in Nigeria in the late nineteenth century. Ironically, it was used to predict the future.'

'And this?'

'A headdress carved by the Baga people in Guinea-Bissau. It's in the form of a woman, and represents motherhood ...'

Sara was shaken from her reverie by Ceri, who had begun to pontificate in full throat. 'It would be laughable if it weren't so goddamned serious,' her friend said. In a short time, Ceri seemed to have advanced from indignation all the way to outrage.

'Sorry, I was miles away,' she said. 'What would be laughable?'

'Our serial killer,' Jamie explained.

'He's like something from a black comedy!' Ceri wailed. 'This maniac wanders into a town where murder's practically non-existent, and some clairvoyant mojo tells him every other person's about to kill somebody. That is, unless he intervenes. Soon, there really are bodies everywhere.'

She took a pull of bourbon and muttered, 'People. They're so stupid.'

'Maybe,' Sara heard herself say, 'but what if he's right?'

Immediately she flushed, realising she had spoken those words out loud. She cursed herself for letting the wine loosen her tongue.

Ceri gawped. 'What do you mean?'

'Oh … it's nothing, really.'

'I'm interested,' Ceri persisted. 'How could he be right?'

Sara drew in a slow breath and tried to recover the situation. 'All I'm saying is, what if someone were about to commit an atrocity and you knew about it?'

'All right,' Ceri said. 'Then what?'

'Well, under those circumstances, stopping that person might be the moral thing to do, right?'

Ceri nodded. 'I agree.'

'You do?'

'Sure. If I could go back and kill Hitler, I would. I might even take a pop at Stalin while I was at it.'

Ceri finished off her bourbon and leaned forward. 'But here's the problem, Sara – I don't have a time machine. And that buffoon can not see the future.'

The word *buffoon* rankled, and Sara heard herself shout: 'You don't know that! Maybe this guy really can see the future.' Her voice was embarrassingly shrill. 'We don't know everything. Maybe we're the stupid people, and he really has saved lives!'

Jamie lay a calming hand on her wrist but Sara shook it off. 'In fact,' she continued, 'maybe by trying to stop him, we're doing incredible damage. What if he could have saved more innocent people, but wasn't able to, because –'

She caught herself in time.

Because what?

What were you about to say, Sara?

She let her words die mid-sentence. Ceri studied her with hooded eyes. Jamie took Sara's hand, and this time she let him.

After several long moments, Ceri snorted dismissively. 'Dr Sara Jones,' she concluded, 'transformed into a ninny through the occult powers of wine.'

Sara flushed with relief. Ceri had just offered her a way to save face. 'Well ... maybe I have had a bit too much,' she agreed, and then laughed. 'You should have seen your expression. You looked at me like I'd gone mad.'

Ceri raised her eyebrows and reached for her cigarettes.

Jamie stretched. 'I think I'll walk Sara home now before she has anything else to drink,' he chuckled. 'One more glass, and who knows what kind of monster she'd defend?'

It was only when Sara was still and quiet that she noticed how the small experiences in her life had changed since she had moved to Wales. Lying naked on her futon, with the duvet pushed to the floor, she could feel the cool late-summer breeze sweep across her body from the open window. She took a deep breath; the quality of the air differed from London's, the oxygen so thick and rich. The evening light was unique too – sharp white moon-glow replacing the orange streetlamps that had flooded her Pimlico flat.

And the quiet! In London, she had slept to the sounds of taxis chugging by, over the white noise of thicker traffic drifting down from Victoria Street. Here in Penweddig, there was no sound at all – except, tonight, for Jamie's rhythmic breathing beside her.

'How are you feeling?' he mumbled softly.

'Better now,' she said. After a moment, she added, 'I was never really drunk, you know. It's just that Ceri has a way of putting things sometimes.'

'I know what you mean. She can get you defending ideas you don't actually believe.'

Jamie took Sara's silence as agreement. 'How long are

you planning to stay here, anyway?'

'Here?'

'In Wales.'

'I'm not sure,' Sara sighed. She reached out an arm, and stoked the rigid muscles of his abdomen with her fingertips. 'Why?'

'Just thinking,' Jamie replied tentatively. 'Either Ceri and I will catch this guy, or Dyfed-Powys will send me packing. Either way, I won't be here forever.'

'I know,' she whispered.

'Do you think you might want to come back to London?' he asked.

'And marry you?' Sara said with unexpected sharpness, but also a small smile playing on her lips.

'I didn't say that,' Jamie said. Seeing her expression in the moonlight, he grinned. 'We could live together, that's all.'

Sara stilled her hand, laying it flat against his warm skin. 'I'm thinking about it,' she said seriously.

Jamie straightened his back against the headboard. 'Really?'

She made a small sound of reassurance; she really had been thinking of it. When she had resumed her affair with Jamie, it had been in panic and uncertainty, in the wake of sedating Eldon Carson. Later, Carson had surprised her by articulating her own concerns, suggesting that he and Jamie represented opposite values in her life – blind comfort versus stark knowledge. Now she had decided he was wrong. Eldon's abilities made him wise beyond his years, but he was not infallible. Sara chose to see both aspects of her life functioning independently of one another.

'If I did move back,' she said pensively, 'it wouldn't be right away. I want to spend the rest of the summer here, and maybe the autumn too.'

214

'That's fine,' Jamie agreed emphatically. 'This is a beautiful time of year.'

Sara cocked her head, as if listening to something just out of range. 'I suppose it is,' she agreed, 'all things considered.'

Ceri Lloyd stopped by on Friday morning while Sara was still in her dressing gown. It was the first time they had seen each other since Sara's wine-fuelled near-confession in her garden. As embarrassed as she was by her lack of control that evening, Sara knew that she had also been harbouring a simmering resentment towards her old friend. Ceri had no right to call Eldon Carson a buffoon.

That petty gripe was wiped away quickly by Ceri's grim expression. One look, and Sara knew that this was not a social call. 'What's the matter?' she asked.

'A body washed ashore near Tanybwlch Beach yesterday,' Ceri replied.

A chill passed through Sara. 'Like the others?'

Ceri shook her head. 'This one had been out to sea for a while, then came ashore at high tide and lodged in the rocks.'

She reached into her pocket. 'Recognise him?'

Sara accepted Ceri's iPhone; the photo had been taken in the morgue. It was of a body from the chest up. Sara felt the shock of recognition, then a flood of pity. 'That's the street person who called himself Daffy.'

'Thought so,' Ceri said, nodding tersely. 'I saw him once at your Centre. They're making dental checks now, so we'll know who he was.'

'You say it wasn't like the others,' Sara said. 'But was it …?'

'Murder? It's being treated as such. He had an artery severed by a broken bottle. Then he fell – or was shoved – into the bay.'

'What's the speculation?'

'There was alcohol in his blood, but not much. We're guessing he'd only started drinking, with some person or persons. Maybe they were drunker than him, took offence at something he said.'

'Cut him and threw him into the sea.' Sara sighed and shook her head.

'They'll want a statement.'

'You're not on the investigation?'

'Thankfully, no. I just promised to show you the photo.'

Sara said, 'I'll visit the station today.' She nodded towards the kettle. 'Cup of tea?'

Ceri shook her head. 'Got to go. Suddenly, this place is full of villains.' Wistfully, she added, 'There wasn't a murder in Aberystwyth for years.'

Sara smiled in sympathy and sadness; guilt rippled through her like waves on the bay. If only her psychic skills were more reliable, she would have been able to read Daffy's future, to protect him, to find those responsible. And then …

And then what?

As she closed the door on Ceri and watched her panda car negotiate the lane, Sara felt a pulse of hostility, this time directed at Eldon Carson. If only he had taught her more, instead of spending weeks on remote viewing games and pointless theory. Then she might have been more a proficient psychic now—one able to see into people's pasts and futures.

It was like torture to think that she might have saved Daffy.

TWENTY

On the last Friday in August, Eldon and Sara sat in the kitchen. The room was lit by only three candles, and in the dim light, Eldon busied himself with some sort of craft. He had cut a small disk from a piece of cardboard, torn a section of the *Guardian* into thin strips, and now was rooting around in Sara's cupboard.

'What are you looking for?' she asked, an agitated edge to her voice.

'Found it,' he said, pulling a bag of flour from a shelf. He poured a quantity of the powder into a mixing bowl and added warm tap water.

'What are you doing, anyway?'

'Making something.'

'You look like a little kid,' she said, 'busy with a craft.'

'I'm an artist,' he said. 'I'm making you some art.'

Eldon dipped a piece of newspaper into the bowl of paste, and wrapped the gummy strip around the cardboard disk. Sara watched him repeat this procedure meticulously, several times, squeezing excess bubbles of paste from his project with his thumb. Eldon had been here for nearly an hour, but had yet even to mention continuing with Sara's psychic practice.

Eventually, she said, 'Eldon?'

He looked up, holding his mucky, dripping hands over the bowl.

'I want to see the past.'

She held his gaze firmly and he stared back unblinkingly. The flicker of flames and shadow made his expression change by the second. 'You mean –'

'My parents' murder. I want to see it. I want you to show me.'

He shook his head softly. 'You're not ready, Miss Sara. Give it time.'

He picked up another piece of paper and dipped it in the bowl, but Sara pounced on his words. 'Eldon, I've been thinking about this a lot. These techniques are only useful to me as far as I can use them to understand my past. I'll never understand anything unless I go back there.'

He smiled reassuringly. 'You will. In time.'

'I want to do it now,' Sara snapped.

He looked at her as a father would look at a spoiled child. 'Okay,' he said, 'I can't stop you. Take yourself there.'

He stared at her. Waited.

Sara started. 'I can't do it on my own!' she said. 'I'm not ready for that.'

'Exactly,' Eldon said with finality. 'You aren't ready. You're a promising psychic – but you're only just beginning.'

She threw herself back in the wooden chair petulantly. 'I am tired of describing pieces of fruit and famous monuments,' she said. 'I want to put this stuff to practical use.'

He looked at her, sprawled across the cushions, and spoke dispassionately: 'You haven't learned to control your emotions yet.'

Sara thumped her hand against the love-seat in frustration.

'You need to develop detachment,' Eldon said.

'How can I learn, if I don't do it?' She swung her legs around to the side of the chair and stood. 'You made a deal with me,' she said. 'I learn to do everything you know how to do, and you …' Sara drew a slow breath. 'You get to be with your own kind. I'm keeping my end of the bargain. Now I want you to keep yours.'

She watched something like hurt flicker through Eldon's eyes. It was fleeting, but so rare it startled her. 'You know I have a point,' she said softly. 'Eventually you'll want to see if I can cope with this. What are we waiting for?'

Twenty minutes passed, during which Eldon cleaned away his mess, washed his hands, and placed the papier mâché disc on the windowsill to dry. Sara had led herself through the relaxation exercises, which had grown almost second-nature to her. Now, she sat across from the American at the kitchen table.

'Seven, seven, three, zero, nine, six, four, two,' he said.

Sara wrote the numbers down on her pad of paper, and was instantly struck by a tingle of apprehension. It was as if the room had grown colder. 'This is wrong,' she breathed.

'How?' Carson asked neutrally.

'The atmosphere. It doesn't feel right.'

'What's wrong with it?'

'I don't know …'

She was starting to breathe erratically. 'Relax!' Carson commanded. He held up a calming hand. 'Just concentrate on the visuals – don't jump ahead of yourself. Describe what you see.'

Sara concentrated. What did she see? 'I see a rectangle, and a smaller rectangle within it. One is grey. The smaller one's light blue.' Sara frowned. 'I'm in the air.'

She could feel breeze now. 'This is a bird's-eye view of a paved surface. A small building. I'd guess some sort of school room.'

'Good,' Carson said. 'Now I want you to drift higher, and look away from the school building.'

'Okay ... there's a river on the other side of the road. A bridge in the distance.'

'Look on your side of the avenue. Can you see the side street to the right?'

'Yes,' Sara said.

'Drift over and tell me what you see.'

Instantly, Sara felt herself moving swiftly through the air. 'It's empty,' she said. 'I'm hovering now – next to a large tree.'

'Drift down.'

Unhampered by a body, Sara floated easily through branches and leaves until suspended six feet above the pavement. She faced a middle-aged man, holding an object wrapped in an overcoat. He glanced about furtively, and Sara sensed his distress. She concentrated on his thoughts.

Suddenly, her sense of apprehension quickened into a vibration of terror. 'You bastard!' she gasped. 'You've brought me to ... to ...'

'Miss Sara, remain professional!' snapped Eldon. 'Do not get emotionally involved with what you see. Simply observe and report.'

'No! I can't.' She felt herself start to tremble. 'Eldon, I can't watch this. I don't want to see what's going to happen!'

She saw the man named Frank Linden Dundas lurch

220

forward, and hurry around the corner onto Quarry Avenue.

'You must watch it,' Eldon countered sternly. 'You cannot choose to see only the things you want to see.'

Sara swallowed hard, and drew a deep breath. 'Okay, I'm … I can go on now.'

'Has he seen the Carpenter boy yet?'

Sara drifted around the corner; Dundas was about halfway down the street, trotting awkwardly. He dropped his overcoat to the pavement, and fumbled with his rifle until the stock snapped to full-size. 'Yes, he's running.'

'Follow him. Tell me what he's thinking.'

Sara quieted her mind, reached out. 'He's not thinking,' she replied. 'He's panicking.'

She directed all her attention to the area around the man's head, and concentrated, searching for thoughts and impressions. 'He has no intention of killing all those people! He wants to shoot … I'm not sure. Someone else.'

'How does it change? Why will he do what he's about to do?'

'I don't know.'

'All right,' Eldon said, 'I want you to speed ahead in time, to the moment before he fires his first shot.'

Before Sara could object, she found herself in a new place, on a street lined with shops. Dundas was frozen in an ungainly trot, raising his shotgun towards a woman. She gripped her son's hand, and was still in mid-scream. Sara reached out with her mind to feel the woman's emotions. Fear, yes, but not dread. She screamed a warning, to alert other shoppers to the man with the gun.

In the second or two since she had opened her mouth, however, the situation had changed, and Dundas was about to kill her.

'What's happening?' Eldon asked.

'Everything's frozen,' Sara replied. 'You said go to the

moment before he fires the first shot. That's where I am.'

'I see,' said Eldon approvingly. 'Now let the scene play out.'

Without Sara's conscious involvement, the scene became animated once more. Sara watched as Dundas discharged his shotgun shell full into the woman's chest, and felt her own chest constrict with horror. She screamed as the woman screamed. She felt her arms flail out, as if they were trying to shove Dundas off his murderous course. Her hand struck a ceramic vase filled with lilies, spilling tepid water across the table like blood. The young boy spun around, propelled by his mother's fall, and was caught between the shoulder blades by the next, close-range shot. Sara felt the violent concussion of his sudden death. She wailed.

'Freeze it there!' Eldon shouted, and Sara clenched her muscles taut.

'Go to the park now,' Eldon said, more quietly. 'Freeze at the moment right after he's killed the old lady.'

Sara found herself suspended above Quarry Park, over a frozen scene of carnage. The elderly woman lay bleeding on the grass, her dog staring at Dundas with terrified eyes. Dundas was in mid-turn, raising the barrel of his gun …

Raising it towards a young mother, and the baby in the carriage.

The baby.

'No!' Sara screamed, and stood, knocking her chair backwards.

'Sara,' Eldon warned steadily.

'Shut up!' she shrieked. 'I won't watch any more. I want it to go away!'

She grabbed at the envelope on the table, now soggy with vase-water, and tore at it, grinding the newspaper photo inside into small, gummy pieces. As Eldon moved around the table to comfort her, she collapsed into wracking sobs.

He took her into his muscular arms. 'It's all right,' he said. 'I'm sorry you had to go through that.'

'Why?' she sputtered, 'Why did I need to –'

'Shhh,' Eldon said. 'It was necessary. You don't have to see any more.'

When she had calmed down, Eldon looked at her sternly, the way her father had once done when she had learned an important lesson. 'Do you understand why you're not ready to face your past?'

'I guess so,' she said meekly.

'Do you think we might do it my way from now on?'

She hung her head, and quietly agreed.

Sara focused on the kitchen clock. It was just after midnight. Eldon Carson was in the living room, fetching his jacket, preparing to leave. She needed to go to bed; all her energy had been flushed away. Waves of chill wafted through her body, and goose bumps had formed on her flesh. When she touched her skin, it felt hot and tender. Sara recognised the symptoms of a mild nervous breakdown.

In the past, she had seen the aftermath of numerous grisly horrors, but never an actual murder. Now, she had done far more than see; the remote viewing state was more visceral than passive witness. Sara had participated in every emotion, felt every pain, heard every thought. Eldon had been right; she had not been ready. She was grateful that he had shielded her from her parents' deaths. He entered the room. 'Will you be all right?' he asked, as he drew on his jacket.

'Fine,' she said. She drew in a trembling breath. 'I'm sorry.'

He smiled understandingly. 'It was something you

needed. Sorry I had to do it like that.'

Sara heard a car driving cautiously down the bumpy lane and tensed. 'Get back!' she whispered. 'Hide in the stable.'

Eldon withdrew through the living room, and Sara, drawing on a reserve of nervous energy beneath her exhaustion, nudged aside the curtains. It was Rhodri's Jaguar. She yelled into the dark living room: 'Leave through the back door – quickly!'

She watched Rhodri get out, remove a small travel bag from the back seat, and skip jauntily up the steps. He pushed open the door, and called, 'Surprise!'

'Rhoddo,' Sara said, in a tone that belied her shock. She kissed him on the cheek, and he hugged her in reply. 'What are you doing here?'

'I was at the aerodrome in Lancashire,' he said. 'I flew in on the company's morning shuttle from Hampshire, and had someone drive up with my car.'

'Why? There's an evening shuttle back to Hampshire, isn't there?'

'For once, I have a weekend free. I couldn't imagine a better way to spend it than with you.'

Sara tried to calm her nerves by willpower alone. She turned and filled the kettle.

'I wondered if you'd be asleep,' he said. 'But I told myself, nine times out of ten, she's doing paperwork at midnight.'

'I don't work nearly that hard,' Sara said.

'Eight times out of ten, then.'

Sara filled the teapot with boiling water, and wondered whether Eldon had managed to escape in time.

Suddenly, from the corner of her eye, she saw him enter the room. It was one shock too many, and she nearly swooned.

'*Nos da*,' Eldon said nonchalantly to Rhodri in a

passable Welsh accent. 'You must be Rhodri. Sara's told me so much about you.' He ignored Sara's mortified stare, and shook her brother's hand, staring firmly into his eyes.

Rhodri blinked, puzzled by the intensity of the young man's appraisal.

After a second, Eldon broke contact. He picked up his soggy papier mâché disc from the window sill, then kissed Sara sweetly on the cheek.

'Good night, darling,' he whispered. 'Get some sleep. You must be exhausted.'

Sara and Rhodri drank their tea in the living room, with the new fluorescent light glaring overhead.

'A local boy!' Rhodri exclaimed. 'I'd never have believed it. I always thought you were such a snob about these things.'

'A snob?'

'With your penchant for English police detectives and such. And this fellow is so young! Who is he?'

'Just a friend.' Sara took too big a swallow of her tea, and felt it burn her throat. Rhodri chuckled naughtily.

She was still breathless with shock and indignation. What had Eldon been playing at? She knew him well enough now to understand he did nothing without a reason, and that he was not prone to practical jokes. Why had he risked revealing himself to Rhodri when he hadn't needed to?

'If you must know,' Sara said, 'I am seeing Jamie again.'

Rhodri's face fell. 'Oh, Sara, no. For heaven's sake, why?'

The strength of her older brother's passion stymied Sara. In a halting voice, she said, 'We've sorted out our differences.'

'Impossible.' Rhodri shook his head decisively. 'The biggest difference is, you're a nice, gentle person and he's an untrustworthy sod.'

'He is not,' Sara countered.

'Then why did he visit me behind your back?'

Sara sighed. 'That's all been straightened out now.'

'Has it?' he asked sceptically.

'Count on it,' she insisted.

Briefly, Sara told her brother about how the limits she had set allowed them to enjoy each other's company without conflict.

'He meant well,' she concluded. 'Once he found out I truly didn't want him turning over our past, he stopped.'

Rhodri raised an eyebrow, but said nothing.

Sara persevered: 'Look,' she said, 'you trust Ceri's judgement don't you? Even she likes Jamie now.'

'Ceri?' Rhodri asked suspiciously. 'She doesn't like anyone.'

'Judge for yourself,' Sara said. 'I'll have them both to dinner tomorrow evening.'

Rhodri looked startled by Sara's suggestion. 'Dinner with the Scotland Yard Inspector?' he said. 'I can barely contain myself.'

'Deal?' Sara asked.

Rhodri considered. 'It might be fun at that. Your Inspector is well-meaning, but easily taunted.' He grinned widely. 'I take it you'd rather I not mention tonight's fellow?'

Sara hesitated. 'In fact, I would prefer that,' she said finally.

'Don't worry,' he replied with a chuckle, 'I'm very good at keeping secrets.'

TWENTY-ONE

Sara spent Saturday morning cooking. She made vegetarian lasagne, a Greek salad, and fruit salad for pudding. While the pasta baked, she and Rhodri took a stroll along the beach. Rhodri wore a pair of leather sandals, and had his chinos rolled up above his ankles. He kicked at pebbles as they strolled, and looked genuinely relaxed.

'You're wasting your bloody time here in Wales,' he said, not for the first time. 'Twenty years ago, neither of us could wait to get out.'

Sara shrugged without concern. 'People change.'

'That they do,' Rhodri agreed.

A strong wave broke on the beach and foamy sea water surged towards their feet. They stepped hastily sideways.

'You don't belong here any more. You should be in London where people need you.' Rhodri arched an eyebrow. 'Poor Andy Turner is absolutely distraught without you.'

Sara shook her head in fond exasperation. 'Andy was my patient for over two years,' she said, 'and he didn't make a single bit of progress. Do you know why? Because there's nothing wrong with him.'

Rhodri laughed. 'There is now. He's working himself into an absolute stupor for me.'

Andrew Turner had been one of Rhodri's closest

friends since they worked in the same marketing department fifteen years earlier. Now, as CEO of Thorndike Aerospace, Rhodri had awarded Andy's consultancy huge contracts, and made his old friend rich.

'What's he working so hard on?' Sara asked.

'The Hampshire Air Show,' Rhodri said. 'It starts Tuesday. It's a major event in the defence industry calendar. All the big arms contractors build hospitality pavilions for their international customers.'

Sara smiled ironically. 'Saudi oil sheikhs, Third World despots …'

'Allies in the war on terror,' Rhodri agreed cheerfully. 'The pavilions are really just big advertisements for the company, with all sorts of flashy presentations and high-tech gadgets. In the past, Thorndike hadn't participated in any significant way; we've always sub-contracted from larger aerospace firms. Now, I'm changing direction, and we're pitching to be the prime contractor on major government contracts.'

'And you need a higher profile,' Sara said.

'Exactly. So this year, we're running our own pavilion, and Andy's company is creating it for us.'

'No wonder he's exhausted,' Sara said.

'We need to make an impression,' Rhodri said, nodding, 'and Andy knows if he cocks it up, I won't be pleased. This is so important I'm driving straight to Hampshire this evening.'

A brother and sister, perhaps seven and five, ran past them in bathing costumes and Crocs. Their footsteps crunched deep into the pebbles. From behind, a mother shouted warnings of caution. Sara could remember similar Sunday afternoons with Rhoddo, and despite their talk of defence contracts and corporate marketing campaigns, she realised she still felt very close to her brother. It was as if the intervening years had not changed them much at all.

'Andy is trying to win me over with flattery. He's planned a special presentation for me to open the pavilion on Tuesday. I'm to emerge through clouds of smoke to the "Ride of the Valkyries".'

Sara laughed. 'Andy is nothing if not subtle.'

By the time they returned home, the mozzarella on top of the lasagne had browned to a lovely finish, and Sara switched off the oven. She uncorked a bottle of wine and poured two large glasses with warm satisfaction, realising that the afternoon was the most enjoyable she'd had for ages.

By dinner-time, the warm glow of Sara's afternoon had evaporated, and was replaced by nagging discomfort. Rhodri, Jamie and Ceri sat with her at the table, in deep discussion. Sara was easily distracted, staring out the kitchen window as if she suspected someone of spying through it. She told herself there was nothing to worry about – it was simply the topic of conversation that was making her feel this way.

'As far as I can remember, Inspector,' Rhodri was saying pointedly, with an unflattering emphasis on Jamie's rank, 'these are fairly close-knit communities around here. Why has it taken so long to find the killer? Someone must have spotted him.'

'Several people have spotted him,' Jamie replied, with good-natured patience. 'Because of his contact with Sara, we had an accurate description three weeks after the first murder, and just days after the last. We can trace several of his movements up until that time; afterwards, he seems to have disappeared.'

'I understand there's been no killing for nearly a month,' said Rhodri.

'That's true,' Ceri cut in. 'One possibility is, the

offender left the area.' She frowned. 'We may not know for certain until a body turns up somewhere else.'

Rhodri turned his attention back to Jamie. 'Then I can't imagine what's keeping you here,' he said pleasantly.

Jamie grinned without humour and speared a cherry tomato with his fork.

Sara straightened her shoulders and tried to get comfortable. She was beginning to question the wisdom of inviting Jamie to dinner. The fact that he had won Ceri over, she told herself, was no proof that he could do the same with Rhoddo.

'Ceri and I are keeping busy,' Jamie said defensively. 'We're working together, trying to trace anyone who may have links to the killer ...'

As Jamie launched into a description of his travails with Ceri, Sara realised that the strain between her brother and her lover had not been what was unsettling her. She felt was as if there was an uninvited presence hovering in the room, watching her. What was it? She tried to relax, and extended her mind ...

Eldon! she thought.

A sensation pulsed inside her head, non-verbal but inarguably real. An acknowledgement that her suspicion was correct. Eldon Carson may not have been present physically, but he was in the room.

'Sara,' Ceri said, responding to her sharp intake of breath, 'are you feeling all right?'

What are you doing? she asked the presence she could not see. *Why are you ... wherever you are?*

Her mind bumped against a sensation like grim laughter.

'I suppose,' Rhodri said languidly to Jamie, 'it would be in your interest to choose the least likely candidates to interview.'

'The least likely?' Jamie asked. 'What are you suggesting?'

'Well,' Rhodri drawled, 'since you want to stay here as long as possible, it would make sense to interview people who would not lead you to the killer.'

'Sara?' Ceri repeated. 'Do you want to lie down?'

'What?' Sara asked, and saw concern on Ceri's face. Jamie and Rhodri had stopped talking.

'You had your eyes closed.'

'Oh. No, I'm fine.'

'I'm sure you didn't mean to be offensive,' Jamie said with a stiff smile.

'Yes, I did,' Rhodri replied. 'I was teasing you.'

Inside her mind, Sara heard Eldon chuckle again. She found being observed like this more than simply unsettling – it was intrusive, a violation.

Go away, she thought sharply. 'I just got tired for a second,' Sara explained to the three pensive faces staring at her. 'I'm all right now.'

His presence remained, like a high-frequency noise that silently strained the nerves. Suddenly, she felt as though she was the victim of a stalker – something Eldon had not made her feel since she had first descended her stairs to find him sitting in her darkened living room. Recently, they had been behaving almost like friends, but this gesture did not feel friendly. She thought of Eldon's powerful build, of his willingness to kill ... and was momentarily afraid.

For the first time, Sara found herself wondering how she would ever get rid of Eldon Carson when the time came. He had made it clear that he wanted to be around her. When he had traded what he had to offer, taught her everything she needed to know, would he go away quietly?

And what could she do about it if he wouldn't?

Sara had just opened the Drop-In Centre for another week, and was arranging chairs when she heard the door downstairs open, close and lock.

'Hello?' she called, and moved to the top of the stairs.

Eldon Carson was halfway up the old, wooden steps. 'What are you doing here?' she gasped. He rarely ventured outside in daylight, and to appear on the promenade, in her Centre, was foolhardy.

'It's okay,' he said. 'I've locked the door, and put up the "Closed" sign. Just don't answer the phone.'

Eldon appeared calm, but his voice was strained, and Sara could sense a flush of angst radiating from him. She looked out the window: the street, wet from the drizzle of this grey day, was quiet.

'What do you think you were doing Saturday evening?' Sara asked tersely. 'You frightened me.'

He looked at her and tried to grin. Sara detected a sadness in his smile, which he was trying to hide. 'I was watching over you,' he said.

'Well, I don't like people eavesdropping on my dinner parties,' she replied. Frowning, she added, 'It was creepy.'

'Creepy?' Eldon laughed sardonically. 'You're going to have to get used to things like that.' He dug into a bag of biscuits. 'Now that you understand that there are more than one way for a person to be present ...'

'I don't care how many ways there are, the simple fact was, you weren't invited! If you have special powers, you also have responsibilities.'

Eldon poured himself a coffee, and added milk to his cup. 'I agree wholeheartedly,' he said darkly.

'Then, at least have the decency to apologise for ruining my evening.'

He sat on the old, sagging sofa. 'I didn't ruin your

evening – and if you thought about it for a minute, you'd realise that. What was really bothering you was the distance you felt between you and your friends.'

Sara shuddered. 'Not this lecture again,' she sighed.

'Sara,' Eldon said, 'I've been there; I know how lonely it is. But trust me: your awareness is expanding. You're seeing things in a way that would have been impossible for you, even a month ago. That can't help but throw the beliefs and actions of your friends into a new light.'

Sara stared sullenly at the floor and said, 'Whatever happened to "Miss Sara"?'

Eldon paused, startled by the question, then chuckled bleakly. 'I think we know each other well enough now to dispense with formality.'

Sara shook her head in surrender, and helped herself to a cup of coffee.

'Your friends are nice people,' he continued, 'but they're not like us.'

Eldon made an effort to shake off his sombre mood; he lifted his bag from the floor and loosened the straps. 'I've finished your gift,' he said.

She looked up. 'What gift?'

'The one I started making in your kitchen.' He leapt from the sofa. 'I want you to wear it. It's a reminder of the things you are able to see, and the things you'll be able to see in time.'

Eldon pulled a small object from his bag, and held out his hand to Sara. In his palm was a papier mâché disk on a leather thong. She accepted it curiously, and looked down – suddenly flushing with the shock of recognition. Eldon had made a beautiful reproduction of his Eye in the Pyramid design. It was exquisitely smooth, delicately painted and varnished to a soft gloss.

'Eldon,' Sara stammered, 'I couldn't possibly wear this.'

'Why not?'

The image ... you know what it represents. It's disturbing.' In her mind's eye, Sara saw a fourteen-year-old boy with his throat cut, and the blackened corpse of Navid Kapadia. She handed the pendant back to him. 'I don't want to hurt your feelings, but I think this is inappropriate.'

In a flash, Eldon's eyes hardened and he tugged his gift from Sara's hand. 'It's completely appropriate,' he countered, his words clipped and harsh. It was the first time he had used such a tone with her. 'The reason you reject it is what makes it appropriate.' He shook his head in exasperation and spoke formally: 'Miss Sara, I have been letting you come to terms with all this at your own pace. That was necessary – but I cannot do it any more.'

He inclined his head towards the sofa, and snapped, 'Sit down.'

Sara stood completely still, her eyes burning into his. 'Why?' she asked.

'Because it's time I made you aware of a few truths.'

Trevor Hughes' living room was a rubbish tip of unclean dishes, leftover food, beer cans, and full ashtrays. Threadbare floral carpet covered the floor in swirls of brown, orange and lime green. The only new objects in the room were a television set and a series of flags and posters in black, white and red. Jamie sat on the edge of a dirty armchair, grateful that Ceri had not been able to join him. Her reactions to Trevor Hughes might have been a liability.

'Mr Hughes,' Jamie said, 'You are a member of a group called Race Riot, is that right?'

The man hesitated, staring at Jamie with deep suspicion. Jamie's eyes drifted up to a poster. *White Pride Worldwide*.

'It's a legal organisation,' he said finally.

'Sadly, yes,' Jamie said, and held out the Photofit of their suspect. 'I'm here to ask if you've seen this man.'

Hughes shifted position with a grunt, and took the picture. He stared at it for a long while. 'Why?'

'He is a suspect, wanted in connection with the recent spate of killings in the area,' Jamie said. 'We believe he may be pretending to be a member of an organisation such as yours, in order to attract allies.'

Hughes stared at him blankly.

'In other words,' Jamie said, 'he may be using someone like you.'

Jamie watched a series of complicated emotions pass across Hughes' putty-like features. He wondered if, in his heart of hearts, this man really thought himself superior to whole other races.

At length, Hughes said, 'Haven't seen him,' and held out the Photofit.

'Then you're lucky,' Jamie replied, taking the picture back. 'Because whoever this man is using is in terrible danger.'

He stared again at the Nazi symbols on the wall. 'Mr Hughes, do you know anything about the Eye in The Pyramid?'

'The what?'

Jamie described the symbol, modified to include the killer's scales of justice.

'Uh-uh,' Hughes said, shaking his shaved head.

Jamie shrugged and rose. He dug into his pocket, and held out his card. 'This is my name, and I've written the number of the Aberystwyth station on the back. If you hear anything you think may be significant, please call me.'

Hughes took the card and tossed it on a small wood-grain laminate table without looking at it. Jamie moved to the door. 'Let me stress this, Mr Hughes: no matter what he says, this man does not believe the things that you believe.'

'I told you, I haven't seen him,' Hughes said, his voice tinged with hostility.

'Nobody's said you have,' Jamie said. He pulled open the door. 'Take care of yourself, Mr Hughes.'

Eldon leaned forward on a plastic chair across from Sara. He sat very close to her, but several inches higher than her position on the sunken cushions of the sofa. He held his papier mâché pendant in both hands, his thumbs rubbing the lacquered surface.

'I didn't give you this gift randomly,' he said with unusual bitterness. 'I'm not a little boy drawing a picture for the girl he's got a crush on. This was intended to make you think.'

Sara stared at him coolly.

'It signifies something,' Eldon went on with sarcastic precision.

'We had a specific deal,' Sara said, her jaw and throat tight. 'You wanted to be around me, and I wanted to learn what you could teach me.' She noted his bleak smile and added, 'For one particular purpose.'

He blew air between his lips derisively 'You might have thought that once,' he said, 'but you don't any more. We're more involved than you can admit. That much was obvious at your dinner party, when you started to wonder how you'd ever get me to go away.'

Before she could check herself, Sara's eyes widened in surprise.

'Did you think I couldn't sense that?' Eldon asked, furrowing his brow in feigned confusion. He dropped the pendant in his lap and spread his hands wide. 'Sometimes, I can't help but wonder if you're tired of me.'

Sara stared at her hands, and twisted a ring. The tap dripped, pinging rhythmically against the aluminium sink. 'You know why I was angry about the dinner party,' she responded in a subdued voice.

'I know,' Eldon agreed, 'but you had no right to feel like that. You threw your lot in with mine the moment you decided not to call the police.'

'That,' Sara countered, 'was because I understood your reasons for killing. But it doesn't mean I have to like what you've done.'

'Oh, for God's sake, Sara,' Eldon barked, 'you can't go on denying everything you don't want to deal with!' He leaned forward and added, 'The gift we possess is not pick-and-mix. Face facts – the more you increase your psychic power, the more like me you're going to become.'

'I'm nothing like you,' Sara said. 'I thought you might understand that by now.' She folded her arms and leaned back in the sofa. 'You know less about me than you've led me to believe.'

Eldon opened his hands in a gesture of truce.

'Okay …' he said softly, 'let me tell you what I know about you. Despite your tendency to stick your head in the sand, I know you're honest. You're also brave, and you have the strength of your convictions.' He smiled tenderly. 'I knew all that about you when I first noticed you. But, at the same time, I saw someone in desperate need – a need only I could meet.' An expression of pain crossed his face and he spoke plaintively: 'What could I do? Leave you in ignorance, knowing who you were and what you were capable of? I understood that you wanted my gifts more desperately than even you knew …'

'That all sounds very worthy,' Sara said with muted irony. 'But you wanted something too.'

He nodded firmly. 'I've never denied my desire to be near you – I didn't lie to you about that. But our trade could never be as simple as you believe. Sara, the gift I have handed you is a poisoned chalice.'

'What's that supposed to mean?'

'It means, there will come a time when it will start demanding things of you.'

Sara stared at him blankly, uncertainty flickering in her eyes. 'Will there, now?' she said defiantly.

'Yes,' he insisted. 'In exactly the same way it demanded things of me. Sara, one day you will find yourself knowing, beyond doubt, that someone is going to commit a terrible crime, unless you stop it.'

He looked at her with piercing eyes. 'On that day, what will you do? I believe you will not run away from that responsibility.'

Sara sat very still, and Eldon held out his pendant once more.

'Soon,' he said, 'the gift I have given you will reveal to you everything you've ever wanted to know about your life. But one day it will also make you a killer.'

He smiled with compassion and anguish, and added, 'Just like me.'

TWENTY-TWO

Eldon Carson gazed upon Sara Jones' shocked features with understanding and pity. He realised all too well that this was the first time she had truly related his experience of being psychic to her own. Until now, Miss Sara's only worry had been learning enough to understand her past. Now, the full truth had hit her, and he understood the plummeting sensation of emotional vertigo she was feeling. It was not unlike his own experience, when he had realised that the fate of Yusuf and Jamila Kapadia lay in his hands.

He watched as Sara forced the fear from her eyes with steely determination. 'No,' she said defiantly. 'I refuse to become what you have become.'

'I don't blame you,' Eldon said with great seriousness. 'It's an awful thing to be – but how will you stop it?'

She thought for several long seconds, as Eldon listened to the tap dripping, and to the buzzing of the noisy electric clock on the wall.

'I'll tell you how I'm going to stop it,' Sara said finally. 'I will resign from the psychic club. From now on, I refuse to accept any more training from you.'

She moved to the sofa and sat defiantly.

Eldon smiled with acute, painful sympathy. 'That won't work,' he replied. 'You've progressed too far.'

Sara's large, hollow eyes stared at him with sullen challenge.

'Think of yourself as a radio scanner. You may not be tuned to quite the right frequency yet, but you're close enough to hear the static. That's enough to keep you from ignoring it.'

After a full minute's silence, Sara rose, and walked to the window of the Centre, looking out at the grey day. 'The street is empty,' she said. 'You can leave without anyone noticing.' She tilted her head towards the exit. 'Please go now. I never want to see you again.'

He stared at her, admiring her composure, her strength ... and her beauty. Eventually, he nodded. 'I promise you'll never see me again,' he said simply. Eldon watched the shock register in her eyes. He took the pendant, which Sara had refused twice, and placed it gently on the counter.

'You didn't need to worry about getting rid of me, you know,' he said. 'I never intended to stay. All I ever wanted was to help you, and feel what it's like to know you.'

Eldon approached her, and held out his hand. When Sara did not flinch, he touched her arm tenderly. 'You've been preparing for this moment all your life,' he said. 'From the day your parents were killed. Some kids might have given up – and that would've ruined their lives. Others might've let the experience twist them into something bitter, less than human. You went into the world and became the person who could get answers. He stared at her with admiration. 'You made yourself into something very rare – a truly responsible person.'

Their gazes locked for several seconds before Sara shook away his hand. Eldon held up his palms in a gesture of concession and farewell. 'I apologise for leaving you to work the rest out for yourself,' he said. 'But it's been an honour to be your teacher.'

Turning, he walked to the door.

'It's not going to happen,' Sara said with quiet conviction.

'Maybe not for a long time,' Eldon replied, turning. 'You should stay with Jamie; he's good for you.'

He stared at her silently for a long time, his expression tender and compassionate.

'Good luck,' he said hoarsely, and descended the stairs.

Eldon Carson had driven Trevor Hughes' car up Penglais Hill with his throat tightly constricted, tears blurring his vision. He wept for many reasons: for the ultimate fate of Sara Jones, because he would never see her again, and for fear that she would end up hating him for what he was about to do.

And he cried for the fear that in less than a week, he might be dead.

When he turned onto the road from Bow Street towards Hughes' house, his self-pity was swamped by an overwhelming prickle of warning. He knew he needed to be on his guard now.

Carson found Hughes pottering aimlessly about the house. A half-smoked cigarette smouldered in an ashtray, and an almost-full bottle of lager sweated onto the top of the blaring television.

'Hi, mate,' Hughes said. He tried to sound relaxed, but tension choked his voice.

Carson sensed immediately that he was nervous, even frightened. He reached into his mind ... there was something else.

It was expectancy. He was waiting for someone.

'How was your morning?' Carson asked, as he stabbed a finger at the television button, killing the din.

'Oh, fine, mate, fine,' Hughes said, his voice rising half an octave. 'What are you going to do this afternoon? You hanging around here, or –'

'Sit down, Trevor,' Carson said, pulling a plastic chair away from the wall and shoving it towards him. 'Right here.'

'Okay, mate … sure,' Hughes said, and sat obediently. He was humouring Carson, stalling for time. 'We can talk, eh? I've been meaning to ask … what lodge of the Klan did you say you're from? I checked out their home page, like.'

Carson stood less than two feet away from Hughes, and looked down at him, straight into his eyes. 'Who was here this morning, Trevor?' he asked slowly.

'Nobody,' Hughes said, too quickly.

Carson nodded, but not in agreement. 'It was Harding, wasn't it?' he asked. 'The Scotland Yard detective.'

'No!'

'He showed you a Photofit,' Carson went on. 'It looked like me, didn't it?'

Hughes hesitated, his thick lip trembling. 'I didn't tell him anything,' he blurted.

Carson walked around Hughes in soft, measured steps, until he was out of his line of sight. 'You don't trust cops, do you?'

'No, mate, of course not.'

'No,' Carson repeated in a whisper.

Hughes tensed. His upper body shuddered and jerked, preparing to spring forward, perhaps to run – but welling terror held him back. Carson laid a hand on Hughes' clammy, bare shoulder. 'Relax, Trevor. Just stay there.'

Hughes allowed his muscles to ease, and began to tremble. 'You just can't trust police,' he said in a wild ramble, ''cos they work for the Government and it answers to Jews. Course, you already know that, 'cos you're with the Klan, right mate?'

'He made you doubt me. Detective Inspector Harding. You believed what he said.'

Sweat trickled down the sides of Trevor's face, getting lost in the folds of his neck. 'I don't know,' he whispered.

Carson reached into his satchel, and withdrew a disposable pen. Reaching over Hughes' shoulder, he carefully drew the Eye in the Pyramid symbol on his forearm. 'Look at that drawing, Trevor,' he said. 'Tell me where you've seen it before.'

Hughes breathed hard and swallowed.

'Did the detective show you a copy of it?'

'No.'

Carson chuckled. 'I guess he didn't trust you enough.'

A car pulled up onto the crumbling tarmac at the front of the house. Two doors opened and clunked shut.

'I'm in here!' Hughes screamed.

A pair of Hughes' skinhead friends fell through the front door at a half-run, to find Carson holding a long knife to their friend's throat.

'Sit down, gentlemen,' Carson said. 'Both of you on the sofa, please.'

Hughes began to blubber. 'Oh shit, oh shit,' he said, 'you should have fucking sneaked up!'

The skinheads stood uncertainly, staring at the situation. 'Sit down,' Trevor screamed, 'or he'll fucking kill me!'

They shuffled to the sofa and sat. Carson reached out and brushed against their minds. He felt no real evil or danger there, only mild malice and garden-variety stupidity. 'You've got a special event on your calendar, haven't you Trevor?' Carson said.

'What?'

'This October. In South London. What is it, Trevor?'

'It – it's Race Riot's March Against the Mosques.'

Carson nodded. 'Let me tell you a story,' he said to the skinheads on the sofa. 'Our friend Trevor here goes to Peckham, right? ... and he spends the day drinking with his chums. By the time the time the march happens, he's very drunk. The march pumps him up – by the end of it, he's unstoppable. Drunk, high on adrenaline and his own white supremacy –'

Carson dug the edge of the knife harder into Hughes' throat and the neo-Nazi cried out.

'And looking for trouble. Sadly, nobody wants to fight. Then he spies a Somali kid at a bus stop. Trevor here calls his friends over. They don't mean anything, they're just having fun ... but they end up crippling the kid.'

'That never happened!' Hughes squealed. 'You just made it up!' With bulging eyes, he looked desperately at his friends. 'He's a fucking serial killer,' he cried, 'stop him!'

Before they could move, Carson had jerked the knife hard through Trevor Hughes' throat – and when Hughes' friends moved, it was to dash wildly from the house to their car, and speed away in a shower of crumbling tarmac.

Carson reached out for Trevor Hughes' lifeless right arm. Underneath his drawing of the symbol, he carefully etched the name of South London teenager Ashkir Shido Caadil, who would now live a long and healthy life.

Recently renovated, the Owen Hotel's dining room aimed at an up-market clientele. It was decorated in shades of cool blue, with heavy velour curtains held back by floral ties. The chairs were ornate, upholstered in rose pink, and the napkins were thick pink linen. Each setting had more cutlery than was necessary.

Although a long-time resident of the area, Ceri Lloyd had never dined at the Owen. Tonight, Jamie Harding was treating her to a working dinner.

They sat next to a large bay window, watching the last of the sun drop behind the bay.

'You don't see sights like that in London,' Ceri said.

'No,' Jamie agreed politely. What did Ceri Lloyd know about London sunsets?

'You've been here a while now,' Ceri said. 'D'you like it enough to want to stay?'

Jamie cocked his head questioningly.

'It's not so strange a notion,' Ceri went on, sounding like a temptress leading a chaste young man to damnation. 'You and Sara are going to stay together, aren't you?'

'I hope so,' Jamie agreed.

'But you're hoping that she'll join you in London.' Ceri fiddled with her cutlery until the pieces were out of order. 'And she might,' she added.

'But you hope she doesn't.'

'Obviously,' Ceri said. 'I know that this has been the grimmest summer we've seen here in years – and yet, having Sara back has made it the happiest one, too … at least for me.'

She looked at Jamie's compassionate smile and frowned. 'I wasn't exactly lonely without her, mind you,' she said defensively. 'I've got good friends, and my job, and I involve myself in politics … Sara's like family.'

'I can understand,' Jamie said. 'I feel rather strongly about her, too.'

'London is no good for her,' Ceri said abruptly. 'She belongs here. And I'll bet Wales would be better for you too. Why live in all that filth when you could have this?' She waved her hand towards the window. 'You'd get a job in CID here, no problem.' Her eyes narrowed, those of a negotiator cutting a deal. 'I'd even help you.'

'Well, that's very kind,' Jamie said. 'I'll – I'll think about it.'

Ceri snorted with derision, and a hint of affection. 'No, you won't.'

Shifting in her chair, she placed her elbows on the table, and looked about, ensuring they were alone. 'The fellow you interviewed this morning,' she continued, lowering her voice. 'What was his name?'

'Hughes,' Jamie replied. 'Trevor Hughes.'

She smiled. 'Even paradise has its drug dealers.'

'Drug dealer *and* Nazi,' Jamie reminded her.

She chortled. 'A busy boy. How did that one go?'

'It was interesting …'

Succinctly, Jamie detailed the contents of his conversation with Hughes, but before he had finished, Ceri interrupted: 'How long did you say he looked at the killer's picture?'

Jamie frowned. 'Maybe ten seconds.'

'That's a long time,' Ceri said.

'It made me suspicious too,' he agreed. 'I tried to frighten him into telling me more, but the man is obstinate. Either that or stupid.'

'Most likely both,' Ceri said. 'I'll bet you were nice to him.'

'I suppose I was polite.'

'That was your mistake. Wish I'd been there.'

The hostess returned with two drinks menus. Ceri and Jamie ordered and paused for her to leave; once she had cleared the room, Ceri said, 'That Hughes character knows way more than he's telling you.'

'I agree,' Jamie said. 'If you really think you can get more out of him than I did, we can go back there after dinner.'

'I'd like that,' Ceri said, and fidgeted in her chair. 'In fact,' she said abruptly, 'you know what? Let's go now.'

'Now?' Jamie said. He had not eaten all day.

When the drinks arrived, Ceri requested the bill.

Jamie's hollow stomach moaned in complaint.

'Drink up, then,' Ceri said enthusiastically. 'I want to pay a visit to Mr Hughes.'

After Eldon had gone, Sara had kept the Centre open, striving for a normality it had proved impossible even to simulate. She had been jittery, and hoping desperately for visitors – people with concrete problems, ones easier to make sense of than her own.

She had imagined trying to tell her troubles to a mental health professional: 'I've been sheltering a psychic serial killer, you see, and he's been teaching me to be psychic too. But now he expects me to go out and start killing people, and I don't really feel like doing that ...'

Throughout the afternoon, Sara had experienced one fit of hysterical laughter and two helpless crying jags. No one had come to relieve her solitude; she had been left alone, her mind churning with thoughts that were absurd, unbelievable, and tenacious.

Now she was home, listening to soft jazz in the glow of candlelight. The music, the light, the scent of cinnamon, were all to exorcise Eldon's spirit from a house still haunted by his presence. There was the chair on which he'd sat. There was the stable, where she'd imprisoned him, and sealed the fate of five people.

Sara had travelled through so many emotions, and now settled on a feeling of profound sadness for Eldon Carson. The task he had assigned himself was lonely, and Sara had become the one person able to identify with him. He had left her with so many questions. Eldon had described how, as a teenager, he had sought out other psychics, and a few had proved genuine. This implied that there were real psychics who had not ended up murdering people. How could he be so certain Sara would follow in his footsteps? Perhaps she really could quit the psychic club.

How psychic was she anyway, without her mentor's guidance? She decided to banish her fear by seeing what she could do alone. She crawled under the stairs and dug out a box of old photo albums, choosing a picture of herself from her early days in London. Upstairs, she slipped it inside an envelope and made herself comfortable on the bed.

'This, Sara,' she said, 'is your target. Your random coordinates are six, three, five, seven, five, nine, two.'

'Now,' she said, 'go and explore it.'

Carson drove east in Trevor Hughes' ancient Ford Escort along the straight, impersonal stretch of motorway that linked South Wales with the south-east of England. His pockets bulged with the wads of cash Hughes had hidden all over his house. Carson observed the speed limit meticulously: he had no intention of wrangling with cops. He would find an anonymous hotel somewhere not too near his destination, and get some rest. Soon, they would be looking for Hughes' car.

What was he driving towards? Death? Imprisonment? The irony, thought Carson, was that this psychic simply did not know. His own future had failed to reveal itself to him. Even if he survived, he would be more thoroughly an exile than before. He had entered Aberystwyth a troubled young man who did not feel at home anywhere – now he was all that and a murderer too. A murderer who would not, could not, stop killing.

And, from now on, he would have to do it without Sara Jones. She would never want to see him again, even if he escaped the worst of his possible fates. Carson felt like someone who had been given a glimpse of paradise, then denied it forever more.

Feeling more miserable than he had ever felt before, he

tuned the radio to a jazz station. Carson had never liked jazz, but it made him think, with bittersweet anguish, of Sara Jones.

The isolated house was dark as the night sky when Ceri pulled her panda car onto Trevor Hughes' crumbling driveway. She and Jamie stepped out with caution. The light from the inside the car threw a milky glow onto the brick wall. They closed their doors and it vanished.

'Does he own a car?' Ceri whispered.

'You'd think,' Jamie replied, 'living out here.'

Ceri moved towards the side of the house, where a carport covered part of the driveway. She saw nothing but the silhouettes of weeds growing through the tarmac, and an abandoned tyre leaning against the wall. 'Was it parked here yesterday?' she asked.

'Strange,' Jamie said. 'No.'

He climbed the cement stairs to the front door and pressed the buzzer. It did not make a sound. He knocked loudly and waited, then knocked again. 'Mr Hughes?'

Silence.

'He's not here.' Jamie noticed that Ceri had not joined him. He called her name.

'Back door's open,' she shouted.

'Unlocked?' Jamie asked, rounding the corner of the house.

'Pushed open,' she replied.

He stared through the open door, and called, 'Mr Hughes, are you in there? It's the police.'

No answer.

Jamie hesitated, and looked at Ceri quizzically. To enter a suspect's house required at least reasonable belief he was home and evading the police. That meant evidence they could use in court – not simply a police inspector's hunch.

Ceri sensed the reason for his hesitation. 'In my book,' she said, 'an open door is probable cause.' She pushed the half-open door wide. 'You want to go in first, or should I?'

Jamie shrugged and entered the sour-smelling kitchen, flipping on the light. He edged into the hallway, and glanced into the living room. He could barely make out the round black shadow of a chair in the centre of the room, with a large figure sprawled over it.

'In here!' he shouted, as he snapped on the light. The bare white bulb flickered overhead. Ceri was already behind him.

They stared at Trevor Hughes' corpse for no more than a second before Jamie yanked out his phone. 'It's Detective Inspector Harding. Please give me CID ...'

Ceri approached the body, and stared at the symbol drawn on its arm. 'Well, well,' she said. 'It looks like the Nazi's guest decided it was time to leave.'

Six, three, five, seven, five, nine, two ...

Sara lay on her bed, eyes closed, hands at her sides, and breathed deeply. She listened to the rustle of the trees outside her window, of the bleating of the sheep in the rear field, and emptied her mind of all thoughts. The fingers of her left hand brushed against the envelope, inside of which was her target.

Herself.

Swiftly, she felt her psychic body hurtling downwards through layers of darkness, a dizzying freefall which slowed gradually, and finally stopped. Sara felt queasy, disoriented, but she was tingling with excitement. She did not know where she'd arrived, but she flushed with something like pride, knowing she was doing it on her own.

The effort was hardly easy. Although she got a distinct

impression that she'd arrived somewhere, Sara could not steady herself enough to figure out where she was. It was like trying to focus on an object after spinning in circles. Gradually, she wrested control over her perceptions, and found herself hovering several feet above a long, narrow strip of …

Of what?

The view was hazy. She could make out a rough surface. Parts of it glowed soft white, as if lit from within. Rarer sections glittered like diamonds, while other patches were dark grey.

'What are you?' she asked aloud.

Then, instinctively, she understood. It wasn't a place at all, but a symbolic path – her life's experiences up until this moment. Some of them bright as new life, others dim as the grave. By focusing on spots in the path, Sara could feel faint vibrations of the moments they represented. There – the sadness she had felt when Aunt Issy sold the B&B and moved away. There – her first time in an operating theatre.

And there – way back – a throbbing red pulse of pain. Sara focused. Forced herself to see. *Don't be afraid, Sara. Face it.*

She reached out.

The horror of returning home. She could vaguely see the fruit and vegetables scattered on the mosaic tiles. Was that blood? She could hear a young woman's voice – Ceri's – like an echo.

Show me more.

The sensations were too indistinct – and Sara could not control them. Damn it. She wasn't strong enough. Her psychic body rose again, away from the pulsing redness. She felt herself separating. Tried to focus. Then she heard a buzzing. Vibrations. Groggily, Sara opened her eyes.

Her phone was ringing.

She fumbled for it, saw it was Ceri and thumbed the screen. 'Hey,' she said thickly. 'What's the matter?'

'You in the house?'

'In my bedroom. I was … sleeping.'

'Come downstairs – it's important. I'm at the door.'

In the kitchen, Ceri's face was a grim mask. Her shoulders sagged wearily. 'We've found where the offender was staying,' she said.

Sara's pulse started to race. 'You've got him?'

Ceri shook her head. 'He's gone. He'd been living with a racist fanatic. Yesterday he killed the guy and fled.'

'Killed him,' Sara repeated flatly.

'Just like the others. So far we haven't identified the name written on the victim's arm, though we're told it's Somali.'

Sara's mind began to whirr. 'Do you know where he's gone?'

'Scenes of Crime found his bag.' Ceri rapidly lit a cigarette. 'Inside were notes and sketches. He's been planning a new murder.'

Sara's pulse raced. 'Who? Where?'

Her friend pulled her close. 'I don't want you to worry. Jamie's notified the Met, and they're getting in touch with the authorities in –'

Sara shook herself away from her friend's grasp. 'Ceri, who's he planning to kill?'

Ceri stared at her friend soberly. 'The offender is on his way to the Hampshire Air Show.'

'What?' Sara gasped.

'I'm so sorry – he's after Rhodri.'

TWENTY-THREE

The town of Weatherby in Hampshire boasted two three-star hotels, a few good pubs, and a large airfield, used by the military and private businesses. Once a year, it became a thriving tourist destination. Cars, taxis and coaches crept along the narrow roads, and streams of pedestrians carried blankets, pillows and folding chairs along the well-tended pavements, all heading towards the Hampshire International Air Show. To locals, the gridlock meant a kind of house arrest. Police requested they stay off the main roads, and they tended to confine themselves to quarters, watching the aerial displays from dormer windows and roof decks. Clusters of police, in cars and on motorcycle and foot, dotted the A road into town, more common than traffic lights.

It was just after ten in the morning and Carson edged Trevor Hughes' car forward, thankful for the police's numbing regime of overwork. He could not sense whether Hughes' body had been found, or, if it had, whether the satchel he had forgotten had been discovered in the exercise room. He was tired. Had he not been driving, he might have been able to lie down and send his mind back to Wales. To be safe, Carson thought, he had to assume that every police officer was searching for him.

Last night, he had changed the registration plates and peeled the swastika and Celtic cross stickers from the bumper. He told himself again this was madness, trying to kill Rhodri Jones at one of the most heavily guarded events of his year … but he also knew it would be his first and only chance.

Time was running out in all directions. Carson had known his days in Aberystwyth were nearly over: the police were close to contacting his host, and Hughes was too stupid not to arouse their interest. This had also set the timetable for Carson's leaving Sara, and Aberystwyth itself – likely with the police in pursuit.

Carson had also sensed that Rhodri Jones would leave Sara's house immediately after her dinner party, and make for a heavily guarded aerodrome in Hampshire. He had considered trying to kill Rhodri before he had left Aberystwyth – but the likely outcome would have been his own capture before getting to Trevor Hughes, and saving a boy from a life-changing injury.

Carson sensed a time limit on Rhodri, too. He knew that he needed to end his life before, or immediately after, his speech at the Air Show. After that would be too late. The Air Show itself would be the first time Carson would be able to gain easy access to the base where Rhodri had imprisoned himself.

Carson checked his watch. It was 10:18; he had left the motor lodge an hour and a half ago. He tapped his fingers nervously on the steering wheel. Rhodri Jones was due to make his presentation in just under forty-five minutes.

By the time he reached the base's car park, a formation of Red Arrows was screaming overhead, the planes trailing red, white and blue smoke. The show was in full tilt, and the lot was full. A giant notice read *Alternate Parking, Follow Signs*. It took another twenty minutes before Carson had joined hundreds of other latecomers in a wide field beyond the perimeter fence. He sprinted past the long stream of visitors walking slowly along a winding path to a barrier, where two guards were stationed. One stood behind a table, checking handbags. The other ripped tickets beside an open gate. He had little doubt that they had been warned to watch out for him. How seriously would they take their jobs? Carson reached his mind out to one of the men, then pulled back as if he had been burned.

These men were Ministry of Defence police.

He stepped back out of the flow of the crowd, and centred himself. He focused on the ticket-taker, concentrating on blanking all suspicion and distrust from the man's mind. He worked at removing all thoughts of stopping a man with his description. Finally, Carson approached the ticket-taker and smiled.

''Scuse me, mate,' he said in a passable East London accent, 'can I get a ticket here?'

The man looked up with alert, intelligent eyes. He stared at Carson for several seconds before shaking his head and saying, 'I'm sorry?'

'I don't have a ticket,' Carson said. 'Can I buy one, please?'

The man paused for several beats before saying, 'Of course.'

Carson sighed mentally in relief as he paid the guard, who ripped a visitor's pass and gave him the stub, along with a pamphlet. He walked calmly through a small village of Portaloos, and rounded the corner onto a weedy path. A jet shrieked through the sky above him as he eased around a clump of tourists and broke into a trot, dodging bodies as he hurried towards the main car park, and beyond that, the Defence Park. With any luck, he would reach the Thorndike Aerospace pavilion minutes before Rhodri Jones' speech.

The aerial performance was in full-throttle as Carson

emerged from the car park into the throng of spectators. In a centre clearing, a vertical-landing jet made a deafening descent. Nearby, a small child cried out and covered her ears, releasing her Winnie the Pooh helium balloon into the sky. Carson squeezed through the crowd, stopping on the periphery to consult the pamphlet he had been given with his ticket. Inside was a map of the grounds: the Defence Park was to the north-west of him, beyond the refreshment stalls and the children's funfair.

This was where security would be the heaviest, and the guards best-prepared to identify him.

The Defence Park was a series of huge cordoned-off spaces, each with an expensive, temporary building surrounded by an arsenal of weapons and their platforms: planes, missile-launchers, armoured vehicles. Each pavilion housed a major player in the Defence industry. Inside, these companies or governments boasted of their high-tech prowess in the art of war, through glittering audio-visual displays, presentations, and lectures. They were not for the general public, but for those international few entrusted with billions of pounds for military procurement. Each required a special invitation to enter.

Carson pushed through the crowds, past families, businessmen and day-trippers, until the Thorndike area was in sight. It was ringed by a waist-high metal fence with smartly jacketed attendants posted at each gate. They wore Thorndike's corporate colours, maroon and white. Inside the enclosure, Carson could see uniformed security officers milling about the displays of the aircraft that Thorndike had been partners in creating.

He approached the pavilion. It looked just as he had envisioned it – he knew every entrance, every security station. Those uniformed guards were for show. The real security wasn't dressed in maroon costumes. Were they armed? Carson couldn't tell.

He glanced at his watch; Rhodri would make his presentation any moment. Behind Carson, the air display was reaching its noisy climax; he imagined he had at least a few minutes. Thorndike would not begin its presentation until the show was over. He leaned against a large metal rubbish bin and focused on the building, trying to tune in to Rhodri Jones' particular frequency. Carson sensed him; he was already inside. He gazed into the crowd milling outside the pavilions and defocused his eyes … who was carrying an invitation from Thorndike?

He concentrated.

There: a man in a Lacoste tennis shirt and chino trousers was approaching. Carson sensed that he was peripherally connected with one of Thorndike's suppliers.

He hurried to intercept the man.

'Excuse me, sir,' he said. 'I'm Andrew Turner, working with Thorndike Aerospace. You're with one of our suppliers, aren't you?'

'Yes,' the man replied, 'from KT Engineering Systems.'

'Of course,' Carson said, trying to affect embarrassment. 'This is a little awkward,' he said, 'but may I check your invitation? We've had a few problems.'

'Sure …' Flustered, the man pulled a neatly folded card from his back pocket. 'What's wrong?'

Carson smiled wearily. 'Miscommunication,' he said. 'Please wait here; I won't be a moment.'

Carson hurried away with the air of a harried junior official, and approached the gate. He handed a young hostess the man's ticket.

'Right through the doors into the waiting area,' she said. 'The presentation will begin in just a moment.'

Carson glanced into the reception area of the pavilion. It was a small holding pen, with two sets of double doors, which led into the theatre. 'I think I'll look around first,' he said.

'You haven't much time,' she warned.

He shrugged and moved towards the display of heavy armaments. Glancing over the barricade, he made eye contact with the troubled-looking man whose ticket he had stolen, and held up a finger: one more minute, just sorting things out …

He knew that the staff entrance was around back. Weaving through the displays of missiles, jets and an enormous mock-up of an aerial reconnaissance craft, he slipped towards the back entrance. It was propped open for ventilation.

He stepped in and found himself in a short, narrow hallway. The walls had been painted with vertiginous maroon-and-white stripes.

To his left, Carson heard the muffled strains of Wagner competing with the murmuring of a waiting crowd. Suddenly, the music cut out, the voices dimmed to a murmur, and the soundtrack of a corporate PR film began. Carson dashed up the hallway until he came to a door. He could hear the sounds of the film behind it.

For a moment, his hand wavered at the handle. The summer had been so unreal, such a flurry of reaction that, after he had determined his incredible course, he had seldom questioned himself. Now his legs were rubbery, and he felt like a frightened child. There was still time to turn and leave. To do anything else would certainly mean capture – at the very least.

He blanked all thoughts from his mind, steeled himself, and opened the door.

'Rhoddo?' Sara said, still gasping for breath. 'Why would he be after Rhoddo?'

Ceri had managed to shuffle her from the kitchen to

the living room, and had placed her in the corner chair. Eldon's chair. 'We just don't know what he's trying to achieve,' she said, 'but he doesn't stand a chance. The Met's been in touch with the Hampshire police, and they're going to get Rhodri out of there. We've also sent them the Photofit of the suspect. He won't even make it onto the grounds.'

Ceri looked into Sara's worried eyes and smiled reassuringly. 'You have to admit, an international trade show for the defence industry is a stupid place to try an assassination.'

'Where's Jamie?' Sara asked abruptly.

'The station,' Ceri whispered soothingly. 'He'll be here as soon as he can.'

Sara stood. 'I've got to call him.' she said.

'Who? Jamie?'

'No! Rhoddo.'

Ceri smiled indulgently. 'He's being well protected, Sara. He's got every police officer in Hampshire looking after him.'

'I've got to talk to him,' Sara cried, leaping from the chair and dashing to the kitchen for her phone. She swiped the screen furiously, and stabbed at Rhodri's name.

From the next room, Ceri listened wordlessly as Sara uttered a savage oath. 'Voicemail,' Sara snapped. 'What is the point of having a mobile if you didn't leave it on?'

She looked at the clock: Rhoddo had turned off his phone because he was already making his presentation. Desperate to know what was happening, she closed her eyes and stretched her mind, reached out ... and a warm fog began to descend over her. Sara was hit by a wall of confusion – interference like a radio band pulling in too many signals at once. Yet, she sensed that Eldon was in there, somewhere – a vague impression. She could read fear, single-mindedness, grim determination ... and danger. Hopeless, unavoidable danger. But for who, Rhodri or Eldon?

Sara's head grew heavy and fell forward.

'Sara!' Ceri cried.

Sara jerked herself awake and cursed. Ceri was at her side, arms around her. 'Come and sit down,' she whispered.

Tears began to well in Sara's eyes. Danger. She could sense no more than danger. And she was helpless to do anything about it.

Carson found himself backstage. A large white screen separated the space from the small stage, and, beyond it, the audience. Carson could see the reverse image of the video projection on the screen; it threw colours against the plasterboard wall at the back of the room. He smelled the sweet chalk of special-effects smoke, which welled from machines as the video reached its triumphalist conclusion. The smoke began to spill backstage, and Carson could see it welling at the bottom edge of the screen, around the legs of two silhouetted figures hunched at its side in stiff anticipation.

One of them was Rhodri Jones.

Carson started to breathe heavily, and groped for the knife in his boot.

'Sir?' said a voice in an insistent stage-whisper. 'You're not supposed to be back here.'

Carson saw a uniformed Thorndike employee bustling towards him. Over the loudspeaker, he heard the dramatic opening strains of the 'Ride of the Valkyries'.

She placed a hand on his elbow. 'Let's go into the hall.'

'I'm a friend of Rhoddo's,' he said, motioning to Rhodri. 'He said I should wait for him.'

The smoke drifted in wispy tendrils and a pre-taped announcer's voice boomed through the hall: 'Ladies and gentlemen, please welcome the Chief Executive of Thorndike Aerospace, Mr Rhodri Jones.'

The crowd applauded dutifully.

Carson looked up sharply to see Rhodri disappear around the screen. Carson flung the woman's arm back and she stumbled. He reached into his boot and withdrew his knife. At the side of the screen, Andrew Turner turned in surprise. Carson dashed towards the stage, knocking Turner and leaping into the thick fog.

Carson heard Rhodri's amplified voice sound through the hall as he leapt from the smoke onto the platform. The lights made spots well before his eyes. He located Rhodri gripping a lectern at the far side of the stage. Suddenly, two sets of doors at the back of the hall burst open, and a string of armed police officers charged down the stairs towards him.

Rhodri's voice faltered in confusion. Nervously, he adjusted his microphone. Feedback wailed as Carson leapt for him, and in a single movement clutched him to his chest, pressing his knife to Rhodri's throat.

The herd of police stopped, and jerked their weapons towards the pair. People in the crowd shrieked and tried to scatter. 'I'll cut his throat,' Carson screamed. 'Don't come any closer.'

'Just relax, son,' Rhodri muttered in a steady and remarkably calm voice. 'Don't do anything foolish.'

'Have you heard from Glyn Thomas lately?' Carson muttered under his breath.

Rhodri's facade of composure broke. 'What?' he gasped.

'Drop the knife!' an officer bellowed. 'There's no way to get out of this.'

'Glyn Thomas, remember?' Carson said. 'Your old

friend.'

'Who are you?' Rhodri whispered.

'Look at me,' Carson said, and eased the knife's pressure on Rhodri's throat. Rhodri eased his head around slowly, straining to see his assailant. His brow furrowed, then recognition flashed in his eyes. 'You!' he said. 'You were at my sister's house. You were … who are you?'

Carson smiled sardonically. 'I'm your just desserts,' he said, and jerked his knife upwards to Rhodri's throat.

Rhodri took advantage of the looser grip to throw himself backwards; his assailant had barely sliced into his flesh before the snipers responded to the gap Rhodri had made.

The first of many bullets shattered Carson's ribcage, and he was blown backwards towards the white screen, now marred by bullet holes and spattered points of blood.

TWENTY-FOUR

Jamie Harding strode through Sara's kitchen; she had leapt off the love-seat before he had made it to the living room.

'Jamie!' she cried, dashing towards him.

He caught her in his arms; she was gasping for breath, her muscles twitching from tension. 'Where is he?' Sara wailed. 'What's happened?'

Jamie squeezed her tightly. 'Don't worry,' he said. 'I've just heard Rhodri is fine.'

Sara registered this fact with relief. 'The killer,' she blurted. 'Was he ...?'

'Shhhh.' Jamie held a finger near her lips.

She felt herself go limp in his arms and began to sob. 'He didn't show?' she asked with desperate hope.

'Oh, he was there, all right,' Jamie said. 'Our message was almost too late. The MoD police couldn't prevent Rhodri from taking the stage.'

He looked into Sara's anguished face and realised she was in no condition to hear the details. 'I'm not sure what happened,' he lied, 'but they stopped him.'

'Where is he?' she cried. 'The killer!'

'The Armed Response Unit got him.'

Sara released a low groan. *Oh my God*, she thought. 'You mean he's ...?'

Jamie squeezed her even tighter. 'That's right,' he said

with a broad smile. 'It's all over now.'

Sara tossed her head back and released a loud wail. The bright Indian-summer sun glared through the window into her eyes and she clenched them, causing stars to sparkle. Her head swooned, and she felt herself falling, falling against Jamie's chest, into blackness.

'You shouldn't be alone this evening,' Ceri said, as she bustled about Sara's living room, straightening things she had already straightened. It was two hours after Sara had come round from her blackout. Jamie and Ceri had both stayed with her, bringing her tea, trying to get her to eat, and making countless telephone calls to determine what had happened at the Hampshire air base. Rhodri, they had learned, had been treated for a flesh wound by an on-site doctor, and had refused to go to the hospital. He had spent time with the police, giving them a statement, and then demanded a Thorndike town car to take him home.

'I could stay,' Jamie offered, too quickly. After a second's hesitation, he added, 'That is, if you want me to.'

Sara took a sip of tea and shuddered. Ceri had turned on the heating, even though the early-September afternoon was warm. The room smelt of hot dust. 'Thanks,' she said, 'but no.'

Jamie gave her a parental look that asked, *Are you sure that's wise*?

At the same moment, Ceri frowned and said, 'I think you're in shock.'

'I really want to be alone,' Sara insisted to Jamie, then smiled bleakly at Ceri. 'And who's the doctor here?' she asked.

'You should have company,' said Ceri.

'I should have a hot bath,' Sara replied. 'Then I'll ring Rhoddo. I really don't want you breathing down my neck when I talk to him.'

'Oh,' Jamie said, taken aback.

'Right,' Ceri added sympathetically. 'Of course. We'll leave now – and then I'll look in on you later.'

'If you do,' Sara said, 'I won't answer. I'd really like to be alone.'

Ceri opened her mouth to speak, and then closed it again.

Sara stood, and kissed both friends on the cheek. 'Thank you for looking after me,' she said with finality, 'but I'll ring if I need you.'

Jamie and Ceri left with muttered admonitions to take care of herself. Sara assured them that she would, and watched their cars move in a slow convoy down the potholed track.

When they were gone, she picked up her purse and grabbed her car keys.

Sara drove south through the Brecon Beacons. This mountain route was fussier than the coastal road, but never as busy – and far less likely to maroon her behind a slow-moving farm vehicle. Getting out of Wales was never easy.

Traffic on the M4 was flowing well that evening; Sara made good time, pushing her BMW well beyond the speed limit and trying to feel for the presence of police with her mind. As she passed just south of Reading, the sunset was turning the sky crimson. It reminded her of blood, and – not for the first time this evening – images of what Eldon's body must look like now flooded through Sara's mind like nausea. She thought about how easy it would be to veer onto one of the A roads and head towards Weatherby, where Eldon lay.

And then what? Ask to visit his corpse?

It was not until Sara got past the M25, just before 10 p.m., that her journey slowed to a crawl. Getting into

London was as hard as getting out of Mid-Wales. By the time Sara was edging along the Hammersmith Flyover, she had more or less banished all of her imagined images of Eldon's bloody body on a mortuary slab. And yet, she admitted to herself, she was not driving to Rhoddo's house out of concern for her brother's well-being – doctors had already said he was fine – but simply to find out everything she could about Eldon Carson. After all, Rhoddo knew how he had died, as well as what he had said before he'd died. He might even know why Eldon had targeted him in the first place.

God knew, Sara couldn't intuit any of the answers, no matter how hard she had tried on her journey.

She was, she told herself, a pathetic psychic.

Certainly, her psychic powers had not allowed her to foresee the van that was ahead of her on the Marylebone Road. Sara remained unaware of its presence until the very moment she slammed into its rear bumper. The left front side of her car crumpled, and she felt the airbag slam against her like a wrecking ball.

Sara cried out and struggled from the car. Looking at the vehicle she had hit, she was at first relieved to see that she had only damaged the bumper. Then her heart sank when she noticed she'd hit a *white* van. Every middle class prejudice Sara held about men in white vans kicked in, and told her that she was in for a time-consuming fleecing.

She stared at the driver's door, which glowed orange under the streetlamps, and waited for him to emerge. Cars honked and swerved around her.

Sara felt a momentary flutter of hope when a middle-aged woman climbed down from the cabin. The woman looked nice enough, with her neatly-ponytailed hair and her pretty knit jumper. Then she spoke.

'What the *fuck*?' White Van Woman shouted.

'I am so sorry,' Sara hollered over the din of the street; they stood in the left-hand lane as traffic funnelled around them. 'I simply didn't see you.'

'No shit,' the woman said. She looked Sara over, then squinted at her crumpled BMW. She made a calculation, and suddenly her hand shot to her neck. 'Bloody hell, I think I've got whiplash!'

Sara groaned: *oh, please don't.* The woman tried to gauge her reaction to this performance.

Sara raised her voice: 'Are you really going to do this?'

'I'm injured,' the woman insisted.

Placing her hand gently on the woman's arm, Sara guided her across the bus lane to the pavement alongside Baker Street Station. She leaned in close to the woman's ear. 'I don't have time for you to have whiplash,' she explained. 'I need to be somewhere.'

White Van Woman blinked incredulously and gestured to their vehicles. It was going to take quite some time to sort out this mess, regardless of personal injury claims.

But Sara had been telling the truth; she did not have the time to do this. 'Do you have an Uber app on your phone?' Sara asked.

'What?'

'An Uber app.'

'Er – yeah.'

'Then here's what we're going to do,' Sara said. 'You're going to find me an Uber – I need to get to Islington.'

The woman began to object. Sara silenced her with a raised finger. 'While you do that,' she continued, 'I'm going to fetch the title to my car and sign it. When the Uber gets here, I will give you the title, and leave.'

The woman shook her head, as if she didn't understand.

'You will own my car – but you will have to get it off this street. Do we have a deal?'

White Van Woman squinted at Sara suspiciously. Even second-hand, the BMW was worth more than ten grand, and the woman was trying to guess the nature of whatever con Sara might be running.

'You're going to give me your car?' she asked.

Sara moved back onto the road, wrenched open the passenger's door and removed the title, as well as a pen and her purse, from the glove compartment. 'Here is the title,' she said, returning to the pavement. Opening her purse, Sara rifled through the cash. 'And here is two hundred and forty pounds. That's all I have, but it should cover the towing. You can pay for the repairs yourself.'

Sara heard a police siren in the distance and wondered if it was heading towards them.

'One more thing,' she added. 'When I leave here, our business will be done. You can tell the police whatever you like, and if they ring me, I'll back you up … but you will not claim to have whiplash.'

The woman pondered, and her suspicion eased in the face of this bizarre good fortune. She shrugged and said, 'Go on, then – fill out the title.'

Producing her phone, she added, 'You're going to Islington, right?'

The Uber took Sara to the pavement in front of Rhodri's house. She stabbed the buzzer and rapped her knuckles on the black, high-gloss wood.

There was no answer.

She tried again; Rhodri did not respond. Sara frowned, tried to stretch her mind through the wooden door, through the cold, empty halls … She was certain he was home, more certain than she had ever been about anything in her life.

She glanced up at the bedroom window. 'Rhoddo!' she called.

After another moment's hesitation, Sara dug in her handbag for her cluster of secondary keys, and isolated the three necessary to enter her brother's house. Inside, the foyer was cool. Rhoddo's burglar alarm did not trill. All Sara could hear was the strong, precise clacking of the grandfather clock, and the wild thudding of her own heart.

'Rhoddo?' she called. Her tightly-controlled voice wavered.

She flicked on the hallway light and noticed Rhodri's umbrella stand had toppled over. Thin switches of willow and leather crops were scattered across the mosaic floor. Cautiously, Sara stepped over them, and peered into the sitting room. Rhodri's jacket, tie and trousers lay neatly over the arm of the sofa. Further into the room, a black leather skirt lay discarded on the floor, like a skinned hide flung to rot where it had landed.

In the gilt-framed mirror over the mantelpiece, Sara could see the polished wooden stairway behind her. Somehow, the act of concentrating on it sharpened not only her eyesight, but her hearing. Faintly, from upstairs, she heard the repetitive patter of music. She swallowed, felt a wave of irrational dread, and walked towards it.

Up on the landing, a ripped pair of black panties lay lifelessly next to a thin willow cane. On the peach wall there was a small smear of blood.

The music came from Rhodri's bedroom. The electronic buzz of an acid house track.

'Rhodri,' Sara said in a low voice, 'I am coming upstairs.'

She leapt up the remaining few stairs. The door was open a crack, but the room was dark. She pushed the glossy white wood with the flat of her palm. Something was blocking the way. Fear welled inside her, and she felt fifteen again. She threw herself shoulder-first into the door. On the other side, she heard a muffled thud, and a weak groan.

Sara squeezed through the gap, stumbling over Rhodri's bare legs. She released a guttural wail: he was sprawled on the glossy floorboards, wearing only an unbuttoned white shirt without cufflinks, and jockey shorts. His skin was as white as the garments he wore. Whiter – the clothes had been stained bloody, deep red splashes spreading outward through the white linen.

Sara switched on the overhead light. Rhodri was bleeding from deep slice to his left wrist. A small, blood-sticky razor blade lay at his side. The music thrummed repetitively from a speaker dock in the corner.

'Sara, help me,' he whispered. 'I don't want to die.'

'Rhoddo …'

'I thought I did – I mean … I'm in trouble, Sara. Help me.'

Gasping, trying to calm her breathing, Sara bent down and examined her brother's wound. It was obvious that Rhodri had meant to kill himself: many would-be suicides slashed across their wrists, which was enough to hurt a lot, but usually not enough for significant blood loss. Rhodri had sliced downwards, deeply – but, fortunately, he had missed the vein, cutting alongside rather than through it.

Still, he had lost a lot of blood, and without immediate treatment, he would die. Sara's mind reeled. She had left her medical kit in Wales … but she could bandage the wound with a bed sheet.

'Oh, Rhoddo,' she said through angry tears, 'you're so stupid. I'm going to bandage you up, then I'll call 999, okay?'

'No!' he gasped. 'Don't call anyone … nobody can know.'

'Rhoddo,' she said, standing, 'you need to see a doctor!'

'You're a doctor,' he whispered. 'Help me.'

She needed to staunch the flow. The screech of the music made it hard to think. She reached to the corner, stabbed Rhoddo's iPhone into silence, then looked frantically towards the unmade bed ... and gasped. All thoughts of creating a tourniquet were lost as she gaped at the motionless figure that lay tangled in the sheets.

She closed her eyes. 'Oh my God, Rhoddo,' she whispered in sickened horror. 'Oh, my God.'

The prostitute was dead. She lay curled naked in a foetal position, the skin of her buttocks a war-zone of welts. Her head was twisted at an odd angle.

'I didn't mean to kill her,' Rhodri moaned. 'Oh, Sara, I'm so sorry. You've got to help me. There's nobody else we can call. Just don't let me die!'

What should I do? Sara asked herself. The train of indulgence she had ridden with her brother all these years had suddenly run out of track. Rhodri needed a blood transfusion. He would either face the authorities or bleed to death – and either way, the life he knew was over.

Sara felt herself swoon, and shook her head sharply to ward off a fainting spell. An odd sensation pricked at her, as if trying to compel her to slip into blackness. She fought it, and worked to dull her emotions. She grabbed the edge of a sheet, tore at it with her teeth, and ripped a strip. She moved back to her brother, and crouched down beside him, taking his icy cold arm.

'Rhodri, you've got to tell me what happened.'

'I don't know!' he whimpered. 'I don't know what happened.'

'You need to think,' she cried, winding the strip around his forearm.

At this touch, Sara's vision began to shimmer. She slumped down to the floor, suddenly unable to control herself. The bedroom about her began to grow very bright, then faded. She felt herself falling through layers of blackness.

Sara was tuning in ... tuning in to her brother Rhodri. And suddenly, at long last, her search drew to an end.

Suddenly, she understood everything.

It is the previous week. Sara finds herself hovering above the harbour in Aberystwyth. The distorted reflection of the moon ripples in Cardigan bay. Ahead, by a broken sea-rail, two men stand.

Steadily, Sara drifts closer.

'It's down there,' she hears one man say. 'See that crack?'

She doesn't recognise him.

'Where?' the other fellow asks, and Sara gasps. *My God*, she thinks ... *that's Daffy!*

'You're not close enough. You've got to move in.' The man tugs at Daffy's jacket.

This is the night Daffy died – Sara is sure of it.

She feels the same breathless horror rush upon her that she experienced in her visions of Shrewsbury. But she is more in control now. She steadies herself. She doesn't know why this vision has come, but she knows she has to watch.

'I can't see it,' Daffy is saying. 'I don't know where it is ...'

Sara watches the man push Daffy towards the break in the rail, kicking expertly at his calves. She sees Daffy fall onto his knees, hears him scream.

'Shut the fuck up!'

A bottle cracks the back of Daffy's skull, and the assailant shoves him to the cement, savagely breaking the bottle against his face. Now, Sara hears herself scream. From somewhere, Rhodri cries out in response, but the man assaulting Daffy pays no heed.

Stop it, Sara! Watch. Just watch.

So she watches. She watches impotently, as the man uses the broken bottle to cut into Daffy's arteries, and then kicks him over the edge of the seawall, into the tide.

The man watches Daffy bob and float. Then suddenly …

She edges a little farther back in time.

Daylight in Aberystwyth. The platform at the train station. Passengers exit the two coaches from Shrewsbury. Tourists weighed down by backpacks larger than their backs, students blowing into town for the new term, a woman back from holiday, her suitcase adorned with a tag from Gatwick.

Passengers for Birmingham wait to board. A woman clutches her young son while Daddy folds the pushchair. A businessman checks his watch and taps a small date book against his thigh.

Against a brick wall, removed from the small crowd, two men sit on a bench. Sara can drift close without anyone noticing, because here, she is pure spirit. She looks carefully.

She recognises one as the man she has just seen murder Daffy. The man who will murder Daffy somewhere later in time.

The other man is Rhodri.

When is this? Sara thinks, and knows the answer. This is last Thursday – the day before her brother appeared in Penweddig. A day he had claimed to be in London.

The two men speak quietly, their voices camouflaged by the noises of the station. Sara can hear them perfectly.

'You know he's in town?' Rhodri asks.

'Oh, he's in town,' the man replies with a smirk. 'I even know where he sleeps. There's a wooden shelter on the seafront.'

'I don't care where he sleeps,' snaps Rhodri. 'I don't want to know anything about him.'

'Fine, fine,' the man says with a dismissive wave. 'You got the money?'

'Of course I've got it,' Rhodri replies, then chuckles sardonically. 'You can even keep the bag it's in. Quality bag, that.'

From somewhere in the distance – from the other time she occupies – Sara hears her brother cry out to her. She must wake up and help him, he says. 'Please,' he says, 'please.' He is dying.

But Sara cannot wake up. Once again, she tumbles through blackness, backwards.

It is early summer, London, and Rhodri is afraid, a fear like anguish – tortured, indignant rage that time could be so cruel as to unearth this relic from days long buried. That was a different Rhodri, he wants to scream. Why are you here? Why are you the same?

But this man is not the same. No – he's weak. The years have faded him, used him cruelly, and this foul little shit is no match for Rhodri fucking Jones. You can tear him apart, Rhoddo, no problem.

The blackmailer who calls himself Daffy stands – stands out, incongruous – in the hallway of Rhodri's house. 'You owe me this, Rhoddo,' he says, his voice high and wavering, uncertain, 'you owe me a life. It's taken me years to realise I have a right to this.'

'You have a right to nothing,' Rhodri spits, his voice just as scared, but more deadly. 'You're the reason my life went off the rails, and the fact that I pulled it back on track again is no thanks to you. If you hadn't run, I'd have killed you then and there.'

Daffy breathes in staccato jerks. He thinks Rhoddo will strike him, but all Rhoddo says is, 'I wish I had.'

Daffy begins to weep, like the terrified young man he was, like a small transgressor turned victim who has paid too high a price for youthful misjudgements. 'Please,' he screams, 'I'm desperate. I can't live like this any more!'

'Then you can die,' Rhodri hisses. 'Just don't do it in my bloody house.'

'Everyone will know!' Daffy shrieks. 'I'll tell them and you'll be finished. You'll be in prison!'

Rhodri is trembling now, patches of sweat staining his shirt at the armpits, the odour of his cologne thick in the air. 'I would strongly suggest,' he whispers through gritted teeth, 'that you kill yourself tonight. It will be less painful than if I have it done for you.'

Daffy's face contorts in silent, wracking sobs and he drops to the floor, his hot tears and phlegm smearing across the cold mosaic. Rhodri kicks him, hard, in the ribs.

'Get out, Glyn,' he snarls. 'Or I'll kill you now.'

TWENTY-FIVE

Sara's head lolled groggily as she fought her way to consciousness. She sucked a deep breath through her mouth, into her constricted chest, lungs burning from inhaling Rhodri's sharp cologne. She was pressed against his chest. Coughing, she hoisted up her head in a clumsy jerk; her brother's eyes were opened, staring blankly at the plaster moulding on the pristine white bedroom ceiling.

'Daffy,' she breathed. 'Daffy was Glyn Thomas, wasn't he? Wasn't he?'

Rhodri's head nodded slowly.

'And you had him killed.'

'Sara,' Rhodri whispered faintly, 'I'll explain. I promise I will. Just help me now. Please. I'm so weak.'

'Why did you kill Daffy?' Sara asked.

Rhodri's eyelids fluttered and closed. 'He wanted … to hurt me.'

'He was trying to blackmail you,' Sara said. 'Tell me why, Rhodri.'

Rhodri shook his head from side to side, faintly. 'He was disturbed. Mentally un … sound'

For the first time ever, a dreadful thought crept into Sara's mind, outflanking her conscious logic with a darker certainty. She felt horrified, as if it made her unclean to acknowledge what she was thinking.

'What did you do to make him blackmail you?' she whispered, dreading the answer. 'When we were young, when it all happened. What did you do?'

Rhodri's lips moved, but he said nothing.

She heard the Islington traffic shudder and grind in the distance. They were so far from Wales, so removed from their past. And yet, it was all here, all now, all vivid in front of her. An uncontrollable tingling shimmered through Sara's body, leaving in its wake a floating numbness, as if she'd been anaesthetised.

She rolled off Rhodri and pushed herself up, until she was sitting upright. Her new-found lightness made her head swirl, but she forced herself to take a strong breath. She stared at the bandage on the side of his neck, where Eldon had sliced him.

'Rhodri,' she said in a unflinching voice, 'I want you to tell me the truth.'

She reached out to grasp his cold, dying arm, but then her voice broke as she sobbed, 'Who murdered our parents?'

Rhoddo sings at the top of his voice as he flies his motor scooter over twisty little lanes. His Walkman plays the same trance track that Duncan had shared just minutes ago. Rhodri is high on everything.

Trees and hedgerows flash by, and there's light and love in all of them. When Rhoddo breathes, there is steam in the frosty winter air, and the steam glows brightly. Duncan Kraig understands what love is – something his father never could, not in a million, trillion years. Glyn says Rhoddo's dad is just a pain in the arse who doesn't comprehend the majesty of what's happening in Artist's Valley.

'Majesty' is one of Duncan's words. Glyn's been using it a lot lately.

Rhoddo feels pretty majestic too, as he fishtails the motor scooter on the gravel drive and swaggers into the house. He knows from the car that the old man's home, working upstairs, and hopes he just stays there.

Trouble is, he doesn't.

'Rhodri,' calls the voice. 'Get up here – I want to see you.' In Rhoddo's head it sounds like bubbles underwater, and he giggles.

Rhoddo peels off his jacket and sheds it in the hallway. Duncan Kraig says, 'Just be cool about stuff. Say yeah, okay, and do what you want to anyway.' Duncan's really brilliant, but then he's never had to fight with Rhodri Jones Senior.

Speak of the devil and he stomps downstairs. 'It's still school hours,' Daddy shouts. This is the way it always starts. 'What are you doing home? I'll bet I know who you've been out with!'

He looks at Rhodri with just the weirdest expression, and Rhodri laughs and laughs. 'What have you taken?' he demands in a low, horrified drawl, shaking Rhoddo by the shoulders. 'Tell me! What sort of drugs are you on?'

Drugs? How terribly quaint. What does Daddy know about drugs?

But, Jesus – Rhoddo must look worse than he thought. There's part of him, deep down inside somewhere, that's thinking really straight, that's lucid and articulate, and this part watches his father watching him, and realises maybe it wasn't so smart to come home right now. It observes his dad shake him and shake him, and notices how this begins to irritate the non-watching part of Rhoddo, who suddenly feels like sleep. You don't want to be shaken when you're sleepy. So he pushes, lashes out. 'Get off me!' he shouts.

The lucid part of Rhoddo that's watching braces itself.

Daddy swears, grabs at him, and Rhoddo tries to fight, but his arms aren't working so well now. They're like windmills in a gale. Daddy grabs him easily, and frog-marches him upstairs, pushing, jerking his arms, lecturing all the while. Rhoddo's legs are rubbery.

Daddy throws him on the bed, slams the door, locks it from the outside.

He put on that lock a while ago. It's so insulting that Rhoddo hasn't been able to admit it to Glyn. He hears Daddy stomp upstairs again, and Rhoddo falls into the strangest sleep.

He dreams of every fight he's ever had with his father. He observes years of pursed lips, glaring eyes, disapproval. 'You're coddling the boy,' say his dreams. 'Stop coddling him.' Jesus, a lifetime of that – like a prison! And now what? It's just going to get worse. No more Artists Valley for Rhoddo Jones.

He's numb when he wakes up, but he knows what he's going to do. It's all so clear now, that this situation cannot be allowed to go on. Rhoddo's place is with Duncan and his friends.

Sara shook her head, gasping, repeating the words, 'No … no, no, I can't, I can't …'

The certainty was so terrible, the dread so tangible, the moment so close and she couldn't, wouldn't face it. She needed to cry; she wanted to run. There were two times, two horrors playing out before her. Which horror should she choose?

But Sara couldn't choose because the visions did not stop. She was in young Rhoddo's mind as he climbed off his bed.

And there's no thinking needed now. Rhoddo is going to want his gloves – but they're balled up in his jacket downstairs. Never mind, there's a spare pair in the drawer under the bed. So, with gloved hands, he edges his window open, and squeezes out onto the flat roof extension. He drops to the cold, dead grass – but he's still not too well co-ordinated. He falls.

'Shit!' he hisses, and a burst of steam shoots from his mouth like light. Blankly, he slinks around the house, enters the kitchen, and eases the jangling keys from their hook.

Daddy's shotgun is in the shed.

Getting the freezing-cold gun is easy, but the cartridges will be harder. The old man keeps them in the hall cupboard, at the foot of the stairs which lead to his loft office. No sneakiness or subtlety possible there. The assault's got to be full-frontal. Dead on.

Rhoddo returns to the kitchen and walks up the stairs to the first floor. But carefully – his legs aren't so steady right now. The shotgun cocked over one arm, he pulls open the cupboard door and fumbles with a dusty box of shells.

'Kay?' his father calls. 'That you? Go see Rhodri. He's in his room, and I think you should go take a look at him –'

His father appears at the top of the stairs, and gasps, mid-sentence. Slowly Rhoddo aims. He pulls the trigger and his father is flung backwards. So is he. There was more recoil than he'd expected, and it's hurt his shoulder. He catches his balance and stands still for a moment, trying to think. He doesn't know whether to shoot Daddy again – he's never done this before – so he reloads just in case, and creeps upstairs. Looking at the body makes him feel ill.

Rhoddo clumps down the stairs in slow, careful steps, like a pallbearer. As he reaches the bottom, the front door yawns open. A rush of chill air sweeps over him. His mother gazes at him stupidly, squinting into the darkness after the brightness of the day outside. He can't let her see what's upstairs. He can't let her face what had to happen.

The noise is deafening. He hopes none of his neighbours have heard. When Mummy falls, he doesn't look at her; instead, he watches the fruit and vegetables. The paper bag rips, and they scatter. The oranges roll the farthest.

'You murdered them,' Sara whispered, horror ripping at her stomach like swallowed glass. 'You murdered our parents, and then you framed Glyn Thomas.'

'Sara,' Rhodri whispered, 'I will explain it all to you, I swear.'

Sara stood, feeling a cold, penetrating clarity for the first time ever. 'I don't need your explanations, Rhodri,' she said. 'There's nothing you can tell me that I can't see for myself.'

She knew that her words were true. She could see anything she wanted to see.

'Please,' Rhodri begged.

'Rhodri,' Sara said coldly, a sheet of icy anger spreading inside her, 'you've had twenty years to explain yourself. Instead, you lied, and used me to cover up for your perversions.'

Rhodri's blue hand twitched, as if he wanted to reach out to her. 'I couldn't tell you the truth,' he said, 'because I didn't want to hurt you. I love you, Sara, I've always loved you.'

'You don't love anyone, Rhodri,' Sara spat. 'And the person you hate most of all is yourself.'

'Yes! Yes, I hate myself,' Rhodri whispered faintly. 'I want to be a new person. Please, Sara … don't let me die.'

Sara looked at the telephone that sat next to the bed, next to the corpse of another of Rhodri's victims. She could still ring for an ambulance, she knew. There was still time to save her brother's life.

In a flash, Eldon Carson's words rang through her mind: 'There's only a small number of people in any one place who do all the damage ... they're like cancer, eating away at the rest of us.'

She looked back at Rhodri and knew that he was, and always had been, one of those cancers. For years, Sara had buried her distaste towards his dark habits and excused his excesses, blaming them on the tragedy of their parents' deaths. Now, the irony that weaved through her years of compassion seemed pathetic and bitter. Suddenly, there was no pain involved in watching her brother die. He was not, had never been, the person she had thought he was; he was a stranger whose only link to Sara was that he had murdered her parents. And now he was leaving this earth. There was a certain rightness to that; in a few moments more, the world would be a slightly cleaner place.

'I'm so sorry,' Rhodri said faintly.

Sara stood. 'Goodbye, Rhodri,' she whispered, the harshness of her tone now distorted by sadness, and stepped quietly towards the door. She turned off the light and squeezed through the gap between her brother's body and the door jamb.

EPILOGUE

Out on the street, sleet splattered the pavement in wet pellets. From Jamie's old leather sofa, Sara looked through the bay window, up at the sheet-white sky; London's most threatening skies always turned pale, she had noticed. Grey was a colour for minor-league weather, but white meant business. She half-listened to the icy droplets thrum against the roof of Andy Turner's Town Car, as Andy played with a string of tinsel from the Christmas tree and reminisced about Rhodri's funeral.

'Don't get me wrong,' he said. 'Highgate Cemetery is stunning. And with its history, and all the famous bodies ... well, you didn't make a bad choice. But what I had in mind could have been magnificent!' Andy sighed with regret. 'If only you'd let me use the helicopter.'

'Rhoddo didn't want to be cremated,' Sara reminded him. 'He always wanted a burial at Highgate.'

Absently, Andy taunted Ego with the tinsel. No longer a sprightly kitten, Ego watched from the arm of Andy's chair with interest, but did not pounce.

'Imagine it, though,' Andy continued. 'You could have cremated Rhodri first, then held a massive funeral in Aberystwyth.'

'Massive?' Sara said. 'There aren't enough people.'

'Every Thorndike employee would have come,' Andy insisted. 'Anyway, at the funeral's moving climax –

which I would have written myself – a helicopter would appear in the sky and land to the sound of –'

'Wagner?' Sara interrupted.

'Something appropriate,' Andy said. 'You and Jamie would have taken Rhodri's remains and climbed ceremoniously on board. There'd be a short flight to Cadair Idris, and as you hovered over its summit, you'd open the urn and let Rhodri drift on the mountain's breezes, to settle across its majestic slopes.'

He held open his hands. 'Can't you see how breathtaking that would have been?'

Jamie emerged from the kitchen with a tray of mugs: Lady Grey tea for Andy, coffee for himself and Sara. 'How would anyone know how breathtaking it was?' he asked. 'I mean, if only Sara and I were there to see it happen?'

'Simple,' Andy replied. 'I would have been on a second helicopter with a camera crew.'

Over his third cup of Lady Grey, Andy peered at the range of tribal masks and aboriginal paintings that Sara had affixed to Jamie's walls. 'It's nice to see them again,' he said. 'It reminds me of all those pleasant hours I spent in your office. I do miss having therapy with you.'

'You never needed therapy to start with,' Sara said.

'Well,' Andy demurred, 'maybe I've just missed talking to you.'

Sara smiled. Returning his gaze to the wall, Andy added, 'I'm surprised you managed to squeeze your art collection into such a small space.'

'I didn't,' Sara said. 'Most of it's now in boxes at a friend's house.'

Sara had put her home on the market the day after Rhodri's death, then moved in with Ceri to avoid any morbidly curious ghouls posing as homebuyers. Ceri had ordered around-the-clock police protection to ward off the journalists, photographers and TV crews that descended on Penweddig. They still speculated, of course. On television, in the papers, and over the Internet, rumour had been rife that Rhodri's air show assailant, the late Eldon Carson, had also been responsible for the murders in Aberystwyth.

The police and Home Office denied it. Officially, the Aberystwyth killer was still at large.

Although her house had not yet sold, Sara left Aberystwyth in late autumn. With her quest for understanding at an end, she found she no longer wanted to stay in Mid-Wales, a place so filled with tragic memories, both new and old. Besides, she was needed here in London; Rhodri had named Sara executor of his will. As it turned out, she was also its sole beneficiary. Rhodri left her his entire estate – house, furnishings, a lump sum from his pension, and a substantial portfolio of investments. There was also a large life insurance policy, but it was very likely to be nullified by his suicide. Negotiations with the insurers were ongoing. Sara guessed it would take the better part of a year before the lawyers finally released any of the money, but she had already promised the family of Maja Bosco – the young woman Rhodri had killed – a sizeable chunk of the proceeds.

'Are you planning to stay here in Brixton?' Andy asked.

Jamie caressed Sara's arm. 'Maybe,' he said.

'Probably not,' she countered. 'This flat was okay when Jamie was a bachelor, but for both of us, it'll be a bit small.'

'What about Rhodri's house?' Andy suggested. 'It's big enough for the two of you, as well as any new addition to the family.'

Sara shuddered. 'No thanks ... I've lived with ghosts

for long enough.'

Andy turned to Jamie. 'And what do you plan to do?' he asked. 'I mean, now that you've quit the Met?'

Jamie pursed his lips. 'I'm thinking about Human Rights Law,' he said. 'I've been looking at universities online. It's not clear-cut. My undergrad degree's in Criminology, so I might have to get a graduate diploma in Law before doing an MA.'

'I'm sure you'll find a way to save the world.' Andy said, and looked at Sara. 'I suppose you can do anything you want now.'

He meant, *with all of Rhodri's money*.

'What I want is to work,' Sara said. 'But not on Harley Street; not now, anyway. Maybe I'll volunteer somewhere ... it depends on who's looking for someone like me.'

'Every mental health organisation in London is looking for someone like you,' Andy told her. 'Choose the one you want, and I'll get you the job.'

Sara laughed. 'How?'

Andy shrugged. 'Most organisations can be bribed with an offer of free consultation and a healthy dose of sponsorship.'

'Don't make promises you might regret,' Sara said. 'Besides, there's no need for any of us to rush.' She reached across and squeezed Jamie's hand. 'We've got time.'

Sara and Jamie had planned to take the Tube into the West End for a spot of Christmas shopping after Andy left. Although it was Saturday, Andy was on his way to his office; he offered them a lift into town. 'You don't want to walk to the station,' he said. 'It's still wetter than Wales out there.'

The boutique offices of Andrew Turner & Associates

were located in a building near the London Library, so Andy dropped off Sara and Jamie outside Fortnum and Mason. They walked the short distance to Piccadilly Circus, and then onto Regent Street. In a crowded cosmetics shop, Sara bought a bag of pricey bath bombs to send to her nursing and social worker friends in Aberystwyth. The American twenty-something behind the counter chatted to her with well-rehearsed enthusiasm – but Sara sensed her yearning to go home for Christmas. Sara pressed deeper into the woman's thoughts. Home was in Minneapolis, and her parents were going through an ugly divorce.

In a menswear shop, Jamie surveyed a stack of jumpers. Over the course of the day, the garments had become dishevelled, and a staff member reached in front of him to straighten them. The staffer showed nothing but professional competence, but Sara could sense his resentment towards Jamie. That was unfair – Jamie hadn't messed up the sweaters.

Everywhere they went, Sara could feel the frustration, confusion, tiredness, and occasional joy of the holiday shoppers. The gift that Eldon Carson had bestowed upon her had not gone away. In fact, as Eldon had predicted, her powers had strengthened, even in the short time she had been living in London. Sara could now get a strong sense of the thoughts and feelings of most of the people she came into contact with, although she had not yet received any tangible glimpses into the future.

That is, until later on that afternoon, when she and Jamie were weaving through the throngs on Oxford Street.

The sleet had died away by then, but the sky was still threateningly white. Sara spotted a homeless man sitting on a wet stone bench in front of Selfridges. Suddenly, she felt as though she could see into his soul. Perhaps the strong connection was because he reminded her of Glyn Thomas, the man she had hated unjustly for so many years, and whose death she had failed to prevent.

Or maybe it was just because she thought she could help him.

In a flash, Sara knew a lot about this man. She knew his name – Ken Salter – and she knew that, unlike many homeless people, Salter was not mentally ill. He genuinely wanted to get back on his feet. The trouble was, Ken Salter had a drinking problem, and an explosive temper. It was a bad combination.

As soon as she realised this, Sara's head began to tingle. She placed a steadying hand against the shop's window.

'You okay?' Jamie asked.

'Fine,' Sara said. 'Just give me a moment.'

Instantly, Sara saw a freezing cold midwinter night … and a homeless shelter on fire.

'We could get sushi,' Jamie suggested. 'Sit down for a minute.'

Sara silenced him with a raised hand. Suddenly, she was witnessing the argument, hours before that fateful night, when staff at the shelter refused Salter a bed. He was drunk and belligerent – he took the rejection badly, staggering into the freezing air with curses, then returning in the small hours with a jug of petrol, some rags, and a lighter.

Before dawn, seventeen people were dead.

Or would be dead. Two years from now.

Slowly, Sara came to her senses, and shook her head. Since the end of summer, she had agonised over this moment, over what she would do when such a vision hit her. Sara had decided that Eldon's extreme method was not the only way open to her. She was a psychiatrist. She had to believe that people could change.

Ken Salter was shuffling away now. Sara ran after him. 'Ken!' she cried. 'Ken, wait.'

'Sara?' Jamie called.

Salter turned suspiciously. 'How d'you know my name?'

She got close enough to smell him, and forced herself closer. 'I used to work at a soup kitchen,' Sara lied. Where did this man eat? She reached into his mind. 'On Tottenham Court Road. You know, in the church.'

'Oh … yeah,' said the man, 'I remember you.'

Sara noticed that Jamie had gravitated to her side. She suggested he get a table at the sushi place in Selfridges, and promised to join him shortly. Once Jamie left, Sara bought Salter a wrap from Marks and Spencer's Food Hall, and he ate it on his bench.

'You still work at the church?' Salter asked her.

'No,' Sara said, 'but I still help people.'

'How?'

'I help them with their emotions,' she explained. 'I'm a doctor. I talk to people, and it makes them feel better.'

Through a mouthful of chicken, Salter said, 'That's great, but I feel fine.'

'Do you want to get off the street?' she asked.

He shrugged.

'I could help you to do that.'

Salter tilted his head. 'How?'

'You'll have to see me again to find out.' Sara opened her purse and pulled out twenty pounds. 'Take this,' she said. 'I'll come back at 10 a.m., Monday morning, and give you some more. But only if you promise to talk to me.'

Salter took the note and looked at it appraisingly. Then he stuffed it in his coat pocket. 'OK,' he agreed.

'It's a deal,' Sara said with a smile.

Her smile was genuine; she felt a pulse of exhilaration.

Maybe, Sara thought, this was what Eldon's gift had prepared her for. In a breathless rush of confidence, Sara truly believed she could steer this man away from his anger – away from that horrible moment two years from now, when his drunken fury would take all those lives. Working together, they would create a new, different future for him. She would accomplish what her psychic mentor had never even tried to do – and in the process, she would prove Eldon Carson wrong.

Sara bid goodbye to her new client, reminding him about Monday. As she made her way through the department store crowds, she reached under her blouse and fingered the papier mâché pendant she wore there. She hoped with all her heart she could change Ken Salter for the better.

Because, if she couldn't, she feared she might have to kill him.

The Mismade Girl

When Alice Seagrove is found dead, a name carved into her body, old memories are stirred up for DI Hal Luchewski. The name is that of a murdered sex offender – and the man who killed him, convicted in Hal's first ever murder case, has just been released from prison.

As he digs deeper, Hal discovers multiple links between Dr Seagrove, the recently released killer Nino Gaudiano, and Nino's long-missing daughter Louisa. Hal must tread a fine line as he digs into the secrets of several people involved in both cases – and time is running out.

Meanwhile, Hal's convoluted personal life is strained, as his relationship with boyfriend Stevie is on the rocks and he has to deal with revelations about his world-famous father...

The Black Path

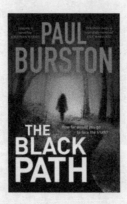

*S*ometimes Helen wonders if Owen isn't the only one living in a war zone. She feels the violence all around her. She reads about it in the papers. It feeds her dreams and fills her days with a sense of dread. Try as she might, she can't escape the feeling that something terrible is about to happen.

Then one night on the troubled streets of her home town, Helen is rescued from a fight by a woman who will change her life forever. Siân is everything Helen isn't – confident, glamorous, fearless. But there's something else about her – a connection that cements their friendship and makes Helen question everything she's ever known.

And when her husband returns home, altered in a way she can't understand, she is forced to draw on an inner strength she never knew she had.

As bitter truths are uncovered, Helen must finally face her fears and the one place which has haunted her since childhood – the Black Path.

LONGLISTED FOR THE GUARDIAN'S 'NOT THE BOOKER PRIZE'

For more information about
Terence Bailey
and other **Accent Press** titles
please visit
www.accentpress.co.uk